"CARE TO MAKE A WAGER?"

Her eyes narrowed. Clearly she wasn't ready to trust him. "What kind of wager?"

"How about this? There's going to be a dirt dance in the arena after the rodeo tonight. If I guess right the first time, you'll promise to go with me."

"And if you don't?"

"That's up to you. I could buy you dinner."

"Forget it. Either way, I'll be too tired to dance or eat. And I'll be busy after the rodeo, loading the bulls for the drive home."

"Then I'll make it easy for you. If I can pick Whirlwind on the first guess, you'll give me twenty minutes of your time—just to talk to you."

"And if you lose?"

"Whatever you want. Your call."

JANET DAILEY

WHIRLWIND

ZEBRA BOOKS
KENSINGTON PUBLISHING CORP.
www.kensingtonbooks.com

ZEBRA BOOKS are published by

Kensington Publishing Corp.
119 West 40th Street
New York, NY 10018

All Kensington titles, imprints, and distributed lines are available at special quantity discounts for bulk purchases for sales promotion, premiums, fundraising, educational, or institutional use.

Special book excerpts or customized printings can also be created to fit specific needs. For details, write or phone the office of the Kensington Sales Manager: Attn.: Sales Department. Kensington Publishing Corp., 119 West 40th Street, New York, NY 10018. Phone: 1-800-221-2647.

Zebra and the Z logo Reg. U.S. Pat. & TM Off.

First Kensington Books Hardcover Printing: September 2020
First Zebra Books Mass-Market Paperback Printing: July 2021
ISBN-13: 978-1-4201-5094-0
ISBN-10: 1-4201-5094-4

ISBN-13: 978-1-4201-5097-1 (eBook)
ISBN-10: 1-4201-5097-9 (eBook)

10 9 8 7 6 5 4 3 2 1

Printed in the United States of America

CHAPTER ONE

Kingman, Arizona
Summer

LEXIE CHAMPION PULLED OFF HER SUNGLASSES, WIPED THE lenses on the hem of her rumpled denim shirt, and slipped them into her pocket. Her eyes were gritty from the dusty desert wind that swept across the rodeo grounds, picking up the odors of manure, barbecue, popcorn, tobacco smoke, and diesel fumes—a mélange that, to Lexie, was as familiar as any air she'd ever breathed.

From the midway beyond the bleachers, her ears caught the music of a carousel. It blended with the bawl of cattle and the blare of the rodeo announcer's voice as the rodeo's opening ceremony began.

They'd driven most of the night to get here—she and the foreman, Ruben Diego, with four bucking bulls in the long gooseneck trailer. They'd arrived at the Mohave County Fairgrounds late last night and loosed the bulls down the chute into one of the holding pens. After giving their charges water and bull chow in rubber feed tubs, the two of them had crashed across the front and back seats of the heavy-duty pickup for a few hours of sleep.

Now it was late in the day. The strains of the national anthem from the arena told her that the Kingsmen Pro Rodeo, was about to get underway. The bull riding event would be last on the two-hour program. Before then, there should be time to relax, get some barbecue, maybe even change the clothes she'd driven and slept in. But Lexie was too wired to rest. All she wanted was to be right here, with her bulls. After the threatening message she'd received last week, she needed to know that the precious animals were safe.

Ruben had gone off to the midway for food and sodas. She'd told him there was no need to bring her anything, but he probably would. Ruben, a full-blooded member of the Tohono O'odham tribe, might be an employee of the Alamo Canyon Ranch, but he treated Lexie and her sister Tess as if they were his own daughters.

Alone for the moment, she leaned against the six-foot portable steel fence, resting a boot on one of the lower rungs as she gazed across the complex of pens and gates. Here the rodeo bulls, trucked in by stock contractors like the Champion family, waited to be herded through the maze of chutes, rigged with a flank strap and bull rope, mounted, and set loose to buck.

Until the instant a rider's weight settled onto their backs, most of the animals were calm. They were bred and raised to do one job—buck that annoying cowboy off into the dust. They knew what to expect and what to do. But at up to a ton in weight, with the agility of star athletes, they were amazingly powerful, incredibly dangerous. And in the arena, at any adrenaline-charged moment, the most amiable bull could turn murderous.

Nobody knew that better than Lexie.

Her thoughts flew back to the cryptic note she'd found tucked beneath the truck's windshield when she'd driven into Ajo for groceries last week. Written in crude block letters on a page torn from a yellow pad, it had been there when she'd come out of the store. Its simple message had sent a chill up her spine.

YOUR FAMILY OWES ME. IT'S PAYBACK TIME.

Even the memory made her shiver. Had the message been a prank? Her first impulse had been to scan the parking lot for someone who might have left it. But she'd seen no one, not even a familiar vehicle. Impulsively, she'd crumpled the page and tossed it into a trash receptacle. If anybody was watching, she wanted them to know she wasn't scared.

Later, after realizing she'd destroyed evidence, Lexie had regretted the act. But nothing could erase the image of that message from her mind—the letters pressed hard into the yellow paper, as if in pure hatred. Why did this person think her family owed him—or her? And what did they mean by *payback*?

She'd told no one yet. Not Tess or their stepmother, Callie; not even Ruben. Why cause worry over what was bound to be an empty threat? But she wasn't about to leave her bulls if there was any chance someone might harm them.

"Well, lookee here! Howdy, honey!" The slurring voice made Lexie jump. The cowhand who'd crept up behind her was dirty, unshaven, and, as her late father would've said, as big as a barn door. His clothes and breath reeked of cheap whiskey.

"You're a purty little thing with that long yellow hair." He loomed over her. "I was thinkin' maybe you're one o' them buckle bunnies. I got a buckle right here if you want to see it." His dirty hand tugged at the ordinary Western-style belt buckle and unfastened it. "You'll like what I got underneath it even better."

Until now, Lexie had merely been annoyed. She'd dealt with drunks at other rodeos. But now a cold fear crept over her. She was alone out here, where nobody could hear her scream over the sounds of the rodeo. The man had her backed against the fence, and he was big enough to easily overpower her. There was a pistol under the front seat of the truck, but it was parked in the lot reserved for rigs, too far away to be of any use.

She glared up at the big man, trying not to show fear. "I'm not a buckle bunny," she said. "And you're drunk. I don't like drunks. Neither does my boyfriend. If you're smart, you'll leave before he gets back here."

The boyfriend part was a lie, but it was the only defense she had. Unfortunately, the way the man's yellow-toothed grin widened told her it wasn't enough. She'd told Ruben to take his time getting back; but even if he were to show up now, the 150-pound foreman was pushing sixty. Without a weapon, he'd be no match for the hulking brute, and there was no one else in sight. Lexie was on her own.

Crouching against the steel fence, she prepared to defend herself. The big man was staggering drunk and appeared slow. A strike in a vital spot—his groin or his eyes—might disable him long enough for her to get away.

"C'mon, honey. You'll like it once we git started." He lunged for her, the move fast but awkward. Lexie had been poised to spring at him, boots kicking, fingers clawing, but her instincts took over. She dodged to one side as he lurched forward, stumbled over his own feet and crashed full force into the tubular steel rails of the fence. Stunned, he grunted and staggered backward, blood flowing from his nose. His legs folded beneath him as he collapsed in the dust.

As the man curled onto his side, moaning and cradling his bloodied nose, Lexie whipped out her cell phone. She didn't have the number for fairground security, but a 9-1-1 call should get some kind of help.

She was about to punch in the number when, from a short distance behind her, came the sound of . . . *clapping*.

Startled, she turned to see the rangy figure of a man striding toward her from around the far end of the fence. Moving fast, he came within speaking distance. "That was some show. Remind me never to tangle with Miss Lexie Champion."

It startled her again, hearing her name. But she wasn't about to lower her guard. "I could've used some help," she said, glaring up at him. He was a shade under six feet tall, compactly muscled, and dressed in weathered cowboy clothes. The only distinguishing feature of his outfit was the silver PBR prize buckle that fastened his belt. The man was a bull rider, evidently a good one, and he looked the part.

His grin widened. "If I'd shown up thirty seconds sooner, I'd have decked the bastard for you. But by the time I saw you, there was no need. I couldn't have done a better job myself." He swept off his battered Resistol hat and extended a hand. "Shane Tully. I took a chance on finding you here. It looks like I arrived just in time. If that jerk hadn't fallen against the fence, you'd have needed some help."

Lexie accepted the confident handshake. His palm was cool against her own, the skin as tough as boot leather. *Shane Tully*. The name rang a bell in her memory, albeit a faint one. He was a regular on the PBR circuit, his rank just moving into the top twenty. This year he was a serious contender for the finals in Las Vegas.

The man on the ground moaned and stirred. "Broke my friggin' nose," he muttered. "Need help . . ."

"Let's get you on your feet, pal." Handing Lexie his hat, Tully crouched behind him and worked his hands under the big man's arms. Some pushing and lifting got the drunk upright. Tully took a clean white handkerchief out of his pocket and laid it on the man's bleeding nose. "Keep it," he said. "This'll teach you not to make unwelcome advances to ladies. There's a first-aid station on the midway, by the Ferris wheel. Can you make it that far on your own, or should we call security?"

The man swore under his breath and shuffled off, one hand clutching the handkerchief to his nose. Lexie kept her eyes on him until he'd gained a safe distance. Only then did she turn to face the bull rider.

She knew he probably wasn't here to compete. This rodeo was sanctioned by the Professional Rodeo Cowboys Association, or PRCA. The cowboys coming here would compete in bronc riding, calf roping, and other events including bull riding. In 1992, the leading bull riders had broken away from the PRCA and formed their own elite organization, the Professional Bull Riders, or PBR. Only the best could compete in their hugely popular events around the country. Membership, for both riders and bucking bulls, was by invitation.

Which might have something to do with the reason Shane Tully had come to find her.

"You still haven't told me what you're doing here, Mr. Tully," she said, handing him the hat.

"It's Shane, and I can't say you've given me much of a chance."

He smiled with his mouth. His features struck Lexie as more rugged than handsome—deep-set brown eyes, a long jaw ending in a square chin, and a scar, like a thin slash with two stitch marks, running down his left cheek.

He had the look of a man who'd been through some rough times, but Lexie guessed that he wasn't much older than twenty-five or twenty-six. With a few notable exceptions, bull riding was a young man's sport. Older bodies couldn't take the punishment.

"I'm giving you a chance to tell me now." She folded her arms, waiting.

His gaze flickered past her, into the holding pen where the four bulls milled like star athletes loosening up for the big game. Then his eyes, warmer now with flecks of copper, met hers again. "I was in the neighborhood," he said, "and I thought I'd stop by and check out your bull, see how he bucks—maybe give myself an edge if I happen to draw him later."

Lexie didn't have to ask which bull he was talking about. That would be Whirlwind, the rankest bull the Alamo Canyon Ranch had ever produced—the bull that, after twenty-three times out of the chute, had yet to be ridden to the eight-second whistle—the bull that had just been selected to join the PBR circuit.

"So let's see you pick him out of the lineup."

Lexie Champion challenged Shane with her words, her voice, and her no-nonsense expression. She was pretty without being a glamour girl—lean and tanned, with cornflower eyes and sun-streaked blond hair, swept back into a single braid. Shane liked her looks, and he enjoyed a challenge. It might be interesting to see how far around the bases he could get with her. But one thing at a time. Right now, he was here to check out a bull for his boss and, if the animal looked good, to pass on an offer.

He'd done his homework, but he stalled on purpose, taking his time as he studied the four bulls in the sawdust-floored holding pen. They were fine animals—descended, like all rodeo bulls, from Brahma and longhorn crosses, to produce a distinct breed—the American Bucking Bull—with massive bodies and the typical hump above the shoulders. Matching yellow I.D. tags hung from their ears. Their horns had been blunted at the ends to lessen any injury to the rider. But Shane knew firsthand how much damage even blunted horns could do.

One of the bulls was speckled white, one a deeper color, almost silver, with mottling around the neck and shoulders. One was a dark brindle, and one coal black except for a white streak down his face. For a dozen years, the Champion family had been breeding PRCA rodeo bulls. Their stock carried the bloodline of Oscar, the great bucking bull of the 1970s who'd passed on his traits to his many descendants.

When it came to bucking bulls, bloodline was every-thing—that's what Brock Tolman, Shane's boss and mentor, always said. That truth hit home as Shane studied the four superb animals. They were well-proportioned and in prime condition. But only one of them had that extra edge, the spark to kindle the fire of greatness.

Even if he hadn't seen the photographs, Shane could have picked Whirlwind from out of a hundred bulls. But he was playing a game with the uppity Miss Lexie Champion—and he was enjoying it.

"Well?" she demanded. "Can you point him out?"

"Care to make a wager?" he asked.

Her eyes narrowed. Clearly, she wasn't ready to trust him. "What kind of wager?"

"How about this? There's going to be a dirt dance in the arena after the rodeo tonight. If I guess right the first time, you'll promise to go with me."

"And if you don't?"

"That's up to you. I could buy you dinner."

"Forget it. Either way, I'll be too tired to dance or eat. And I'll be busy after the rodeo, loading the bulls for the drive home."

"Then I'll make it easy for you. If I can pick Whirlwind on the first guess, you'll give me twenty minutes of your time—just to talk to you."

"And if you lose?"

"Whatever you want. Your call."

"Fine. If you guess wrong, you can shovel out the trailer before we load the bulls for the drive home."

Shane laughed. "You drive a hard bargain, lady."

A smile dimpled her cheek. "You said it was my call. So knock yourself out."

Shane made a show of studying the bulls, taking his time. "That black one's a standout. He's massive. Plenty of power. With that white blaze down his face, he reminds me of Chicken on a Chain. Ever see that monster bull buck? He was meaner than hell, both in and out of the arena."

"Only on TV, a few years ago. He was a powerhouse. So do you think the black one is Whirlwind?"

"Nope." Shane kept looking. "And the brindle—he's sharp. Great conformation. But no, it's not him either."

That left the white and gray bulls, their patterns similar, as if their hides had been randomly spattered with black paint. The larger, whiter, one—with a bit of fat on him—was chewing cud, swishing at a fly with his tail. The gray bull, slightly smaller but just as powerful, was alert and restless, ears pricking toward the sounds in the arena, legs shifting, dancing, almost catlike in their precision. His body, a mass of muscle as thick and solid as a tree trunk, strained against the gate, as if he couldn't wait to get out there and buck.

"Hello, Whirlwind," Shane said, grinning as he pointed. "I can hardly wait to ride you." *And not just you,* Shane thought, then gave himself a mental slap. He was out of line, even if it was only in his mind.

"The clock is running on your twenty minutes," Lexie said. "So get talking."

Shane took a deep breath, feeling awkward as hell. "First of all, I wanted to tell you how sorry I am about your brother. I knew Jack—not well, but everybody was his friend. He was the best kind of cowboy and the best kind of man."

Did the words sound rehearsed? They were, in the sense that he'd put some thought into them. He'd been in the stands at last year's National Finals Rodeo when all-around cowboy Jack Champion had been stomped and killed after tumbling off an 1,800-pound bucking bull. He knew she'd been there, too, watching with her father and sister when it happened. There were no words for what they must have felt that night—or for what she must be feeling right now.

* * *

"Yes, Jack was the best," Lexie murmured, struggling against the pain that was still raw after more than six months. Shane Tully sounded sincere enough, but he couldn't even imagine what Jack's death had cost the family. Jack had been their golden hope, their future, the one who would take his father's place and guide the ranch to new prosperity.

And, of course, they had all loved him.

"Is your family doing all right?" he asked.

"We're muddling along," Lexie said. "Jack's death made national news, but you may not have heard that our father passed away this spring."

"Lord, no. I'm sorry." His surprise sounded genuine.

"It was cancer. He'd been sick for a long time." Lexie had learned to sound detached when she talked about it, as if the linked tragedies had happened to people in a movie or characters in a book. "But Jack's death was the final blow. After that, it was as if he'd lost the will to live."

"Again, I'm sorry. I wish I had better words to tell you. But know that I mean it." He paused to watch the bulls for a moment. "So who's running the ranch now?"

"My sister Tess and I, along with Dad's second wife, who manages things in the house. Ruben, our foreman, is a lot of help, too. Things aren't easy, but we're doing all right. We grew up working on the ranch. Tess chose to stay there and help Dad. I was on my way to a college degree in ranch management and animal husbandry before I quit to come home and help. Cash is in short supply, but we're hoping that if Whirlwind can bring in some serious prize money—"

She broke off, stopping the heedless flood of words. What was she doing—letting down her guard to a charming stranger who was asking too many questions? Bad idea.

Even if he was just being sympathetic, her family problems were nobody's business.

"Why am I telling you all this?" she said. "I barely know you. And I thought our deal involved *you* talking to *me*. Maybe you should start by telling me what you're really doing here."

He gave her an easy smile. One front tooth was slightly crooked. The small imperfection lent his features a roguish look. Lexie willed herself to ignore the flip-flopping sensation in her chest. He was too smooth. Too confident.

"As I told you, I came to check out Whirlwind," he said. "I'll be watching him later this evening, but maybe you can tell me what to look for. How does he buck?"

"Why should I tell you anything? The more cowboys he can buck off—cowboys like you—the better his stats will be. If you're in the stands when he comes out of that chute, you'll see for yourself. I will tell you one thing. Whirlwind is just five years old. He's only been on the PRCA circuit a year. But he's not just strong. He's as smart as a fox. He knows tricks that most buckers take half a lifetime to learn, if they ever do. Remember that if you ever climb on his back."

She glanced at her watch, vaguely uneasy. Shane Tully had made it his mission to find her. But he had yet to tell her what he really wanted.

"Your time's almost up," she said. "If you've got anything else to say, you'd better say it fast."

He nodded, his mouth compressed into a thin line. "Just one question," he said. "Have you ever thought of selling Whirlwind? I'm in touch with an interested buyer. He says you can name your price."

"What?" Lexie's jaw dropped. Then the outrage boiled up in her, hot and seething. He'd played her, right into his hands. She battled the urge to punch the man hard enough to break bones in his smug, handsome face.

"Just listen," he said. "You've told me your ranch is struggling. What you could get for this bull would solve a lot of your problems. Think about it, at least. Talk it over with your sister." He fished a business card out of his pocket and thrust it toward her. "Here's how you can reach me."

Lexie snatched the card from his hand, ripped it, tossed it down, and stomped it into the dust. "I don't need to think about it!" she snapped. "And I certainly don't need to talk it over with Tess. Whirlwind is family! He's our hope for the future."

She gasped, almost choking, as a sudden thought struck her. "Who sent you?" she demanded. "Who's making the offer? If it's that snake in the grass, Brock Tolman, you can tell him that Whirlwind isn't for sale. Not now, not ever, and not for any price, especially to him. I wouldn't sell that man a mangy, three-legged dog!"

Lexie waited for a response to her question. When it didn't come, she knew she'd been right. Rancher and stock contractor Brock Tolman had been a thorn in the side of the Champion family for years—ever since he'd snatched away a piece of valuable land from Lexie's father, who'd been negotiating a bank loan to buy it. Brock Tolman might have his cash, his big ranch, and his herd of prime bucking bulls, but there was one thing he would never get his hands on: Whirlwind.

And now he had this slick-talking cowboy doing his dirty work.

She gave him a cold look. "Your time's up, mister. But let me give you some friendly advice. Working for Tolman is like selling your soul. He'll take everything from you and kick you out when he's done."

"I'll keep that in mind." Shane Tully's voice was flat, his expression unreadable.

"You do that," Lexie said. "Now get going. I don't ever want to see you around our bulls again."

He turned away, walked a few steps, then paused and glanced back over his shoulder. "Thank you for your time," he said with a tip of his hat. Then, lengthening his loose, easy stride, he moved off down the line of holding pens.

The next time Lexie looked in that direction, Shane Tully was gone. At least he'd been polite, she told herself—in fact his manner had been downright winning. And he did have nice eyes. When he smiled, they almost sparkled.

But he'd taken advantage of her trusting nature, and she'd let him. When would she ever learn?

Ruben showed up a few minutes later. Short and square built, with the black eyes and sharp-boned features of his people, he'd been a bull rider himself in his youth, when the sport was far less glamourous than now. He still limped from injuries he'd suffered—broken bones badly set. But nobody knew more about cattle, especially bucking bulls, than Ruben Diego.

"I brought you some barbecue and fries." He held out a grease-stained paper bag and a can of diet soda.

"Thanks." Lexie still wasn't hungry, but she knew better than to reject a kindness. She reached for the food, then had another thought. "If you don't mind holding on to it a little longer, I could use a restroom before I eat. There's one on the midway. I'll be right back."

Without waiting for a reply, she dashed off. The midway wasn't far, and, as luck would have it, there was no line inside the women's restroom. Lexie finished in the stall, washed her hands, and splashed her dusty face with water.

Drying her hands on her jeans, she stepped outside, then

stopped as if she'd run into a wall. Her pulse slammed. Not a dozen feet away, half-screened by the passing crowd, she saw Shane, talking face-to-face with the drunk who'd tried to assault her.

Had they seen her? Thinking fast, she ducked around the corner of the building that housed the restrooms. Peering back the way she'd come, she could see the two men and catch most of their conversation.

As Lexie watched, Shane took several bills out of his wallet and handed them to the big man, who sported a fresh dressing on his nose.

"Count it if you want," Shane said. "It's all there, what we agreed on."

"Well, it's not enough," the big man whined. "Breaking my damned nose wasn't part of the plan. You were supposed to rescue the little bitch before I made a move."

Shaking his head, Shane handed the man two more bills. "That should cover the damages. Now go and get lost. You never saw me, understand?"

As the two men separated and melted into the crowd, Lexie sagged against the brick wall. Her heart was pounding. Tears of fury blurred her vision. The drunk, Shane's all-too-timely appearance, and their "friendly" conversation were all part of someone's plan. She'd been set up and played like a twelve-string banjo—and she hated it.

But Lexie wasn't just annoyed. She was puzzled, and a little scared. Last week she'd found a threatening note on her windshield. Today a charming cowboy had gone to a lot of trouble to win her confidence and pump her for information.

Was there a connection? Was someone trying to scare her, or was the danger real?

CHAPTER TWO

SHANE WANDERED DOWN THE MIDWAY, KILLING TIME AND feeling lower than a snake's belly. He'd done exactly what Brock wanted him to. Even though the staged rescue hadn't gone as planned, he'd managed to break the ice with Lexie. He'd gotten a close look at Whirlwind and learned about conditions at her ranch. He'd even let her know that he had a buyer for the bull if her family was interested. After that, with her discovery that he was working for Brock, things had fallen apart fast. He'd be surprised if the woman ever spoke to him again.

Brock couldn't fault him for effort. But right now, Shane didn't like himself much. Lexie Champion wasn't just pretty. She was honest, passionate, and smart. And he'd played her in a way that was downright insulting.

He glanced at the time on his cell phone, scrolled to Brock's number and prepared to give his boss an accounting.

Brock picked up on the second ring. "So how did it go?" His deep, throaty voice would have done credit to a *Star Wars* villain.

"Not as good as we'd hoped," Shane said. "The bull

looks world-class. I'll know more when I've seen him buck. But she's not interested in selling."

"That's no surprise. Anything else I should know?"

Shane took a breath, knowing Brock wouldn't be pleased with the next bit of news. "Just this. She guessed that I was fronting for you. And she wants you to know that she wouldn't sell you a mangy, three-legged dog."

The connection went silent for an instant. Then Brock's laughter boomed through the phone. "Those Champions have always had it in for me. The old man would've spat in my eye if he'd dared. And he's passed his venom down to his daughters. But I'm not giving up, and neither should you. One way or another, we're going to get our hands on that bull."

After the call ended, Shane wandered aimlessly along the crowded midway, past the booths selling barbecue, hot dogs, cotton candy, funnel cakes, and fried ice cream, past the souvenir stands, and the carnival rides. From the arena beyond the gate, he could hear the rodeo—the cheers of the crowd and the blare of the announcer's voice. He already had his ticket, a pricey first-row spot where he could get a good look at the bulls. But the drama of the past half hour and the phone call to Brock had left him on edge. He needed time to unwind before taking his seat.

At least Brock had taken Lexie's refusal in stride. Even after ten years on the Tolman Ranch, Shane couldn't predict how the boss would react. Brock could be kind and generous—as he'd been when he'd taken in a scrawny, homeless teenager, put him to work, and, when Shane had shown the drive and the talent, given him the chance to ride bulls. Everything Shane had and was, he owed to Brock Tolman; and he'd repaid the man the only way he could—with his loyalty.

18 *Janet Dailey*

But Brock could also be cold and ruthless, especially when it was the only way to get what he wanted. A lifetime aficionado of bull riding, Brock had retired on his investments almost a dozen years ago with enough money to stock his ranch with the quality bucking bulls he bought, bred, and delivered by the trailer load to big rodeo events.

But there was one thing Brock had never possessed—a bull with true star power, a bull with the heart and fight to stand beside champions like Blueberry Wine, Little Yellow Jacket, Bushwacker, and Bodacious.

Did Whirlwind have that kind of potential?

That's what Shane was here to find out.

Forty-five minutes later, with the sunset fading behind him and a cold beer in his belly, Shane presented his ticket at the gate, picked up a printed program, and made his way to the front row. The lights had come on above the arena, glaring bright against the deepening sky. Dust motes glittered like specks of gold in the air. Insects swarmed and fluttered overhead. The day had been hot enough to melt asphalt, but with the sun gone, the air was pleasantly cool.

The barrel racing event was just winding down, the barrels being cleared away and the winners receiving their trophies. Bull riding would be next. Shane's seat gave him a good view of the chutes at the end of the arena. The first two bulls of the ten that would buck tonight were being moved into place behind the gates.

A glance at the program confirmed that neither of the starters would be Whirlwind. He was scheduled last, which made sense. The fact that he'd been unridden in twenty-three consecutive outs had already gained him some celebrity. No one would be leaving the stands early.

Shane scanned the list of riders. He recognized about half the names from his own days in the PRCA. The others were new, probably young hopefuls.

The safety crew had entered the arena—a mounted roper and three men known as bullfighters. Dressed in loose-fitting athletic gear to cover their protective vests, the bullfighters were the unsung heroes of the sport. It was their job to distract the bull and help the downed rider get away. In the old days, this dangerous work had been done by clowns. Clown makeup was still an option, but the bullfighters were serious athletes as well as trained paramedics. Countless riders owed their lives to these men.

A hush fell over the crowd as the loudspeaker introduced the next event. Shane took a small but powerful pair of binoculars from his pocket and trained them on the bucking chutes. Behind the first gate he recognized the black bull that Lexie had brought to the rodeo. And there was Lexie on the fence, all in blue, keeping out of the way as the rider, wearing fringed chaps, a helmet with a face mask, a protective vest, and a glove on his left hand, straddled the chute, lowered himself onto the bull's back and waited for help pulling the rope tight.

Shane was here to watch bulls, he reminded himself. Still, for a moment, he kept the binoculars focused on Lexie, admiring her unconscious grace as she waited in tense anticipation for the gate to open. He wouldn't mind getting to know her better. But after today's encounter, he'd be lucky to get within a dozen yards of the woman.

Pulling his attention back to the event, Shane checked the program again. The rider was a friend—an experienced cowboy and a good man, with a wife and new baby to support. As the announcer's voice boomed out the rider's name and the name of the bull, he silently wished them both a good ride and a high score.

"Out of chute number one, ladies and gentlemen, we have Cory Jarman on Renegade!"

The gate swung open. The black bull exploded into the arena. As he leaped, kicked, and spun, putting on a spectacular show, the rider gripped the handhold on the rope. His right arm remained high and free, pumping with the bull's motion. His blunted spurs dug into the bull's loose hide. *Good job, Cory*, Shane thought as the eight-second whistle sounded. The combined score for bull and rider should be well into the eighties.

Then something went wrong. With Renegade still bucking wildly, Cory slid off the left side, twisting his gloved hand in the bull rope. Caught fast, he was dragged along by one arm against a spinning, jumping monster determined to shake him loose.

The bullfighters had leaped into action. Two of them sprang in front of the bull, trying to distract him and slow him down while the third man moved in close to support Cory and try to work his hand free.

In a scene that Shane would remember as a slow-motion nightmare, a sudden twisting move by the bull ripped the glove off Cory's hand. Before the bullfighter could yank him to safety, Cory's legs gave way. He slid under the pounding hooves. Each second it took for the bullfighters to drive Renegade off the rider and out the exit chute seemed to pass like an eternity. When the gate closed behind the black bull, Cory lay crumpled in the dust, barely moving as the paramedics rushed out to stabilize him, ease him onto a transport board, and carry him out of the arena. Moments later, the wail of an ambulance siren confirmed that he was seriously hurt.

Damn! Rotten luck. He could be out for the season. And with a young family to support.

Even with the improvements in safety gear, injuries were a given in this dangerous sport. Veteran bull riders wore scars like medals and carried memories of the bones they'd broken—limbs, ribs, backs, and shoulders. Shane had known riders to wrap fractured bones with duct tape so they could stay in competition, enduring awful pain for the sake of that eight-second ride and the chance for prize money.

The show would go on. The next bull was already in the chute, waiting to buck. But Shane couldn't help worrying about his friend. And he couldn't help thinking about Lexie and how she'd watched her brother die in the arena less than a year ago. The wreck that she'd just witnessed had probably brought it all back. That she was here now, with her family's bulls, showed what a tough woman she was.

He trained his binoculars on her, sharpening the focus. She was still on the fence, her spine rigid, her mouth set in a firm line, as if she were fighting tears. She wasn't going anywhere.

Shane watched the next eight bulls, including the brindle and the white, spotted animal that Lexie had brought to the competition. The Alamo Canyon bulls were the best of the lot, showing their Oscar-linked bloodline mixed with the feisty heritage of the British White Park cattle, removed to America during World War II for safekeeping.

Unfortunately, both bulls bucked off their young riders out of the gate. If Whirlwind did the same, there'd be only the briefest chance for Shane to see how he performed.

Whirlwind would be next. The rider's name rang a bell, though Shane didn't know him. Jay Walking Bird had a decent record in the PRCA. He had a chance to do what

Shane wanted—stay on the bull long enough to put on a good show.

Even without the binoculars, Shane had no trouble seeing the bull in the chute. Still riderless, he was slamming sideways against the gate, shaking his blunted horns.

Rank. That was the word for a bull with a lot of fight in him. And *rank* was the word for Whirlwind.

Jay Walking Bird lowered himself onto the bull's back, bracing himself while a man outside the chute pulled his rope to tighten it around the bull's body. This was a dangerous time. A bull could slam a rider's leg against the inside of the chute, hard enough to break bone. Shane knew this because it had happened to him last year. He'd ridden the beast anyway, in terrible pain, and racked up a score of 88.6, his best ever. The men used a long wooden wedge against the side of the chute to hold the bull steady while the rider made the final adjustments in the rope and gripped the handhold.

At Walking Bird's nod, the gate swung open. Whirlwind blasted out. *Dynamite on four legs* was the description that struck Shane's mind. He could see how the bull had gotten his name.

Shane tended to lump bucking bulls into three categories—leapers, kickers, and spinners. Whirlwind combined high kicks and leaps with a blinding spin that churned up dust clouds around him.

Bushwacker . . . Cochise, maybe . . . even Bodacious. Shane searched his memory for bulls with that kind of power. Whirlwind was smaller than those monsters, maybe 1,700 pounds. But he owned that arena.

His hindquarters kicked so high that his body was almost vertical. Still, Walking Bird hung on, gripping the rope with his right hand. Three seconds . . . four seconds. The bull came down spinning to the left like a tornado as he kept on bucking. Five seconds . . . Six . . . Abruptly, to Shane's amazement, Whirlwind made a subtle shift of direction. Walking Bird, who'd been leaning away from his hand, had no time to adjust. Pulled into the spin, he went flying off the right side, just short of the eight-second whistle. Only the quick action of a bullfighter, throwing himself almost onto the bull's horns, saved the rider from being trampled. Tossed into the air, the bullfighter landed hard and came up limping. By then, Walking Bird had scrambled up the fence, and Whirlwind was roped and headed out the gate.

Good show. Shane glanced up at the posted score. Forty-five points for the bull, zero for the rider. Cory's high score had given him first place.

And knowing about Whirlwind's spin-and-switch trick would come in handy for Shane if he happened to draw the bull in PBR competition.

Lexie was gone from the fence. Shane knew better than to look for her. He'd only be wasting his time. There was no way she'd want to talk to him.

He would call Brock later with a report on Whirlwind's performance. But first he wanted to drive to the hospital, find out how Cory was doing, and let him know that he'd won the event—and the needed prize money.

Without waiting for the awards, he left his seat, made his way out of the arena, and headed for his truck.

The four bulls had been returned to the holding pen behind the rodeo arena. As usual, they were given time to eat and settle down before being loaded for the drive back to the ranch.

"If you don't mind keeping an eye on them, I'd like to

take the truck and go to the hospital," Lexie told Ruben. "Cory and his wife are friends from school. I don't want to leave town without checking on him."

"No problem. I'll get some rest. We can load when you get back. I'll help you unhitch the trailer."

Leaving the foreman dozing in a lounge chair by the trailer, Lexie exited the fairgrounds and followed the signs that marked the way to the hospital. Her hands gripped the steering wheel as she battled the emotions she'd held in check since Cory Jarman's injury. The wreck—as such incidents were called—had happened right in front of her. As Renegade's hooves had trampled the young rider, the indelible memory of her brother's death had crushed her with fresh weight. She'd strangled the scream in her throat, willing herself to remain in place, rigid and stoic, showing no emotion. That was a rule of the sport—no matter what was happening in the arena—or inside your head—you cowboyed up and put on a brave face.

It shouldn't trouble her that Cory had been hurt by one of her bulls. Riders assumed the risk, and bulls were praised for following their nature. Bodacious, one of the rankest buckers of all, had injured so many riders, mostly by bucking them over his head, that he was retired early and had since been awarded the greatest recognition for a bull—the PBR Brand of Honor.

Still, she couldn't help feeling guilt for the elements of fate that had brought Cory and Renegade together for a ride that had ended in disaster.

She shrugged off her misgivings as she pulled into the hospital parking lot and found a space for the truck. She wasn't here to rail at fate or cast blame. She was here to offer comfort and support.

Cory and his wife, Rianne, had been Lexie's friends and

classmates all the way through school. Even in kindergarten, she couldn't remember a time when they hadn't loved each other. They'd married young, had hard times with money and with their efforts to have a family. But with the birth of their baby boy, Rowdy, and the upswing in Cory's rodeo career, things were finally looking good for them.

Now this.

At the reception desk, Lexie got directions to Cory's room. "Don't plan to stay long," she was told at the nurses' station. "He's on some heavy pain medication. He needs to stay quiet."

Something in the nurse's tone deepened Lexie's fears. She braced herself for the worst as she checked each room number she passed in the long hallway. She'd gone less than halfway when, at the far end, she saw a familiar figure step out of a room and close the door softly behind her—a petite woman with short, strawberry blond hair. It was Rianne.

They recognized each other at the same time. Rianne hurried toward Lexie, distress showing in her expression as she came closer. Stumbling slightly, she flung herself into Lexie's arms. Lexie could feel her trembling.

"I'm so sorry, Rianne," she murmured. "Is there anything I can do?"

Rianne shook her head. "I'm just glad you're here. Cory's with a friend right now, so I'm having a break, trying to take all this in. Come on down to the waiting area. We can talk there."

Outside the elevators was a small space with a couch and chairs, vending machines, and a rack of well-worn magazines.

"Where's Rowdy?" Lexie asked as they settled on the sofa. Her friend was dry-eyed, but the strain of holding back tears showed in her face.

"My mom's got him. She took him so I could come with Cory, and we could have a little vacation after his ride." She shook her head. "That's how I happened to be here. Did you see it, Lexie?"

"I was right there, next to the chutes. It was my bull."

"Oh, God. First Jack and now this." Rianne fumbled for Lexie's hand. Lexie reached out and clasped the tension-knotted fingers.

"How bad is it?" she asked, trying to sound positive. "Cory's a tough guy. He's been hurt before and bounced right back."

Rianne shook her head. "His vest and helmet saved his life. But he's got three crushed vertebrae in his lower back." She took a deep, sucking breath, like a drowning person coming up for air. "He . . . can't move his legs."

Cory lay on his back with his head resting on a pillow. The blanket that covered his body concealed a rigid form beneath, like a brace. An IV drip was attached to one hand. A catheter bag hung by a clip on the side of the mattress.

Seated in a folding chair beside the bed, Shane knew better than to look too closely or ask the wrong questions. "That was a pretty good pounding you took tonight," he said, making a deliberate understatement.

Cory grinned, drifting in and out of lucidity. The nurse had mentioned that he was on heavy painkillers. "That bull was a pretty rough customer. But it wasn't his fault. If I hadn't caught my hand . . ." His voice faded for the space of a long breath. "Don't worry," he said. "I've been beat up before. I'll be back on the circuit before you know it—even if I have to patch myself together with duct tape."

"Sure you will." Shane forced the words from his mouth

and the smile on his face, knowing that both were lies. He hadn't talked privately with Cory's wife, but he'd seen the stricken look on her face before she left them. Something was terribly wrong.

"Did anybody tell you that your ride won first place?" he asked, changing the subject. "Eighty-six point two. That's damn fine riding."

"Great bucking, too. That bull racked up a good score."

"Is there anything I can do while you're laid up?" Shane asked.

"Yeah . . ." Cory was beginning to drift again. "Could you make sure Rianne gets the check? Should be a nice one, and she'll need it for . . . the baby . . ."

"You bet. I'll see that she gets it tonight," Shane said, but he needn't have spoken. Cory's eyes had closed. His breathing deepened as he sank into an opioid-induced slumber. Shane rose from the chair and walked out of the room, closing the door behind him. He would go back to the rodeo grounds, pick up the check, and drop it off here, with Cory's wife. That done, he would head back to Tucson and the small guest house he occupied on the Tolman Ranch.

As he walked down the hall toward the elevator, he couldn't help wondering how Cory and his wife were going to manage. Unless they had a ranch or some other job, rodeo riders tended to live from check to check. Some basic insurance was included with PRCA membership, but it wouldn't cover everything. And with a new baby and an injured husband needing her, Rianne would have a difficult time working.

It wasn't his problem, Shane reminded himself. But he couldn't help worrying. No way did this young family deserve what had happened tonight. But that was the nature of rodeo. People got hurt. One bad wreck, and it could be him, lying broken and useless in a hospital bed somewhere. And he wouldn't expect any damned sympathy.

Rianne was close to the breaking point. Lexie sat on the couch with a supporting arm around her friend's shoulders, letting her talk out her fears.

"I've never had to be strong, Lexie. I've always assumed that Cory would take care of me and our kids. Now . . ." Her voice shook. "I love him, but what if I can't deal with this? What if I don't have what it takes?"

Lexie's arm tightened around the quivering shoulders. "You don't have to be strong all at once. All you have to do is get through one day at a time. You'll find that you're a lot tougher than you think."

Did her words carry any meaning, Lexie wondered, or were they just platitudes from books she'd read and movies she'd seen? Having lost her mother in childhood and her father and brother recently, she knew about coping with tragedy—but unlike Rianne, she hadn't been needed by anyone. It had been Tess, her sober, responsible sister, who'd taken the reins of the ranch and the stewardship of everything on it. And even that would be nothing like taking care of a helpless baby and a crippled husband.

Crippled. The ugly word sent a chill up her spine.

"What if he never recovers? What if he never walks again?" Sobs broke in Rianne's throat. "Rodeo is all he knows. It's his life!"

"You and Rowdy are his life," Lexie said. "And you don't know that he won't walk. You told me yourself that the doctors will be doing an MRI as soon as he's stable. Maybe they'll find something that—"

"No." Rianne set her jaw in a determined thrust. "I'm not getting my hopes up. This is what it is, and the sooner I accept it—"

She broke off, suddenly seizing Lexie's arm. "Listen to me, Lexie. Men like Cory and your brother, Jack, they're addicted to the rush of this crazy sport. It's like a drug. They couldn't stop if they wanted to. There's always one more rodeo, one more bull, one more eight-second ride. It's too late for me, but not for you. Whatever you do, don't lose your head and marry one of them, or you could find yourself right where I am now."

Before Lexie could reply, a man walked out of the hallway, the overhead light casting his shadow across the floor. Lexie's gaze traveled upward from a pair of dusty boots and jeans-clad legs to a shiny, silver PBR buckle. Her heart dropped as she raised her head. Shane Tully was standing in front of her.

A startled look flashed across his face, but he swiftly masked it and turned his attention toward Rianne. "Cory went to sleep," he said. "He should be fine for a while if you need a break."

"No." Rianne stood. "If he wakes up, I don't want him to be alone. I'll go back."

Lexie stood as well. "I won't disturb him," she said. "Tell him I came by. You have my number. I'll check back with you. Meanwhile, call me if you need anything, Rianne—anything at all."

"Thanks for offering. I'll manage. If I can't, I guess I'll have to learn." Rianne turned to Shane. "Thank you for coming by. Forgive me for not introducing you to my friend. I'm too muddle-headed to remember your name."

"It's all right. Miss Champion and I have met," Shane said. "I promised Cory I'd bring you his prize check. I'll go and pick it up now." He glanced at Lexie, tilting one sooty eyebrow. "If you're leaving, Miss Champion, I'll walk you to the parking lot."

"Fine." Lexie had a few choice words to say to the man, but not here. She would wait for a better time and place.

Rianne had left them to go back to her husband. They stood side by side, waiting for the elevator to arrive.

"I didn't know you were friends with Cory and his wife," Shane said, breaking the awkward silence.

"The three of us were in the same class, all the way from kindergarten through high school. How do you know them?"

"I know Cory from the rodeo circuit. Her, I just met. Tough break. I hope he's not out for the season."

"You don't know? He didn't tell you?"

"Tell me what?" His eyebrows came together in a worried frown. "What's wrong with him?"

"According to Rianne, he can't feel his legs."

His throat moved. He muttered something under his breath—most likely a curse—as the elevator stopped and the doors slid open. An elderly man using a walker exited and made his way into the waiting area. Shane and Lexie made room for him to pass before stepping inside.

"They'll be doing an MRI." Lexie continued the conversation as the elevator door closed. "There's always a chance the doctors will find something they can fix, like a pinched nerve."

"Or not." His voice was flat with cynicism. Lexie knew he'd seen a lot of bad injuries. Well, so had she, and she wasn't ready to give up hope.

She was readying a reply when the elevator stopped, the

door opened on the hospital lobby, and he changed the subject.

"That bull of yours was pretty impressive tonight."

"Whirlwind is always impressive." Lexie kept her voice level, her expression neutral. But the memory of how Shane had tried to deceive her rekindled a blaze of anger. She held it in check while they were still in the building.

"For a second there, I thought Jay Walking Bird was going to last on him," he said.

"Walking Bird's a good rider. But you saw what happened."

"There'll be even better riders in the PBR. And better bulls."

"I know. But Whirlwind will learn. He'll get tougher and smarter."

The double doors opened automatically. He stayed by her side as they passed through, headed for the visitor parking lot.

"Lexie," he said, slowing his pace, "I hope you won't hold what happened today against me. I should've told you up front that I was working for Tolman."

"Then why didn't you?" She kept on walking. "Didn't Brock Tolman tell you how much my family hates him?"

"Not exactly. But I had a pretty good idea of how things stood."

She stopped and turned to face him. "So was it your idea or your boss's to have that drunk come on to me so you could rush to my rescue?"

"What?"

It was all Lexie could do to keep from slapping that innocent look off his face. "Don't play dumb with me. I saw you on the midway, paying the man off. You paid him extra for getting his nose busted. So whose idea was it?"

He hesitated, a faint smile playing around his mouth. Did he think this was funny?

"Do you have any idea how scared I was?" she demanded.

"He wouldn't have hurt you. He wasn't even drunk, just splashed with some cheap whiskey."

Lexie's simmering anger boiled over. "I didn't know that. I thought I was about to be raped, or maybe worse. I was getting ready to fight for my life when that brute stumbled into the fence."

He exhaled, shaking his head. "All right. It was a stupid idea that got out of hand. I just wanted to meet you and pass on my boss's offer to buy your bull. I figured if I'd come to your rescue, you'd be more inclined to listen."

"It was more than a stupid idea. It was a low-down, dirty trick."

"Agreed." His expression relaxed into a charming grin. "So now that we've got that out of the way, I'm hoping you'll let me buy you a beer and apologize."

The man had *cojones*. She had to give him that. But turning him down would be the greatest pleasure she'd had all day.

"My foreman's waiting for me," she said. "We've got four bulls to load and drive home. I need to go now. But even if I had time to spare, I wouldn't drink with you if you were the last man on earth!"

"Copy that." He laughed. "But this game isn't over. I'll be seeing you around, Miss Lexie Champion. You *and* that bull of yours."

Lexie pretended not to hear him as she strode away. But her cheeks were burning. Shane Tully's brassy self-confidence riled her. He was cocky and arrogant—everything she disliked in a man. But the attraction was there, like a deep, sensual tingling beneath her skin. That attraction made her feel weak and vulnerable when she wanted to be strong—like her sister Tess, who could handle any crisis and stand up to any man.

But never mind. The rodeo was over. She was going home. And if she encountered Shane again on the PBR circuit, all she had to do was ignore him. That would be easy enough—wouldn't it?

CHAPTER THREE

By the time the darkness paled above the desert hills, the journey was nearly over. Lexie was at the wheel now, with Ruben asleep in the back seat. Driving south along the two-lane ribbon of highway, she watched the morning light steal over the Sonoran Desert, casting the armies of tall saguaro into long shadows and turning the barbed spines of teddy bear cholla to glistening silver. Here and there, stands of ironwood, mesquite, and paloverde dotted the landscape with clumps of bright olive green.

The flowering season was at an end. The brilliant hues of blooming cactus, the golden riot of brittlebush, and the orange blaze of mallows and poppies had faded. Here and there, spikes of ocotillo still sported drooping red flags, but otherwise, the colors of the southwest Arizona desert had softened into muted shades of green and gray, with stretches of mountain—bare rocks looking like broken chunks of chocolate—jutting out of the landscape.

Lexie yawned and twisted the kinks out of her neck. She was tempted to stop and get out of the truck to stretch her cramped legs, but Ruben was sleeping soundly, and the ranch was less than an hour away—nestled in a grassy mountain meadowland between the boundaries of federal wilderness and the Tohono O'odham reservation.

The ranch had been in Lexie's family since her great-grandfather's generation. In the old days they'd run ten thousand head of Hereford cattle in the canyons, foothills, and open desert below, paying money to the Bureau of Land Management for grazing permits. But those prosperous times had passed as the government canceled the grazing leases and converted the desert to protected wilderness, leaving only privately owned ranchland for the Champions and other cattle-raising families.

With less than seven hundred acres available for grazing, it had been Lexie's father, Bert Champion, who'd come up with the idea of bucking stock. He'd used some of the cash from selling off his herd to buy a pair of retired bucking bulls, half brothers, with a pedigree going back to the great Oscar, and a dozen heifers from the White Park British line. Learning the business through trial and error, breeding the best animals, raising the calves, choosing the most promising two-year-old buckers, and training them for rodeo work had taken, literally, years. All the hard work, money, patience, and hope were just beginning to pay off. The tragedy was that Bert wouldn't be here to see it. And neither would his only son, Jack. Only Bert's daughters were left to carry on the legacy.

With the sun coming up behind her, Lexie took the hard-packed dirt road that cut off the highway to the left, toward the pass that overlooked the ranch. The spot was more than familiar. Every school day for years, she, her sisters, and her brother had waited there for the bus into Ajo. They'd waited again after school for someone from the ranch to pick them up. It was an easy drive in a pickup or SUV. But towing a long trailer, loaded with animals, up the narrow, winding road and down the other side was something else again.

She slowed the truck to a crawl over the washboard surface, mindful of the precious cargo behind her. A sudden bump or lurch could be enough to injure a bull's leg. There was another approach to the ranch, a graded road that cut across the reservation to the east, but since it added two hours to the time from Kingman, Lexie had chosen the more direct route.

"Want me to drive?" Ruben had awakened and was sitting up in back.

"No, I can make it home. It's not much farther."

"Fine." Ruben was a man of few words. He'd come to work for the Champions seventeen years ago, when Lexie was a little girl. Widowed now, he was an elder in his tribe. He had two married daughters living on the reservation, but his home, for years, had been a small converted trailer on the ranch. His needs were simple, his loyalties beyond question.

A roadrunner sprinted ahead of the truck and vanished behind a clump of prickly pear cactus. Dust as fine as face powder billowed from under the wheels of the rig, coating the windows. Heat waves shimmered above the horizon. Even the morning was hot. The rest of the day was bound to be a scorcher.

But with luck, the weather was about to change. In the southern sky, the first thready clouds were moving north from the Mexican highlands—a sign that the summer storms would soon begin.

"Monsoon." Ruben gazed out the dusty side window.

"Looks like it might be coming early. Good," Lexie agreed. The yearly monsoon season meant green grass in the pastures for the bulls and horses and the thirty head of beef cattle the ranch still raised. One less worry. But there was no shortage of other concerns.

As the road wound its way toward the pass, she struggled to push aside the issues she'd left behind in Kingman— Cory's terrible injury and his wife's worries; Brock Tolman's scheme to get his grasping hands on her prize bull; and the all-too-charming cowboy who worked for her enemy—the cowboy whose face and voice and laugh had claimed a permanent spot in her memory, whether she wanted him there or not.

Forget him, she told herself. *The man's already proven he can't be trusted. And you've already got enough on your plate!*

That plate was truly full. Her father's death had left the ranch with an almost weekly slate of summer rodeos under contract. Lexie had taken on the task of getting the bulls to the venues, with Ruben's help, leaving Tess to manage the ranch. The burden of responsibility was beginning to wear on both sisters, but especially on Tess, whose biggest worry was keeping the ranch solvent.

And then there was the menacing note she'd found on her windshield. Was it a joke, or was the ranch really under threat? What if she'd been wrong, keeping its disturbing contents to herself?

A raven, perched on a dead cholla stump, flapped away as the truck approached. Some of the locals believed ravens were bad luck. But Lexie, who was as local as anybody, had been to college and didn't hold with superstition.

Her hands gripped the steering wheel as she negotiated the last steep switchback. With a long breath of relief, she crested the pass and started the descent into the high valley, an oasis of rolling yellow grassland, fed by seasonal springs and deep wells.

Glancing down from the top of the narrow road, she could see the sprawling tile-roofed ranch house, with its enclosed patio and the large satellite dish on the roof. The house was framed by grassy pastures on the west and a complex of corrals, outbuildings, and a windmill on the east. Three properties shared the valley. The Alamo Canyon Ranch—named long ago for a place that was now federal land—was the largest. The much smaller ranch next door belonged to their neighbor, Aaron Frye, who also managed the third property. Owned by a Phoenix investment company, it was used for growing hay.

Only now, with home in sight, did Lexie realize how tired and hungry she was. All she wanted to do was sit down to a plate of Callie's scrambled eggs, hash browns, and bacon with black beans, scrub down in the shower, and crawl into bed for a few hours of blessed sleep.

But that wasn't going to happen. The bulls would have to be unloaded, watered, and fed their ration of high-protein Total Bull feed. Then Tess would want to brief her on everything that had happened at the ranch while she was gone. And Lexie could also expect to be grilled about the trip to the rodeo in Kingman. Maybe this would also be a good time to tell her sister about the threatening message. Sleep would have to wait.

"Something's wrong." Ruben's voice startled her out of her musings.

"What? Where?"

"Down there. Outside."

Lexie might have looked, but she was negotiating the last switch-back turn on the road down to the ranch. "What do you see?" she asked.

"People in the yard. Nobody working."

Lexie felt her stomach clench. Was it more bad news for

the family? Maybe something had happened to Val, her middle sister. Val had left home at seventeen and never been back to the ranch, not even for funerals. She'd sent a lavish floral piece for Jack's service, nothing for her father's.

Or maybe something had happened to Tess, or to Callie.

"Can you see who's there?" she asked Ruben.

He paused a moment to study the scene below. "Your sister and Callie. And those two boys you hired. Both the dogs. And Mr. Frye's truck just drove in."

All present or accounted for. So maybe it was Val after all. Wild, beautiful, laughing Val, who'd never wanted to stay on the ranch. Death tended to strike in threes—another old superstition Lexie refused to believe. But she'd known it to happen.

Sick with impending dread, she drove into the yard and pulled the trailer up to the loading chute. No matter what else was happening, the welfare of the bulls had to come first.

As Lexie climbed wearily out of the truck, Tess came striding toward her. Whip-lean and long-legged, she was nearing thirty, her loose-blowing dark hair already threaded with silver. Nine years ago, her fiancé had died in Afghanistan. It was as if part of her had died with him, leaving nothing behind but strength, toughness, and a sense of responsibility that had driven her like a lash after her father's death.

Pausing on her way to the truck, Tess barked an order at Chet and Ryder, the two hired boys. "Put some food out for those bulls and check their water. Then you can help Ruben unload and get to work cleaning the trailer."

The teens hurried to do as they'd been told. They were good kids, high school rodeo riders with PRCA dreams. For them, working on a bull ranch was a dream job, even if it involved a lot of manure shoveling. Next year, after they graduated, they'd be paying their dues and trying their luck on the circuit.

The two border collies, old dogs, lolling on the porch, got up and followed the boys to the corral. They knew where the action would be, and they still enjoyed being part of it.

Inside the trailer, the bulls were snorting, lowing, and pushing at the gates of their stalls. They recognized the smells and sounds of home, and they were impatient for the freedom of the pasture.

Tess beckoned to Lexie. "Come on. We can talk over breakfast. You, too, Ruben, as soon as the bulls are unloaded. We've got a problem on our hands."

Lexie fell into step beside her sister. "What's wrong? Did you get some bad news?"

"Not news. Just bad. A few of those two-year-old bulls in the upper pasture got out through an open gate in the night. We rounded up four of them by moonlight. But we lost one."

At least no more family members were dead, as Lexie had feared. But the loss of an animal was disaster enough. "Which one?" Lexie asked.

"The red one," Tess said. "The best one."

Lexie groaned, remembering the young bull that had shown so much spunk and promise the first time he was bucked in the corral with a weighted dummy on his back.

"He stumbled over the edge of that big dry arroyo." Tess's voice was emotionless, as if she'd chosen not to feel. "It looked like he broke at least one front leg and went down. Then the coyotes moved in."

"Oh, no . . ." Lexie shuddered, helpless to blot out the images that flooded her mind.

"At least the coyotes made enough noise to scare the other bulls. They stuck together and stayed away from the edge. Aaron heard the racket from his place and called me. I put the red bull out of its misery. Aaron and the boys helped me round up the rest."

Glancing into the blinding blue sky, Lexie saw vultures flocking above the arroyo. Without heavy equipment, there'd be no way to remove the bull's carcass or even to bury it in the arroyo's rocky bottom, and the meat would be too far gone to butcher. There was nothing to do but leave it for the scavengers. What an awful waste of a promising animal.

"The bull's gone. There's nothing to be done about that," Tess said. "But there's got to be an accounting for how that gate was left open."

"Could the bulls have pushed the gate and broken it?"

"It wasn't broken. It was unlocked, and that gate opens inward. It had to be open far enough for the bulls to get out. Either it was left that way, or somebody opened it."

"The boys?" Lexie spoke the first possibility that came to mind. The two teens were young, and boys would be boys. They could have been distracted enough to leave a gate open.

Tess shook her head. "It wasn't them. They haven't been near that pasture in the last couple of days. I've been here and had my eye on them the whole time."

"Even at night?" The boys slept in the bunkhouse. Sneaking out would be easy enough. What if they'd wanted to practice riding the two-year-old bulls? Teenage boys were crazy enough to try anything.

Tess shook her head. "They were dead to the world when I woke them to help round up the bulls. And they were in tears when they saw what had happened to the red one. I can't believe they had anything to do with opening that gate."

So who would do such a thing? Lexie couldn't answer that question. But she'd made a serious mistake, dismissing the note on the truck as a harmless prank. Maybe if she'd shared the warning and put the ranch on alert, last night's tragedy wouldn't have happened.

Right now, there was just one thing Lexie knew for certain. She needed to tell her ranch family everything she knew.

The ranch house had been designed and built after World War II by Lexie's great-grandfather, Winthrop Ashford. Times had been prosperous then, with the post-war economy booming and cattle by the thousands grazing the desert landscape—eating grass and shitting money as Winthrop had been fond of saying. Winthrop, who'd married late in life, had spared no expense in designing a home for his pretty young bride. The house was built in the Spanish style, pale stucco with a tile roof and an inner patio with an adjoining wing of bedrooms. Massive beams crossed the ceiling, with Mexican tiles on the floors and counters and stained glass in the windows. A cavernous fireplace took up one wall of the living room—a fireplace that was little used due to the hot climate and shortage of firewood.

Sadly, an elegant house couldn't make up for a life of isolation. After less than three years of marriage, Winthrop's wife had fled with her cowboy lover, leaving the old man with their son, a boy named Andrew. Andrew had married and fathered one child—a beautiful daughter named Isabel, who'd become Bert Champion's first wife and the mother of his children.

The bones of the old house were still beautiful, but the surfaces showed the ravages of time and benign neglect. The heavy dining room table where the family shared their meals was marred with a patina of nicks, burns, scratches, and stains. No one had bothered to replace the tablecloths that had worn out more than a generation ago. The dishes were chipped and mismatched. But the food was abundant, the company honest and caring. Wasn't that what counted?

Lexie washed her hands at the sink before pulling out her chair and sitting down in her usual spot. Bert's chair, at the head of the table, was empty. His absence was too keenly felt for anyone to sit in his place.

Tess sat across from Lexie. Next to her, their neighbor, Aaron Frye, who'd stuck around for breakfast, was already filling his plate with bacon, eggs, and potatoes.

"Now this is what I call a breakfast! An old loner like me doesn't get this kind of treat very often." He squirted ketchup onto his hash browns. A stocky man in late middle age, with thinning hair and a craggy face, sun-seared below the hat line, he'd lived a bachelor's existence for as long as Lexie could remember. If he'd ever had a wife, she'd died or left. The lonely mountain valley was hard on women, with the possible exception of the Champion sisters who'd grown up here.

And Callie.

Bert's second wife, now his widow, set a plate of fresh, hot biscuits on the table before slipping into the place closest to the kitchen. At fifty, she was still attractive. Her short, graying curls framed a face that was, like her ample figure, all womanly softness. This morning she was dressed in a fresh white blouse and denim skirt. Her earrings, turquoise studs framed in Navajo silver, heightened the blue in her eyes.

Lexie had been a toddler when her mother died in a riding accident. Coming into the family six months later, Callie had embraced Bert's four motherless children as her own. Lexie could barely remember her real mother, but Callie had been there, warm and wise and supportive through all her growing-up years. She'd never taken to ranch work, but she was a fine cook, and her cheerful, easygoing outlook had transformed the house into a welcoming home.

Three years ago, after Bert had been diagnosed with inoperable prostate cancer, she'd become his nurse. Even when pain had made him rail and curse and fling dishes of food against the wall, she'd remained patient and devoted. His death had set her free, but there'd been no talk of her leaving. Callie was family, and this was her home.

"So how was the rodeo, Lexie?" She dabbed a bit of homemade strawberry jam on a warm biscuit.

"Fine, mostly. The bulls did their job. Whirlwind bucked off a good rider." Should she launch into an account of everything else that had happened in Kingman—most of it bad? Not yet, she decided. Her sister was dealing with enough trauma. If anything, Tess would want to talk about who might have opened the gate to the bull pasture.

"Fine, *mostly?*" Callie asked. "Did something happen?"

"Nothing that can't wait," Lexie said.

Ruben walked in, his face and hands damp from washing at the outside pump. The boys would have told him about the lost bull. That would account for the somber look on his face—gaze lowered, jaw set—as he took his seat and dished a modest amount of food onto his plate. His arrival completed the ranch family at the table. The two hired boys would have their breakfast in the kitchen after the morning chores were done.

Aaron took a second helping of bacon. "Man, you should've heard those coyotes last night. Made a racket fit to raise the dead. Good thing I decided to call you, Tess."

"Yes, thank you for that." Tess looked drained, her breakfast barely touched. Lexie imagined the toll it had taken on her sister, having to shoot that spirited young bull to end its torment.

Tess took a sip of black coffee and cleared her throat. "All we can do now is make sure it doesn't happen again," she said in a level voice. "Any suggestions?"

"Those coyotes are bound to come back," Aaron said. "I could lend the boys a couple of rifles and let them pick the varmints off. They might enjoy that."

"They might. But the boys have other work," Tess said. "As for coyotes, there'll always be more, and they'll do what they were born to do. If an animal's injured or weak, they'll attack it. Our job is to keep our cattle safe."

"We could put chains and padlocks on the gates," Lexie suggested. "But it seems to me that what we need most is to find out who's responsible."

"I know we've pretty well cleared the boys," Aaron said. "My bet is that some of those bucks on the res got a hankerin' for fresh beef. When they snuck over to get some, things got out of hand, and they took off."

Ruben had been quietly eating his breakfast. Now he laid down his fork and fixed his gaze on Aaron. "I will ask around," he said. "But my people aren't cattle thieves. Even if they were, they wouldn't go after a bull. And they wouldn't leave the gate open."

Lexie took a deep breath. It was time. "I think somebody might be trying to hurt us," she said. And she told them about the note she'd found on her windshield.

"So you threw the note away?" Tess shook her head. "What were you thinking, Lexie?"

"I know I should've kept it." Lexie met her sister's earnest gray eyes. "At the time I didn't give it much thought. But what are the odds that the person who wrote the note was the one who opened the gate?"

"I'd bet on it," Tess said. "But who would come all this way in the dark just to cause trouble for us?"

"Maybe somebody who was being paid," Lexie said as the puzzle came together in her mind.

"Paid?" Tess's mouth tightened. "You've been watching too much late-night TV, girl. Who would pay someone good money to hurt us?"

"Brock Tolman," Lexie said. "He wants to buy Whirlwind. And it wouldn't surprise me if he wanted the ranch, too."

Shane drove his ten-year-old Chevy pickup under the wrought-iron gate and up the half-mile-long driveway to the heart of the 9,000-acre Tolman Ranch. The ranch's outer landscape was untouched desert, where sixty-year-old saguaros with upraised arms towered over natural gardens of cactus, paloverdes, boulders, and a spring with a waterfall that nourished birds and animals. Driving through on his way to the house, Shane had seen deer, foxes, and javelinas out here, as well as hawks and golden eagles.

A quarter mile in, the land opened into grassy pastures with stout metal fencing, where the pedigreed Tolman bucking bulls grazed and exercised. Other pastures held cows and calves, heifers, and younger bulls. On the far side of the pastures were corrals and chutes, a stable and paddock for horses, a hay barn, equipment sheds, and a small arena.

The house, set on a low rise, was a rambling structure of wood, stone, and glass. The broad, covered porch that wrapped around two sides offered a view of the pastures and the bulls that were Brock Tolman's passion. In his twenties he'd invested a modest inherited fortune into high-tech stocks. He'd made enough money to retire in his thirties and do what he'd always wanted to do—raise bucking bulls.

As Shane drove up to the house, Brock rose from his chair on the porch and set the bottle of Michelob Gold he was holding on a side table. At the age of forty, he was a muscular 6'4" with chiseled features and a close-clipped beard, and he moved like a man who wouldn't step aside for anybody.

Shane had long since learned that Brock was exceedingly private. He'd been married and divorced years ago, but he never spoke of it. And any women in his life were kept discreetly out of the picture.

"I take it you didn't make any more progress with the Champion girl." He stood on the edge of the porch and waited for Shane to join him.

"That depends on what you call 'progress.' I turned on the charm, but she wasn't buying what I was selling."

"Well, sit down and tell me about it, if there's anything to tell." Brock motioned to the empty leather chair next to his. As if summoned by some secret signal, the old man who served as his cook and butler appeared with an open beer, which he handed to Shane before shuffling back into the house.

"You owe me for one thing." Shane took a long swallow of the cold liquid. "When she saw through that stunt with the drunk coming on to her, I took the blame for it. I didn't tell her it was your idea."

Brock laughed. "Well, it was worth a try. I take it she wasn't too happy."

"She said it was a dirty, low-down trick. And I agreed with her. Don't underestimate Lexie Champion, Brock. She's smart and tough. Nobody's going to charm her into selling that bull." He took a moment to give Brock a quick rundown of what had happened in the hospital and in the parking lot.

Brock's eyes narrowed. "You like her, don't you?"

Shane shrugged. "What's not to like? She's got a mind and a heart to go with that pretty face. And the next time you want to try playing her for a fool, you can get yourself another boy."

Brock laughed again—a sinister Santa sort of laugh, coming from deep in his chest. "Good Lord, you don't just like her. You've fallen for the girl. She's got you wrapped around her pretty finger—which makes you no use to me at all. So let's talk about the bull—Whirlwind. What did you really think of him? Is he superstar material?"

"He puts on a great show. But we won't know that for sure until we see how he does with world-class riders. If he can buck off the likes of J.B. or the Brazilians, or give them spectacular scores if they stay on, then we'll know he's something special."

Brock frowned. "And then, naturally, his worth will go up. You're talking fifty thousand dollars at least, maybe twice that."

"You can afford it—but I'm betting the Champion sisters won't sell. If he turns out to be a top bull, they'll be able to retire and live on his stud fees."

"We'll see." Brock's fingers drummed on the arm of the chair. Shane could sense his mind working. "Here's what I'm thinking," he said. "You're bound to run into Miss

Lexie Champion and Whirlwind on the PBR circuit. I'm not asking you to seduce the girl or play any tricks. But if she agrees to sell me that bull, for any reason, and we strike a deal, there's a twenty-thousand-dollar bonus in it for you. No strings attached. How does that sound to you?"

Shane drained the last of his beer. How could a man walk away from an offer like that? With his old truck as a trade-in, $20,000 would go a long way toward buying the new truck he wanted. But as usual, there was something Machiavellian about Brock's proposal. He was dangling the cash as bait, knowing that acceptance would plant a seed in Shane's mind. Anytime he happened to be with Lexie, whether he wanted to or not, he'd be thinking about the money and how to get it.

Brock was, in effect, asking him to sell his soul for $20,000—money he might or might not ever receive.

But then, hadn't he sold his soul already?

"Well, what do you say?" Brock demanded.

Shane stood, leaving his beer on the side table. "I hope you won't mind if I think about it," he said.

"Of course not. Take all the time you want." Brock rose. "Will you be around for dinner tonight? I'm having some friends over. They'd enjoy meeting a real bull rider, especially one who's made the top twenty."

"Thanks, but I'm pretty beat after the drive." Shane was also in no mood to be paraded in front of Brock's friends like a trained pony. "I'm going to work out and shower. Then maybe warm up something in the microwave and watch a little TV."

"Fine. I'll see you in the morning. We'll be bucking some two-year-olds in the arena. I'm thinking in terms of the next futurity event. Maybe you can help me pick the best ones."

"Sure. See you after breakfast." Shane walked back to his truck, climbed inside, and headed for the small guest cabin, one of several, behind the main house. He owed everything he had to Brock Tolman, including the freedom to ride bulls without holding down a nine-to-five job. But Brock's manipulation was wearing on him. Maybe now that he'd made the top echelon of riders, he'd be lucky enough to find a heavy-duty sponsor or win enough prize money to strike out on his own. The thought of leaving Brock made him feel like an ingrate. But sooner or later, it had to happen. He couldn't stay here forever. The toll on his self-respect was becoming too high.

Brock stood on the porch after Shane had left, watching sunset paint the sky with ribbons of fire. His gaze roamed over the pastures, where the bulls he'd bred grazed on fertilized, watered grass that was emerald green year-round.

Most PBR bulls were supplied by the big-name stock contractors, of whom Brock was one. But it wasn't unheard of for a world-class bull to come from a small breeder, like the Alamo Canyon Ranch. If Whirlwind proved to be such a bull, Brock wanted him to carry the Tolman name.

Tolman's Whirlwind. The name resonated in Brock's mind. He wanted that bull the way other men might want a rare painting, a vintage wine, a luxury automobile, or an exquisite woman.

True, the bull could turn out to be simply good. If that was the case, he would still be a welcome acquisition, bringing a new bloodline into the herd. But Brock had a sixth sense about animals. He'd seen Whirlwind buck as a three-year-old at a futurity event and made an offer on the young bull then. But Bert Champion wasn't selling. Now that the speckled gray bull was going into his second season, still unridden after twenty-four outs, Brock's gut, which was seldom wrong, told him that Whirlwind could be the one to carry his ranch and his name to greatness.

Now that Bert was gone and the youngest Champion girl was taking the bulls on the circuit, Brock had hoped that Shane could win her trust as the first step to making a deal. That had been Plan A. Now that it had backfired, it was time for Plan B—impose enough hardship on the Champion family to force them into selling. The plan might involve some skullduggery, but when it came to something he wanted, Brock believed that the end justified the means.

One way or another, Whirlwind would be his.

CHAPTER FOUR

After a supper of chiles rellenos, cornbread, and fresh salad from the garden, Lexie, Tess, and Callie cleaned up the kitchen and settled on the front porch to relax before bedtime. The men had gone—Ruben to his trailer, Aaron home to the small prefab house on his own land, and the boys to take the first watch of the night.

Lexie ached with weariness after being on the road the night before and staying awake most of the day. The other women were tired, too. But no one would sleep well tonight. The fear that whoever had opened the gate would be back to make more trouble had them all on edge.

For now, keeping watch was the only thing they could do. The two boys, mounted and armed with pistols, flashlights, and two-way radios, were already patrolling the fence lines. Ruben, along with Aaron, who'd volunteered his help, would relieve them at midnight and stay out until dawn. It wasn't a permanent solution—for that they would need to find out who was behind the harassment and put a stop to it.

The two border collies, Ranger and Rover, had come up onto the porch. They would stay close to the house at night and bark if any unwelcome person or animal came near.

Lexie scratched Ranger's ears as she watched the full moon rise over the reservation to the east. The air was sultry with the day's lingering heat. Insects fluttered in the darkness. Bats swooped and darted, hunting them on the wing. From somewhere in the distance, a coyote howled. Remembering what had happened last night, Lexie shuddered.

Earlier tonight, after supper, she'd made a call to Rianne. The news hadn't been good.

"Cory's lower back was crushed." Her friend had sounded drained of hope. "He was in surgery all morning. They fused his spine with bolts and screws, but they couldn't save the nerve. He won't be able to use his legs—ever. He's . . . *paralyzed*." Her voice had quivered and broken. "I don't know what to do, Lexie. I have to take care of my baby. How can I take care of *him,* too? I love Cory, but I didn't sign on for this!"

"I know you love him, Rianne. And you're stronger than you think." Lexie knew she was mouthing platitudes. The truth was, she couldn't imagine the strength it would take to face what Rianne was facing. "Is there anything I can do?" she asked, knowing there was nothing.

"Thanks for offering. But I'm going to my mom's tomorrow to take care of the baby. Even after he gets out of the hospital, Cory will be in that special rehab clinic for weeks, maybe for months. I've got a lot to figure out before he comes home."

"You can make this work, Rianne. I know you can." Lexie had doubted the veracity of her own words, but she was doing her best to stay upbeat. "I'll call you. Okay?"

"Sure. Thanks." The call had ended.

Still stroking the dog, Lexie gazed across the yard to the pasture, where the massive forms of the bulls milled and shifted in the moonlight. They seemed restless, snorting, pawing the earth, and tossing their heads. Did they sense danger, or were they just picking up tension from the humans who cared for them?

"I'm thinking we should post a help wanted ad online," Tess said. "With you and Whirlwind going on the PBR circuit, we're going to need at least two new men—one to drive with Ruben and one to drive with you."

"It might not be easy to find the right people in such a short time." Lexie was accustomed to going with Ruben. But since the ranch would be supplying bulls for local rodeos all season, Ruben would have to take them. Lexie would need somebody else to drive and help manage Whirlwind. She couldn't do it alone. But she didn't relish the idea of traveling with a stranger.

"Can't I just take Chet or Ryder?" she asked. "I know they'd love to go to the PBR with me."

"They're too inexperienced. You need somebody who can drive the truck with the trailer and handle any emergency that might come up—like engine trouble or a flat tire, or any problem with the bull. And the boys will be back in school come September. We'll need people who can stay the season." Tess paused, then brightened. "Hey—maybe Aaron would like the job."

"Aaron?" Lexie gave her sister a startled glance. She'd never given Aaron much thought. He was just the neighbor who came around to help and usually stayed for meals. He was capable, and at least he was known and trusted. But did she really want to spend days on the road with him? "Aaron's pretty busy," she said, still hedging. "Do you think he'd do it?"

"Why not? It would be mostly weekends. The boys and I could take care of his place while he's gone. He only has a few animals, and for now, the hay just needs to be watered."

Tess turned to her stepmother. "What do you think, Callie? Should we ask him?"

With no men around, Callie had unbuttoned her blouse halfway to cool herself. She ran a hand through her silvery curls, hesitating a moment before she answered. "I'm sure Aaron could use the cash. He mentioned to me the other day that money was tight. It certainly wouldn't hurt to ask him."

"Then I'll talk to him first thing tomorrow," Tess said. "And maybe Ruben knows somebody who could help drive the big trailer. That would solve both problems. I just hope we'll have the money to keep paying them."

Lexie already knew her sister was worried about money. Bert's illness and other expenses had drained their finances, but it was too early to sell off the thirty head of beef cattle they were raising. Until then, they would have to depend on rodeo earnings.

In the PBR, Whirlwind would bring in $2,400 every time he left the chute. But the expenses—payments on the second truck and trailer, gas, food, lodging, entry fees, and PBR dues would have to come out of that amount. Given that he'd only be bucked once at any event, for a total of maybe twenty times in a season, his earnings would barely be enough to make a difference for the ranch. The only hope for serious cash would be if the bull racked up enough points to put him in the running for prize money.

Lexie had told the others about Brock Tolman's offer to buy Whirlwind. But she hadn't expected anyone to take it seriously—until now.

"Did your cowboy friend mention how much Brock Tolman would be willing to pay for our bull?" Tess asked.

"What?" Lexie's heart plummeted. "No! I didn't let him get that far! How can you even talk about selling Whirlwind, Tess—especially to Brock Tolman?"

"I certainly wouldn't want to sell him," Tess said. "But if it turns out to be the only way to save the ranch, we can't rule it out. This ranch is a business, Lexie. And Whirlwind is an asset, not a pet."

Lexie shot to her feet. "I can't believe you'd say that—or even think it! Whirlwind is going to be the greatest thing that ever happened to this ranch! And we're not selling him—not for anything!"

Fighting tears, she wheeled and stalked into the house, letting the screen door slam shut behind her.

Left on the porch with the dogs, Tess and Callie looked at each other and shook their heads. "Do you think I should go after her?" Tess asked.

"No. Leave her be." Callie began buttoning her blouse. "She's worn-out. She'll be fine in the morning."

"But she won't change her mind about Whirlwind. I just wish I could get her to step into the real world. It's like she's living in this Hollywood movie, where the animal saves the day and everybody lives happily ever after. When is she going to learn that life isn't like that?"

"Learn like you did, you mean?"

"Let's hope not." Tess had been planning her wedding when she'd gotten the call from Mitch's father. She still remembered standing with his family as the flag-draped coffin came off the plane. She'd grown up overnight, and she'd never felt young again.

Callie reached out and patted Tess's hand. "Lexie's strong in her own way. She'll grow up when she has to. Give her time. And give her a chance. For all we know, she could be right about that bull."

"I hope she is right," Tess said. "But if Whirlwind

doesn't bring in some fast money, and Tolman still wants to buy him, we might not have a choice."

In the living room, Lexie paused to wipe away the tears that had sprung to her eyes. Tess always seemed to expect the worst to happen—Lexie understood that, and she understood why. But sell Whirlwind? That would be like selling the house or the land, or even a member of the family.

Struggling to compose herself, she stood in front of the fireplace, gazing up at the family portrait that hung above the mantel. Taken almost a decade ago, it reflected a happier, more innocent time. There was her father—fit and smiling before the slow-moving cancer that had turned him into a shell of a man. Jack stood next to him, handsome and confident, a high school rodeo star at sixteen. And there was Tess at eighteen, her eyes sparkling, her smile radiant with the bloom of her first—and only—love.

Lexie studied her younger self, a gangly sixth-grader with braces, freckles, and dishwater blond hair, still adjusting to her growing body. And Val, a flame-haired, fifteen-year-old stunner, looking as if she were about to bolt out of the picture. She'd always been the restless one, even then.

Only Callie hadn't changed. She might be a little grayer now, with a few more pounds on her voluptuous figure, but her smile was just as warm, her blue eyes just as bright. What would the family have done without her all these years?

An oval photograph, framed in silver filigree, stood on the mantel below the large picture. Isabel Ashford Champion had been a delicate beauty with haunting gray eyes and a mane of strawberry blond curls. Only Val had inherited her looks. The other children were fashioned in the sturdier Champion mode, with strong features and athletic bodies.

Lexie barely remembered her mother. Sometimes, in dreams, she saw a face bending over her, but it was the face in the photograph—the hair, the makeup, even the dangling pearl earrings. Only a flat image of the real woman.

Tess and Callie would be coming in soon. Not wanting to talk to her sister again tonight, Lexie fled down the hall to her room and closed the door. It was early yet, but she'd been mostly awake for two days. She was exhausted. Even with possible danger lurking outside, she had to get some sleep.

After brushing her teeth and undressing, she opened a screened window, switched on the ceiling fan, and crawled into bed. She'd expected to fall asleep right away. Instead, she lay wide-awake in the dark, the events of the past two days running in a loop through her mind—the fake drunk slamming into the fence; Shane Tully rushing to the "rescue," then proceeding to charm information out of her; Cory's body lying broken in the dust; Rianne weeping in the hospital; Shane there, walking her to her truck, still working his charm—and she, still resisting.

At the end of the week, she'd be driving Whirlwind to Albuquerque for his first PBR event. Would Shane be there? Would he be up to his old tricks, pushing his boss's agenda? What would she do if she saw him again?

But Shane was the least of her concerns, Lexie reminded herself. The most important thing was making sure Whirlwind was in prime condition to rack up points from the judges.

Drifting now, she thought of the threat to the ranch. What if she'd kept the note and alerted Tess right away? Could they have averted the terrible loss of a young bull? Was the tragedy her fault?

Lexie hadn't gone to view the awful scene in the arroyo. She couldn't even imagine the strength it had taken for Tess to stand on the rim, aim the rifle, and put the poor animal out of its misery. But she would always remember the sight of vultures gathering in the sky overhead, circling lower and lower. . . .

With the image of black wings floating in her mind, she drifted into a sleep so sound that even the distant rumble of thunder failed to wake her.

Early Friday morning of that week, Lexie and Aaron hitched the two-stall gooseneck trailer behind the late-model Ford Ranger pickup and backed it up to the chute.

Loading Whirlwind had never been a problem. The bull had been trained to go up the ramp, and he knew the drill. In fact, he almost seemed to look forward to road trips and the chance to buck. But today, his first trip alone, he was snorting and tossing, rolling his eyes from side to side, visibly stressed. Ruben, who was helping, had to touch his flank with the Hot-Shot—a low-voltage taser for handling large animals. The slight jolt sent him bolting into the stall.

Lexie was worried about him. Bulls were a lot like high school boys. Some got along. Others didn't. Friends were comfortable hanging out together. Rivals would fight. Animals that didn't fit in would be, literally, bullied out of the group. Whirlwind was the dominant bull among the mature buckers that the ranch took to rodeos, and he knew his place. But there could be no telling how he'd behave without his companions.

"What if he won't buck?" Lexie voiced her concern over breakfast that morning. "That's been known to happen, when a bull is feeling out of sorts."

"Don't worry, he'll be fine." Ruben spooned black beans over his scrambled eggs. "The new trailer and the bigger crowds will take some getting used to. But once he gets in that arena, with a cowboy on his back, it'll be business as usual."

Ruben had recruited his son-in-law, Pedro, to help him drive four other bulls to Flagstaff. The younger man sat next to him, eating quietly, his gaze lowered.

Lexie wished silently that Ruben could be the one going with her. Aaron, who'd jumped at the chance to go along, was good with the truck and could repair almost anything. But he didn't know much more about bulls than he did about the few steers he raised. And Lexie couldn't imagine what they'd find in common to talk about.

Aaron glanced up at Callie as she bent over the table to replace the empty coffee carafe. "Will you ladies be all right here?" he asked.

"We'll be fine." She paused behind his chair. "We haven't had anybody come onto the place since that gate was opened. If we do, the boys will be here, and Tess is a dead shot." She chuckled. "Me, I'm pretty handy with a broom, or that poker by the fireplace. And I can scream to high heaven. So put your worries to rest."

"Don't worry about your place either, Aaron. We'll take care of everything." Tess had finished her breakfast. Rising from her chair, she gathered up her empty dishes to take to the kitchen before going outside to check the trailers and see the bulls off.

Callie had packed two coolers with sandwiches, cold

sodas, and oatmeal raisin cookies to take in the trucks. Ruben grabbed one; Aaron carried the other and stowed it behind the front seat. "Want me to drive first?" he asked.

"No, I'll take it for a while. That switchback road up to the pass is tricky with a trailer." Lexie checked Whirlwind to see whether he was settling. The bull was still snorting, tossing his head, and rolling his eyes. Not good. But maybe the familiar motion of the ride would calm him.

As a safety precaution, the two trailers would go up the road separately. Lexie and Aaron would be leaving first. After the smaller trailer had reached the top, the larger one would start out. Ruben had made countless drives up the winding road with a loaded trailer. Lexie had no cause to worry about him or the bulls.

They started out slowly, rolling out of the ranch gate and onto the hard-packed gravel road. Lexie gripped the wheel, keeping the tires away from the edge as the truck pulled the trailer up the narrow switchbacks. With eyes narrowed behind her sunglasses, she focused all her attention on steering the rig over the pass and down the other side without jostling its precious cargo.

When they finally reached paved road, they made a quick stop to check on Whirlwind. The bull was safe but still agitated.

"Will he be all right?" Aaron asked.

"He should be fine. He's just missing his buddies," Lexie said. "Driving on smooth roads should help settle him."

Looking back toward the pass, Lexie could see no sign of Ruben and the long trailer. Maybe they'd had some delay—a problem with the truck or with one of the bulls. Or maybe they'd just needed a little more time.

Stop worrying! she told herself.

Would the ranch be safe, with just Tess, Callie, and the two boys to watch the place? There'd been no sign of trouble for days. But what if the person who'd opened the gate was just waiting for a chance like this, to make more devilish mischief?

Stop worrying! Just do your job!

Starting up again, they headed northeast, mostly by back roads, to Albuquerque. The monsoon had arrived, with its afternoon showers. The light rains had settled the dust, leaving the humid air smelling of rain and damp earth. Seeds were sprouting on the desert, poking up tiny green heads.

As the wheels rolled along the paved road, with the radio playing country music, Lexie began to relax a little. She'd known Aaron Frye as a neighbor for as long as she could remember, but she'd never spent time alone with him. She'd expected some awkwardness, but he was courteous, helpful, and didn't try to fill the silence with small talk. Maybe driving with him wouldn't be so bad after all.

At least the trip wouldn't be too long. When it came to transporting PBR bulls, there were strict rules for their care. The animals could be trailered and on the road for no more than ten hours per day in trailers with air-ride suspension and six to ten inches of soft sawdust on the floor. For most events, the PBR tried to book bulls that lived within that range. For longer drives, the PBR had contracts with facilities that had pens for feeding, watering, and keeping the bulls overnight. But since Albuquerque was within the maximum range, there'd be no need for a long rest stop.

So far so good, Lexie told herself. Now she could focus on just one responsibility: Whirlwind.

* * *

Tess stood next to Callie on the front porch, watching the heavy-duty pickup, its trailer loaded with four bulls, head up the first steep grade. Worry nibbled at the edges of her awareness. Ruben was a skilled driver, and he'd pulled the trailer up that winding road more times than she could count. Still, just this once, she couldn't help wondering if it might have been safer to send him the longer way, on the straight road that crossed the reservation to the east.

But her choice made sense. Hauling the bulls across the res would have added more than two hours to the drive, pushing the time over the limit. Regulations dictated that the bulls get an overnight break, which would turn a one-day trip into a two-day haul.

Everything would be all right, Tess assured herself. This trip would be no different from the others. But in the back of her mind, Lexie's threatening note, and the haunting vision of the young bull dying in the arroyo, reminded her that things had changed. Everything in her beloved world—the land, the animals, and the people—had been put at risk.

And if Brock Tolman was behind the threat, damn him to hell!

Holding her breath, she watched the truck climb the switch-backs to the pass, pulling the trailer with the four bulls, each one weighing more than 1,500 pounds, along with feed and gear. The engine roared; the tires gripped the gravel road.

And then, on the sharpest and steepest part of the road, it happened.

With a pop like a gunshot, the truck's right front tire blew out. The truck sagged toward the outside edge of the road, twisting the hitch and tilting the trailer with it.

Tess's heart leaped into her throat. From the yard, she

could see that Ruben was trying to steer the truck away from the steep edge, but the blown tire was resting on its rim. The bulls were bellowing in terror, their shifting weight making the situation even more perilous. Any moment now, the entire rig could go off the edge. Losing the bulls and the trailer would be disastrous enough. Losing the men would be unthinkable.

"Jump!" Tess screamed, but her voice was lost in the distance. Short of watching the men and animals fall to their death, there was only one thing she could do.

One of the horses the boys had used to herd the bulls into the loading chute was close by, still saddled and bridled. Springing onto its back, Tess shouted at Callie, "Get the boys! Tell them to get ropes and mount up! Hurry!"

Kicking the horse to a gallop, she tore up the road to where the rig was leaning over the edge. She had to get the bulls out of the trailer, both to save them and to lighten the load.

She reached the teetering trailer. There was no room to open the side gate. The bulls would have to go out the back, and she was too high to reach the lock. Looping the horse's reins around her arm, she jumped to the ground. Then, praying for strength, she slid back the bolt and flung open the double doors.

There were four pens inside the trailer, two in front, two in back, with a gate between. The two bulls in back would have to come out first. A quick glance toward the cab told her the men couldn't help her. Ruben was fighting to hold the truck on the road. Pedro was leaning inward, trying to keep his weight off the tilting right side.

Swinging onto the horse again, she backed away from the trailer's open rear and uncoiled the rope. The bulls were in a state of panic. They could easily freeze in fear or throw themselves against the side of the trailer hard enough to send the whole rig toppling.

Renegade, the big black, was one of the bulls in the rear. Looping the rope, Tess leaned in as close as she dared, murmured a quick prayer, and flung the rope over Renegade's horns. With the rope anchored on her saddle, she backed the horse, jerking Renegade's head up hard. The only way for the bull to relieve the discomfort was to back up, which Renegade did, stumbling out the doors—awkwardly since the ramp was missing. Tess was able to shake the rope loose before he wheeled and thundered down the road toward home.

Bulls were herd animals. The second bull backed up on his own and followed Renegade out of the trailer.

A five-foot steel-railed gate separated the front and rear pens. The two remaining bulls were trapped behind it. To free them, Tess would have to open the gate. But she couldn't risk getting crushed as the bulls backed out.

Thinking fast, she dismounted and climbed into the trailer with the rope's end in her hand. The well-trained horse held steady as she tied the rope to a rail and slid back the bolt until it was barely holding the gate closed.

In the saddle again, she backed the horse, yanking the gate open. For the space of a breath, nothing happened— and with the rope tied to the gate, Tess had run out of options. *Please . . .* she begged silently. *Please come out.*

The trailer creaked and shuddered. With a snort of fear, one bull, the brindle, took two steps backward and paused.

Come on . . .

The trailer jiggled again. The bull backed into the empty space behind him and, half turning, jumped out the rear of the trailer. The last bull, a tan brute in his first rodeo season, followed, leaving the trailer empty.

As the two bulls stampeded down the road, where the boys would be waiting to round them up, Tess sagged over the horse's neck, sick with relief. She could only hope the worst was over.

With the weight gone from the trailer, Ruben was able to maneuver the truck back from the edge of the road and drive it, slowly, on the ruined tire and the rim, to the top of the pass where he'd have room to turn around. There, he and Pedro blocked the wheels, found the spare and the jack, and went to work changing the tire. Both men looked pale and shaken, but to their credit, they said nothing about how close they'd just come to death.

Once she'd made sure they were all right, Tess rode back down to the ranch, taking the horse at a walk to calm her nerves. That blowout couldn't have happened at a worse time or place. What if it hadn't been an accident?

But how was that possible? The truck had been at the ranch all week, in plain sight. Someone had been on watch every night. There'd been no barking dogs, no uneasy cattle or horses, no unfamiliar tracks.

By the time she neared the house, the bulls had been rounded up and driven into the paddock. There'd be no getting them back into that trailer today. But there was no question of canceling the ranch's commitment to the rodeo in Flagstaff. Four different, less experienced bulls would have to be loaded for the trip. Maybe it was time to try out Whiplash, the younger brother of Whirlwind. Whiplash, heavier and darker than his brother, was four years old and had done well at some local rodeos. This event would be a good test for him.

As Tess dismounted in the yard and passed the horse off to one of the boys, Callie plunged off the porch and came running across the yard. "Oh, my stars!" She wrapped Tess in her cushiony embrace. "Thank God everybody's all right. I was already planning three more funerals."

Tess eased out of her stepmother's arms. Her knees were so weak she could barely stand. "I think I need to sit down," she said.

"Come on." Callie offered an arm to help her to the porch. "Sit down. I'll get you something cold. A beer?"

"Fine." Tess sank onto a plastic-webbed lounge chair. She could feel her heart slamming against the walls of her chest. Up there on the road, there'd been no time to think, just to act. Only now that she was safe did she realize the magnitude of the danger and how close she, the men, and the bulls had come to dying.

Callie slipped the cold can of Bud Light into her hand. Tess took a long, deep swallow, savoring the icy chill that trickled down her throat.

"Should I try to phone Lexie?" Callie asked. "She'd want to know about this."

"No. Lexie doesn't need the distraction."

"She promised to let you know when they made it to Albuquerque. You could tell her then."

"It'll only worry her," Tess said. "We can tell her what happened when she gets home." Closing her eyes, Tess leaned back in the chair, sipping the cold beer and taking slow, deep breaths. When she opened her eyes again, she could see the truck and trailer crawling down the steep, hairpin road toward the ranch.

Minutes later, the rig rolled into the yard and stopped by the paddock. As Ruben and Pedro climbed out of the cab, Tess got up and strode out to meet them.

Ruben was not one to show emotion. But she could tell he was proud of her. Gratitude and admiration shone in his dark eyes as he spoke. "After we check the rig and get another spare tire out of the shed, we'll be loading more bulls. You can let us know which ones to take. But first, there's something you need to see."

He led her around to the rear of the trailer and opened one of the double doors. The ruined tire lay where it had been tossed, half detached from the bent and useless steel rim.

"Here's where the tire blew." Ruben pointed to direct her gaze. "Take a close look."

The tire was fairly new—Tess would never transport her precious bulls on unsafe tires. But the blowout hole wasn't in the tread, where it would be if the tire had run over something sharp. It was in the sidewall.

"See it?" Ruben asked. "Look close."

"I see it." Tess ran a cautious finger along the edge of the break. The side of the tire had been cut almost through, with a razor blade or a very sharp knife, leaving a layer thin enough to burst under pressure.

The chill that crept over Tess was like a skeletal hand clutching at her heart. Somebody had done this— somebody with access to the truck and the ranch, some- body who could come and go without being seen or heard, even by the dogs. Questions flocked into her mind, like the black-winged vultures circling above the arroyo.

Who was behind this?

Where would they strike next?

How far would they go?

And what would it take to stop them?

CHAPTER FIVE

AT THE FAIRGROUNDS IN ALBUQUERQUE, LEXIE UNLOADED Whirlwind from the trailer, signed him in, and saw him settled, with water and food, in his space amid the complex of pens and chutes.

Before leaving him, she reached between the rails and scratched a special spot behind his ear. Whirlwind closed his eyes, soothed by her touch. Lexie had been there for his birth and watched him grow into a promising young bull. He'd always been her favorite; and now that he was moving into the big league of buckers, it seemed right that she should be here to cheer him on.

As Tess often reminded her, Whirlwind wasn't a pet. He was a powerful brute, bred for a singular purpose—to buck in the arena and, if he proved good enough, to pass on his genes to his future sons and daughters. But for all that, he held a place in Lexie's heart.

As she stepped back from the pen, he snorted and shook his blunted horns. "Don't be nervous, big guy," she murmured. "You'll be safe here tonight. And tomorrow you'll do us all proud."

Walking back through the complex to move and park

the rig, Lexie took in her surroundings. There were at least twenty bulls in the maze of pens and chutes, with more still coming in. Every effort had been made to keep them safe and comfortable. The floors were non-slip rubber, covered with clean sawdust. Bins held food and water. An overhead cover protected the bulls from the sun and weather. Security cameras monitored every inch of space.

And the bulls—they were majestic, all of them in prime condition. They paid Lexie scant attention as she walked past their pens—some dozing or eating, some blowing snot and passing noisy gas, or dropping piles of steaming manure.

Being here, surrounded and handled by people, was routine for these pampered giants. For the most part, they took it calmly, until their turn in the bucking chute, when the rider settled into place and the gate swung open. Then they became eight-second rock stars.

They were world-class, the best of the best, some worth hundreds of thousands of dollars. How would Whirlwind do against such competition? That remained to be seen.

The event would start tomorrow evening at seven o'-clock, with the newer bulls and lower ranking riders. Whirlwind would be one of the starters, his rider to be determined by a draw. If he failed to perform well, he could be cut from PBR competition.

Later in the evening, around eight o'clock, the real stars would come out—some of the top riders and top bucking bulls in the country. Rankings, for both men and animals, were based on cumulative points scored in a season, the national champions to be crowned at the November finals in Las Vegas.

Would Whirlwind be among the elite bulls to compete

in the final rounds? It was far too soon to hope. But it could happen. Lexie could only dream.

After parking the rig in the back lot and bidding Aaron a good night, Lexie perched on the hood of the truck to catch her breath before making the promised call to her sister. She'd reserved a couple of rooms in a cheap motel within walking distance of the fairgrounds, so there'd be no need to unhitch the truck. But even though she was tired, it was too early to check in and go to bed. Whirlwind wouldn't be bucking until tomorrow evening. She had time to kill.

By now, the sun was going down. Fiery clouds spilled across the western sky, bathing the sagebrush flats and towering mesas in shades of rose and amber. Beyond the fairgrounds, the city lights were coming on, like fireflies awakening in the twilight.

The back lot was crowded with trucks, campers, and trailers, some small, others large and luxurious. Some even had living quarters in front with space for bulls in the rear. These were parked in the larger spaces with power and water hookups. Not far away, Lexie noticed one of these— a sleek rig with the TOLMAN RANCH banner emblazoned on the side. A light was on in front, where the living compartment would be. Another Tolman rig, the one that had been used to transport most of the bulls, was parked on the far side of the lot.

Of course, the Tolman bulls would be here. Had Brock Tolman come to the rodeo with them? Had Shane? If she were to run into them, would it be best to confront them, or just ignore them and walk away?

But never mind. The charming cowboy and his scheming

boss could go hang for all she cared. She was here for just one reason, and that reason didn't include a clash with the enemies of her family.

Remembering her promise to call, she found her cell phone in her purse, scrolled to Tess's number. Cell service was spotty at the ranch, but maybe today she'd be lucky.

Her sister answered on the first ring. "Lexie? Is everything all right?" She sounded stressed, but with Tess, that was nothing new.

"Everything's fine," Lexie said. "We got here without a problem. Aaron's done okay. Whirlwind is checked in and settled, and I'm just hanging out in the parking lot."

"Any sign of Brock Tolman?"

"I'm looking at two of his trailers, so I know his bulls are here. But I haven't been inside the arena or anyplace else where I might run into him." She paused. "You sound worried, Tess. Is everything all right at the ranch?"

"Everything's fine. I just heard from Ruben and Pedro. They made it to Flagstaff safely, so all's well."

All's well. Something about the way Tess spoke the words roused Lexie's suspicions that they weren't entirely true. "Is there something you're not telling me?" she asked. "Has there been more trouble?"

"Nothing that can't wait until you get home." Tess's voice was fading. They were losing the signal. "For now, it's been taken care of. Just . . ." Tess hesitated as if weighing her words. "Just be careful. Watch your back—and check every inch of the rig before you leave, okay?"

"Tess—"

"You're cutting out. We'll talk when you get home. Call me if you learn anything new." Tess ended the call before Lexie could ask her any more questions.

"Blast!" Lexie glared down at the silent phone. If Tess

wanted to spare her from worry, she was going about it the wrong way. For a moment, Lexie was tempted to call her sister back and demand to know the truth. But that would only create tension between them. She'd been warned to be careful. But she would be more than careful. She would be looking for answers. If any of those answers were here, she would do her best to find them—even if it meant being civil to Brock Tolman and his all-too-attractive right-hand man.

"Well, if it isn't Miss Lexie Champion!" Lexie's pulse clicked into overdrive as Shane Tully strolled into the bright circle cast by the security light.

Her defenses sprang into place. Shane had a way of making her feel like a fluttery, vulnerable high school sophomore. Her instincts told her to make her excuses and leave. But she'd resolved to get some answers about Brock Tolman's connection to the troubles at the ranch. Here was her chance.

She gave him a smile. "Surprise. I thought I was all alone out here. Then you show up out of nowhere. How did you manage that?"

"I didn't. I'm staying over there in that trailer. When I looked out the window, there you were. I was hoping we'd bump into each other while you were here. But I never figured it would be this easy." He paused, his gaze meeting hers, holding it for an instant before he spoke again. "Are you hungry? I had a pizza delivered a few minutes ago. It's keeping warm in the oven. If you're hungry, you're welcome to come over and share it with me. Call it a peace offering."

A peace offering. The words sounded innocent enough, but they put Lexie on her guard. Given the circumstances, she couldn't afford to trust anyone.

"Where's your boss?" she asked.

"Brock's flying in for the rodeo tomorrow. He pilots his own plane. I drove one trailer and brought a couple of the bulls. Brock's regular driver, who brought the other truck, wanted to stay in a hotel. So how about it? Just you, me, hot pizza, and cold beer—no strings attached."

No strings attached. The first time Lexie had heard that line was the night she'd lost her virginity at a frat party in college. The experience, which had left her feeling cheap and used, had also given her a deep-rooted distrust of handsome, charming men. Men exactly like Shane Tully, who probably had women falling into his bed anytime he wanted.

But turning him down would mean passing up the opportunity to get him talking. She weighed, then rejected the idea of asking him to bring the pizza outside. If she wanted to learn his plans, and perhaps Tolman's, she would need to appear trusting.

She tried to make sure her polite smile wouldn't be seen as a come-on. "I was about to go get a chili dog on the midway. But pizza sounds better. Sure, I'll join you—just for a little while."

He gave her a knowing look. "Relax, Lexie. I just want to share some pizza and small talk. If you start to feel uncomfortable, the door will be a step away."

Heat surged into Lexie's face. His honest response had made her feel like a ninny. Maybe she'd underestimated him.

The smile she gave him probably looked as fake as the last one. "Lead the way," she said.

He ushered her into the front compartment of the long, sleek trailer. Lexie's eyes widened. She'd seen similar models at rodeos and on sales lots, but this was the luxury edition— leather furnishings, granite countertops, a built-in home theater setup, everything state-of-the-art high tech. She couldn't even imagine what the bedroom and bath might look like.

"Bathroom's down the hallway if you want to wash up," he said, as if he'd read her mind again.

"Thanks. I probably smell like a barn."

He grinned. "Don't we all?"

The bathroom was tiny but beautifully appointed, with marble fixtures and a massaging shower. Shane's toothbrush and razor were neatly arranged on the side of the vanity. That small intimacy, seeing his personal things there, sent a faint quiver of awareness through her body.

After washing up and drying her hands on a velvety towel, Lexie couldn't resist a peek into the bedroom. The king-sized bed was covered with a fluffy duvet in a buckskin color. Everything else—including the closet, the shelves, and the dresser—was built into the walls, leaving just enough floor space to stand and dress.

"So what do you think of the place?" Shane's voice, almost in her ear, gave her a start. She turned to find him standing in the hall behind her.

Lexie's cheeks flushed. "I just had to look. It's impressive. I hope you aren't going to tell me it belongs to you."

He laughed. "I could. But I'd be lying. Brock lets me use it sometimes when I haul the bulls."

"You said he was coming in tomorrow?"

"Right. But he'll be renting a car and staying in a fancy hotel. He doesn't like roughing it."

"*This* is roughing it?"

"Only if you're Brock. Come on, the pizza's ready. I hope you like supreme."

A bar with stools divided the kitchen from the sitting

area. Shane had set out two plates with the pizza box between them. As Lexie took a seat, he took two chilled Coronas from the small fridge, passed one to her, and scooped a slice of pizza onto her plate.

"How does that look to you?"

"Good. Thanks." Lexie took a sip of the cold beer, her anxiety easing. Something about Shane's manner made her feel comfortable—not a good thing, she reminded herself. Shane had his own agenda, and it wasn't just to charm her.

"I hope you didn't come alone," he said, making conversation. "Where's your foreman?"

"We had a contract to take bulls to Flagstaff. That job fell to Ruben. But our neighbor, Aaron, offered to come with me. I gave him a break after we unloaded. We have rooms reserved at a place just outside the fairgrounds. I found it online. It was close and cheap. The Twilight Siesta Motel. Do you know it?"

"Oh, good Lord!" Shane shook his head. "Did you see the place before you paid?"

"Only the photos on the computer. It looked okay—and it's not like I could afford a fancy hotel, especially since the ranch is paying for two rooms." She stared at him, puzzled by his dismayed expression. "Why? Is there something I should know?"

He exhaled. "The place is a dump, Lexie. It's worse than a dump. It's a hangout for drug dealers and prostitutes. You can't stay there. It isn't safe."

Feeling like a scolded child, Lexie let his words sink in. She should've known there was a catch to those cheap room rates. But it was too late to change her plans. "I don't have much choice," she said. "I've already paid. And Aaron could already be in his room. What about him? Will he be all right?"

"He should be okay as long as he watches his back and keeps his door locked. But not you. A pretty young woman would be asking for trouble."

"But surely, with Aaron there, right next door, I'll be all right."

"Don't even think about staying there. In fact, you might want to call your friend and warn him about the place."

"I can do that much." Lexie found her phone in her purse. "Is there someplace else I can tell him to go?"

"With the rodeo in town, every room's liable to be booked. But you can at least tell him to be careful."

Lexie scrolled to Aaron's phone number, which she'd added just before the trip. His phone rang once, then again and again before going to voice mail.

Why wasn't he picking up? What if something had happened to him?

Concern growing, she left a brief message. "Aaron, I've heard some scary things about our motel. I need to know you're all right. Be careful, and call me, please."

She ended the call and laid the phone on the table. "Now I'm getting worried," she said. "I told Aaron to leave his phone on in case I needed him."

"Don't panic yet," Shane said. "Maybe he's in the shower. Or maybe he just didn't hear the ring. Give him a few minutes. And eat your pizza. It's getting cold."

Lexie nibbled her pizza slice, her appetite gone. She'd accepted Shane's invitation as a way to get him talking about his boss and any plans involving Whirlwind or the ranch. But things weren't turning out that way.

"You're welcome to stay here," he said. "That leather

love seat makes out into a bed. I'd be fine with sleeping there and letting you have the bedroom."

Lexie's pulse slammed—needlessly, she thought. So far, Shane had been a perfect gentleman. But whatever the reason, she wasn't ready to spend a night in this luxurious bachelor's nest. Sleeping in her truck would be a smarter choice.

He seemed to read her hesitation. His eyes drilled into hers as he spoke. "Let me make one thing clear, Lexie," he said. "I like women. I like them a lot. But I like my women a hundred percent willing. I happen to think you're beautiful. But I would never try to take advantage of you or do anything to make you uncomfortable. Where you spend the night will be your choice. Take your time and let me know."

"Thank you, I will," she murmured. Again, he was a half step ahead of her, disarming her with a show of honesty. But he wasn't being honest about everything—for one thing, his finding her and coming up with a reason to invite her into the trailer seemed almost too much like a plan. Not that he was out to seduce her—if Shane just wanted a woman, there were plenty available. It was more like he was trying to win her confidence in order to manipulate her.

Even his description of the motel could be a ploy. For all she knew, the place might be just fine. Aaron should be able to tell her—if she could reach him on his blasted phone.

"I'm still worried about Aaron," she said. "I won't rest easy until I know he's all right."

"I have a suggestion," Shane said. "If you have the number of the motel, you could call the desk and find out whether he's checked in."

"Not a bad idea. But first I want to try his cell again."

Lexie punched in Aaron's number. As before, the phone rang several times and went to voice mail. After leaving another terse message, she found the number of the motel and made the call.

"Hullo?" A woman with a smoker's rasping voice answered the ring.

"Is this the Twilight Siesta Motel?"

"Sure is, honey. But we're full up tonight. Tomorrow, too." The woman coughed. "Sorry."

"Wait—this is Lexie Champion. I paid for two rooms online and got confirmation. I was just wondering whether my friend had checked in. Aaron Frye?"

There was a pause. Then the woman came back on. "Good-lookin' cowpoke? Plaid shirt? White hair?"

"That would be him." Lexie had never thought of Aaron as good-looking, but a woman close to his own age might see him with different eyes. "I've been trying to reach him, and he doesn't pick up. Has he checked in?"

"Yup. Came in about twenty minutes ago. Said he'd had a few drinks and wanted to sleep 'em off, so not to disturb him." The woman coughed again. "Haven't seen him since I gave him the key, but I'm guessin' he's out like a light."

"So he's all right?"

"Far as I know, honey. Gotta go now. Somebody's here."

Lexie ended the call with a sigh. She'd given Aaron leave to go off on his own, and there was nothing wrong with a grown man having a few drinks in a bar before calling it a night. But, blast him, he could at least have answered her call.

"Is everything all right?" Shane asked.

"It seems to be." Lexie forced a laugh. "I should know

better than to try mothering a man old enough to be my father."

"Your pizza's gone cold. I can warm you up another slice."

"Thanks, but don't bother. I seem to have worried away my appetite." Lexie slipped off the stool and dropped the phone into her purse. "Anyway, it's time I walked back to the pens and checked on Whirlwind. He's like the new kid on the block. I need to make sure he's settled in."

"So you mother-hen bulls as well as old men." Shane chuckled as he rose with her. "How about I walk with you? I could show you around the place, introduce you to a few people—and maybe even a few famous bulls."

"Thanks, I'd like that," Lexie answered without hesitation. Shane could teach her a lot about the inner workings of the PBR. And she hadn't forgotten her promise to Tess—to find out all she could about Brock Tolman and his nefarious schemes.

She would make good use of her time with him.

Shane ushered Lexie outside and locked the door behind them. He knew why Brock had insisted he drive that damned fancy trailer. The boss had known Lexie would be here, and he was still hoping that she would end up in that cushy king-sized bed, sated, satisfied, and agreeable as hell.

Brock's offer of a $20,000 bonus on the purchase of the bull had sounded tempting at first. But seducing a woman for money crossed the line—especially when that woman was Lexie. Mr. Tolman could find himself another stud. And when Brock arrived tomorrow, that was just what Shane planned to say to him.

"I meant to tell you if I saw you—" Lexie walked beside

him as they crossed the lot, weaving their way among the parked rigs. "I called Cory's wife after I got home. The news wasn't good."

"I know," Shane said. "I phoned Cory a couple of days ago. He's being transferred to a rehab facility in Tucson. Not much hope that he'll ever walk, but he needs to learn how to manage using his upper-body strength. His wife and baby are with her folks in Ajo for now. Evidently, she's not taking things too well. Neither is Cory. Can't say I blame either of them."

"What will they do, Shane? I've known Cory most of his life. All he ever wanted was to ride bulls. It's like there's no Plan B." She paused, looking up at him. "What would you do if it happened to you? Have you ever thought about it?"

Shane took a moment to watch the moon, its rim a sliver of gold, rising over the Sandia Mountains. "Getting hurt comes with the job. You know that," he said. "Every bull rider I know is walking around with scars and broken bones. But the other thing—getting disabled or killed— sure we think about it. But it doesn't stop us from living. A lot of the guys have families. You'll see their wives and kids in the stands when they compete. Life becomes more precious when you lay it on the line every week."

"That sounds like something Jack would have said."

Shane could sense the tension in her voice. He remembered how she'd seen her brother die in the arena—falling under the bull's hooves as the bullfighters tried frantically to divert the beast. Shane had been there, too, watching the awful scene from the chutes. Maybe he should have kept his damn fool mouth shut about laying one's life on the line.

"How about you?" she asked. "Do you have a Plan B? Would you ever give it up and stop competing?"

"Only if there was no way I couldn't get on a bull anymore. It's life at a level most people never experience—like riding a lightning bolt across the sky. The sheer terror of it—and the way it feels to face that terror and win—it's a high that no drug can touch."

"I know. Jack felt the same way," Lexie said in a quiet voice. "My dad wanted him to quit and run the ranch. Jack wouldn't hear of it. He had to have that rush."

"But it's not just the rush," Shane said. "There's a purity about it, almost a love—just you and that bull, enemies and comrades, both of you giving it all you've got. Both of you fighting to win. There's nothing like it."

Lexie didn't reply. Maybe he'd said too much—or maybe he'd sounded crazy, trying to tell her how it felt, being on a bull. It was probably just as well that they'd reached the gated enclosure where the bulls were kept.

The security guard recognized Shane and let them through. The overhead lights had been dimmed, but he could see that most of the pens were full. The bulls were drowsing, most of them on their feet, a few lying down. The peaceful scent of fresh hay, warm bodies, and grassy manure lay over them like a soft blanket. In the stillness, Shane could hear the animals breathing, the sound broken by an occasional snort or the shifting of a massive body against steel rails.

"Whirlwind is over this way," Lexie said, moving toward the far corner. Following her, Shane caught sight of the mottled gray bull, moving restlessly in his solitary pen. At their approach, he snorted and tossed his head. His horns, blunted to regulation but still long, clattered against the rails of the pen.

"Oh, dear." Lexie sighed. "I was afraid of this. He's not happy. He doesn't like being alone in a strange place."

"You don't want him happy," Shane said. "You want him mad and cranky and ready to buck the living daylights out of any cowboy who climbs on his back."

"I guess you don't yet know who the rider will be, do you?" she asked. "From what I understand, the drawing won't take place till tomorrow."

"That's right." Shane took a deep breath. It was time to reveal the secret he'd been hiding. "But I do know who'll be riding him. I pulled a few strings, called in a favor."

Who? Her expressive blue eyes asked the question.

"It'll be me, Lexie," he said. "I'll be riding Whirlwind tomorrow."

For an instant, Lexie felt as if the air had been sucked out of her lungs. Then reason began to creep in. Why not Shane? He was an experienced rider—among the top twenty in the rankings. It would be in his best interest to make himself, and Whirlwind, look good.

But there was doubt, too. Shane was working for Brock Tolman, the devil incarnate. What if this was some sort of scheme to make Whirlwind look bad, so that her family might be more inclined to sell him? Or worse, what if Tolman was out to punish the Champions by hurting the bull in some way? How could she trust Tolman's fair-haired boy with her precious bull?

"Don't worry, Lexie." Shane spoke to her fear. "I have too much respect for you, your bull, and myself, to pull any dirty tricks. It'll just be me and Whirlwind out there, both of us doing our damnedest for eight seconds."

Lexie forced a smile she didn't feel. "Then I'll just have to trust you. But I'll be cheering for Whirlwind to dump you in the dirt."

"Understood." Shane grinned. "Meanwhile, I'll make good on my promise to show you around the place. Come on."

His hand rested lightly on the small of her back as he guided her past the bucking chutes and down a long hallway going off to one side, under the arena seats. Conscious of the warm contact, she walked beside him, past offices, storage and locker rooms, to the well-equipped medical room at the end where doctors and therapists worked with injured riders. Even at this hour, there were people here—cowboys on exercise machines, medical staff stocking supplies, and others working late to ready the place for tomorrow. Everyone seemed to know Shane. They greeted him as a friend and wished Lexie good luck with her bull when he introduced her.

Along the hallway, the walls were hung with framed photos of great riders and bulls. Lexie pointed one out. "There's Oscar. He was Whirlwind's great-, great-, however many greats, grandfather."

"I know. I did my homework. Most of these pictures you'll recognize, I'm sure."

"Yes, I do my homework, too." Lexie had devoured magazines, videos, and Web sites devoted to the sport of bull riding and breeding. Most of the great bulls in the pictures— Pearl Harbor, Asteroid, Little Yellow Jacket, Blueberry Wine, Red Rock, and others—were gone now. But their descendants were bucking today, all over the country. The science of bull genetics—the breeding of select cows and bulls to produce superb bucking animals—had come to rule the sport. It was all about bloodlines.

"I've always thought Whirlwind was extraordinary," Lexie said. "But when I look at those bulls out there in the pens, they're all extraordinary. They're all amazing."

"That's true," Shane said. "There are no average bulls in the PBR. And with selective breeding, they're getting bigger, smarter, and more athletic. But now and again you get a bull with that extra spark of greatness—like Sweet Pro's Bruiser, or Smooth Operator, or Cochise. Whether Whirlwind is one of those bulls remains to be seen. Brock believes he is."

"So what does Brock plan to do about that, now that I've told him we won't sell?"

"Brock tends to keep his plans to himself," Shane said. "But when he goes after something, he usually gets it. You might keep that in mind."

Lexie went rigid. She took a step away from him. Until now, she'd been warming toward the handsome bull rider. But his words about Brock Tolman brought reality crashing in on her. Shane Tully was one of the enemy. She couldn't let herself forget that.

She had set out with him to learn more about Brock's plans. But what he'd told her didn't help. It only made her want to get away.

"Thank you for the tour, but I've seen enough," she said. "It's time I got cleaned up and rested for tomorrow. I'll be fine walking back to my truck. No need for an escort."

"I need to go back anyway." Shane fell into step beside her. "My invitation to spend the night still stands. And I promise not to lay an ungentlemanly hand on you."

"Thanks, but I'll be fine in the motel," Lexie said. "After talking to that nice woman, I can't believe the place is as bad as you say it is. I just need to get my duffel out of the truck."

"Don't be an idiot, Lexie. You don't know what you're getting into."

"I'll be fine," she said. "The motel is only a couple of blocks from here. I have the address. It's an easy walk."

"I can't let you do this," he said.

"It's not your choice. Stop fussing like an old mother hen. I'm a big girl. I'll be all right. And if I'm not, Aaron will be right next door."

"Passed out, more than likely," Shane muttered. "Are you really set on doing this?"

"I am," she said.

"Fine." He turned to stand in her path. "But you can't stop me from going with you."

CHAPTER SIX

SHANE HAD OFFERED TO CARRY LEXIE'S DUFFEL TO THE motel. still defiant, she'd insisted on taking it herself, striding along the sidewalk with the strap slung over her shoulder, past shadowed alleys and run-down bars. The woman was as stubborn as a mule and as prickly as a teddy bear cholla. But the dangers he'd warned her about were real. He could hardly walk away and leave her open to robbery, rape, or kidnapping.

He should've known better than to mention Brock. Before that, she'd been almost warm. He'd had hopes of keeping her safe in his trailer for the night. But one word about his boss wanting her bull, and she'd gone on the warpath. Why did her family hate the man so much? It had to be an interesting story. But this was no time to ask.

The Twilight Siesta Motel, a line of dingy white-stuccoed units dating from the 1950s, was set back a dozen yards from the street. Its blinking neon sign was missing the *a* and the *M*. Its crumbling asphalt parking lot was littered around the edges with cigarette butts, used condoms, and a few syringes. Most of the vehicles parked in the spaces outside were battered pickup trucks—probably cowhands, here for the rodeo.

"See, it doesn't look that bad." Lexie's voice rang with false bravado.

"Don't be so sure. It's early yet. Barely ten." Shane followed her to the office, which had a hand-lettered NO VACANCY sign taped to the inside of the dust-spattered window. He opened the door for her and followed her inside.

The woman at the desk, dressed in a faded muumuu, was thin, gray, and weary looking. A cigarette smoldered on a blackened ashtray next to her computer. Lexie presented her ID for the reservation. The woman checked the screen and nodded.

"We got you down for a room all right, honey," she said. "But you paid for a single. Your boyfriend's gonna be twenty bucks extra."

"Oh, but he isn't—" Lexie began before Shane stepped in front of her and slapped a twenty-dollar bill on the counter.

The woman took the money and handed over a key on a heavy chain. "Number seven on the far end. Your goodlookin' cowpoke friend is in number six, right next door. Ain't seen or heard from him since he checked in."

"Thanks." Lexie took the key and stalked out, still carrying her duffel. Shane caught up with her halfway to the room. "You didn't have to pay that woman," she said, glaring up at him. "I can just imagine what she thought!"

"I don't give a damn what she thought," Shane said. "I'm sure she's seen it all and couldn't care less. But I'm not leaving here until I'm a hundred percent sure you'll be safe—even if it means I have to stay all night."

She looked mildly shocked, but then recovered. "I'm sure that won't be necessary," she said.

"Did you bring a gun?"

"No, it's locked in the truck," she said. "Did you bring one?"

"I would have, if I'd known you were going to take off like a blasted runaway heifer. But as long as you aren't alone, nobody's likely to bother you."

"I know how to lock a door and cover a window," she said. "You can go on back to your trailer."

"Not unless you come with me."

"Suit yourself." She stopped outside room number six.

"What are you doing?" he kept his voice low. "Your room is the next one down."

"I know. Be still." She stepped close and pressed her ear to the door. After a moment she stepped away. "Aaron's in there, all right. I'd know that snore anywhere. I heard enough of it on our way here."

"But if he's dead to the world, you can't expect much in the way of protection. Give me the key. I'll open the door."

Shane took the key without waiting for an answer. Opening the door, he felt a rush of warm, stale air, smelling of cigarettes and Pine-Sol. At least someone had tried to disinfect the place.

The window-mounted air conditioner sounded like a threshing machine, but after the first few minutes, it began blowing air that was slightly cool. The décor and the faded, worn furnishings were straight out of the 1960s—psychedelic orange curtains matching the quilted spread on the single, queen-sized bed. A vinyl-covered overstuffed chair, its arms mended with silver duct tape, stood in one corner. The ancient-looking TV had an OUT OF ORDER sign taped to the screen.

Lexie tossed her duffel onto the bed and walked into the bathroom, which was missing its door. Bent hinges hung from the frame, as if the door had been ripped loose.

"There's a dead bug in the toilet," Lexie said, coming back into the room. "But it looks like everything's been wiped down. No bloodstains in the shower."

Catching the joke, Shane gave her a grin. "You don't have to stay here," he said. "It's not too late to go back to the trailer."

She shook her head, her jaw set at the stubborn angle that Shane was coming to recognize. The woman would stay in this godforsaken dump just to prove how tough she was. "You can go," she said. "I'll be fine."

"Thanks all the same, but I think I'll stick around," he said, settling in the armchair. "Things tend to get lively here around midnight. If anything happens, you might be glad to have me here. Now get some rest."

Lexie was bone-tired. But as she moved her duffel to a luggage stand and gazed down at the bed, all the warnings she'd read and heard came back to her—like the item about the bedspread being one of the germiest things in a motel room. Aside from being worn and faded, this one didn't look too bad, but there was no way of knowing when it had last been washed. And what about bedbugs? She could see no sign of them as she pulled back the spread, but her skin crawled at the thought of what could be hiding in that mattress.

She would sleep in her clothes, on top of the sheets, she decided. She could change and shower in the morning, when Shane would be gone. That way, she could avoid the awkwardness of undressing with no privacy.

She brushed her teeth, washed her hands, and splashed her face in the bathroom. When she came out, Shane was standing by the front door. "One last chance to come to your senses and get out of here," he said. "If we wait much longer, it won't be safe outside, even with me along."

For an instant, Lexie was tempted, especially when she imagined sleeping in that luxurious bed. But no, she had her pride. And she had no desire to be beholden to Brock Tolman for the use of his trailer.

"I'll sleep fine right here," she said, turning down the dingy polyester blanket and smoothing the top sheet beneath. "You can leave anytime."

Shane muttered something under his breath and sank back into the chair. Clearly, he was losing patience with her. But it was clear that he wasn't leaving either.

Sitting on the edge of the bed, she kicked off her boots and switched off the bedside lamp. The streetlight outside shone through the closed blinds, giving her a view of Shane, leaning back in the chair with his long legs crossed at the ankles. "Sleep tight," he said.

With a muttered reply, Lexie stretched out on the bed. The mattress was lumpy, the room was too warm, and the AC sounded like an old-fashioned dentist's drill. But she was exhausted. Within a few minutes, she had drifted off.

When Lexie's deep, even breathing told him she was asleep, Shane eased out of the chair, stretched his cramped body, and visited the bathroom. Walking back, he paused at the foot of the bed where Lexie slept in her clothes. Even in the strip-shadowed light of the streetlamp coming through the blind, there was something innocent, almost childlike, about her. Her eyes were closed, her hair tangled on the pillow. She slept with her arms outflung, her soft lips parted. Her denim shirt had come partway unbuttoned, revealing the pale curve of one breast and the lacy edge of her bra.

He turned away before his thoughts could lead him in the wrong direction. Lexie Champion was one of the most exasperating people he'd ever met. But something about her awakened a spark of tenderness in him. She was so open and vulnerable, so real, that he couldn't hold back the urge to protect her—even when his protection was the last thing she wanted.

Walking to the window, he raised a blind slat. Nothing seemed amiss in the parking lot—just people returning to their seedy rooms for the night. But he wasn't going anywhere. There was no way he would leave Lexie unprotected.

Still, as long as things were quiet, it wouldn't hurt to get a little shut-eye himself. He was a light sleeper. The slightest suspicious sound would rouse him—if he could even manage to doze in that miserable, sagging chair.

Resolving to try, he settled himself as best he could and closed his eyes.

A furious pounding on the door jarred Lexie out of sleep. She sat up with a jerk, her heart slamming. Beyond the foot of the bed, Shane was getting out of the chair.

"Open the damn door, Vera!" a drunken voice yelled. "I know you're in there." There was more pounding, then another shout. "I've got a gun! If that son of a bitch is with you, so help me, I'll kill you both!"

"Get down, Lexie!" Shane's voice was an urgent whisper. "Over there, on the far side of the bed!"

Lexie did as she was told, trembling as she crouched behind the bed. The stranger outside had begun to kick the door, cursing with each blow. Peering over the bed, Lexie watched Shane position himself against the wall, next to the door.

"You've got the wrong room, mister," he said, loud enough to be heard through the door. "Get out of here, before I call the police. There's no Vera here."

"Prove it, you bastard. Open the door. If that lyin' bitch is in there with you—"

"I'm calling the police on the count of three." Shane had his phone out. "One . . . two . . ."

"No, don't call the cops." The voice had dropped to a whine. "I'm goin'. But if you see that bitch Vera, tell her I'm gonna kill her if I catch her . . ." The voice faded away.

After a moment, Shane peered cautiously between the blind slats. "He's going away. I can see him headed for the street."

Lexie pushed to her feet. Her heart was still pounding. "Has he really got a gun?"

"I can't tell from here. But anytime a person says he's armed, the safest bet is to believe him."

Lexie forced a laugh, trying to hide how scared she'd been. "I almost felt sorry for the poor man," she said.

"You wouldn't have felt sorry for him if he'd busted his way in here and started shooting. He could've been drunk enough to think you were Vera."

"In that case, I suppose I should thank you for being here and saving my life." She paused, unable to resist a jab. "That is unless the whole thing was another one of your setups."

A stunned expression flickered across his face. Then he gave her a sardonic chuckle. "I'll let that comment slide on the grounds that I deserved it," he said. "Now lie down and go back to sleep. It's too early to start the day."

"What time is it?" she asked.

Shane checked his luminous watch. "Coming up on two-thirty. I could use more rest myself."

"In that sorry excuse for a chair?"

"Yes. Unless you've got a better idea."

Lexie knew what they were each implying. They were both fully dressed. There was no question of impropriety. But the invitation had to come from her.

Stretching out on one side of the bed, she indicated the other side with a gesture. "Come on. There's plenty of room, and I won't bite you."

"You won't? That's news to me," he teased, sitting on the edge of the bed to pull off his boots.

"Let's just go to sleep." She turned onto her side, with her back toward him.

"That's what I'm planning on. But I'll be right here in case our friend—or anybody else—shows up. Sleep tight, Lexie."

The mattress sagged and creaked as he lay down on his side of the bed with his broad shoulders inches from hers. He didn't speak or make a move to touch her, but Lexie tingled with the awareness of him—the heat of his body, the sound of his breathing. By now she knew him well enough to feel safe—Shane was here to protect her, and that included protecting her from himself. Somehow, that made the urge to turn over and reach out to him even more compelling.

But she'd be a fool to make the move. Whether he responded or resisted, she'd be sure to regret it. The situation would be painfully awkward for them both. And the urges she felt were only a passing whim. They would be gone in the morning, Lexie told herself as she closed her eyes and forced herself to lie still, allowing him to settle into sleep.

It didn't take him long. Within minutes, his breathing had slowed. A velvety snore, its cadence as soothing as the purr of a cat, rumbled in his throat.

Lulled by the sound, and by the sense of safety his nearness gave her, Lexie drifted back into sleep.

From the dark depths of her slumber, her memory spun a too-familiar dream.

She was in the arena—not watching from the stands this time, but standing on the beaten earth, dressed in bullfighter gear, preparing to move in and do her job.

Jack was in the chutes, climbing aboard Train Wreck, a rank 1,800-pound yellow bull with a string of injured riders behind him. Snotty, foul tempered, and mad at the world, he was the last bull she'd wanted her brother to draw.

She could hear Train Wreck snorting and grunting in the chute, banging against the sides. Somebody cursed. Then she saw the flicker of movement as Jack nodded, and the gate swung open.

Lexie held her breath as the monster bull kicked and bucked, raising clouds of dust every time his hooves struck the ground. Jack gripped the rope with his gloved left hand, keeping his right arm clear as the rules dictated. The timer seemed to crawl. Four seconds . . . five, six . . .

The bull spun left, flinging Jack hard to one side. Leaning crazily, he managed to keep his hold. At the eight-second whistle, he let go and flew free, landing with a bone-breaking crunch in the dirt. As the bullfighters moved in, he struggled to his knees.

Lexie, in her bullfighter gear, jumped in front of the bull, desperate to divert him. But Train Wreck, still bucking, couldn't be stopped. His kicking back legs struck Jack in the head and came down on his body, crushing him into the dirt. Screams tore out of her. No, Jack! No! No . . .

"Lexie!" Someone was clasping her shoulders, shaking her gently. "Wake up, Lexie. You're dreaming."

Still gasping and whimpering, she opened her eyes. Shane was looking down at her. Even in the semidarkness, she could see the worried expression on his face.

"It's all right," he murmured, releasing his grip on her shoulders. "You're safe."

She shook her head. "Not me. Jack."

"The accident."

Lexie sighed. "If that's what you want to call it. I keep hoping the dream will go away. But it keeps coming back. This time, I was right there with him, and I couldn't stop what was happening."

"Nobody could have stopped it. I was waiting my turn in the next chute. We all tried to stop it and get Jack out of the way. But it happened so fast, and that bull was like a runaway locomotive. I can't even imagine what your family went through, watching it happen. A memory like that doesn't just go away, Lexie. Maybe it never will."

A shudder passed through her body. She blinked back an unwelcome surge of tears. "I tell myself Jack would want me to be strong like my sister Tess. I've never seen her break—not even when Jack died. She just moves ahead and does what needs to be done. Why can't I be like—?"

She stopped talking and stared up at him. "Why am I telling you all this? I barely know you. And you certainly don't . . ." Her voice quivered and broke as the tears began to flow. "You don't care to listen to my whining."

His breath eased out in a long moment of silence. "I think we know each other well enough," he said, propping himself on one arm. "And I care more than you might think. Come here, Lexie. You strike me as a girl who could use a good spooning. And we could both use more sleep." He patted the space he'd made next to him.

Her only response was a startled look. Had she misunderstood him—or had he just invited her to snuggle?

"Don't worry," he said. "If I were going to take advantage of you, it would be in a classier setting than this godforsaken dump of a motel room."

Something in his manner made her want to trust him. And why not? Right now, she was a sobbing mess, hardly a woman any man would want to seduce.

Pushing caution aside, she moved next to him, her back spooned lightly against his body.

"There." He rested an arm across her waist. "If you need more room, just roll aside—or give me a shove. I won't take it personally. Now close your eyes and go to sleep. You're safe, Lexie. No more bad dreams."

Lexie sighed and willed herself to relax. She did feel safe. But safc wasn't thc only thing she felt. Every inch of her body tingled with the awareness of his masculine presence. She could tell Shane was making sure not to touch her in an intimate way. Even where his hips cradled her rump, the contact was light and through layers of clothing. But that didn't seem to matter. Forbidden thoughts swirled like hot sparks in her mind. If she stayed here much longer, she would be on fire.

She mustn't do this.

Straightening her body, she rolled back onto her side of the bed.

"Are you all right?" He rose onto one elbow. His eyes twinkled with amusement in the half light.

"You said that if I moved, you wouldn't take it personally."

"That's right." He smiled—a devil's smile, she thought. "Lexie, you're a beautiful, intriguing woman. I don't know what's going to happen between us, but whatever it is, it's not going to happen here."

"What makes you think anything's going to happen between us?"

"I'll take the Fifth Amendment on that."

Lexie settled back onto the lumpy pillow, gazing up at a crack on the ceiling. Sleep was out of the question now. Maybe it was time she carried out the task she'd set for herself—to learn more about Shane and his boss.

"I've spilled most of my life story to you," she said. "Why don't you return the favor? I don't know anything about you except that you ride bulls, and you work for that sneaking, lying scumbag—"

"Whoa. No need to get riled up. I'll tell you whatever you want to know. My past is the traditional hard-luck story. No family to speak of. My dad went to prison for armed robbery. A cop got shot, not by him, but he's doing life in Texas. My mother died when I was twelve, and I got kicked into the foster system. At sixteen I took off on my own. Wanted to ride bulls, any way I could. A hired man found me hiding in Brock Tolman's hay shed. That sneaking, lying scumbag, as you call him, took me under his wing, gave me a job and a chance to ride. I know the man's not perfect, Lexie, but I owe him everything I've got."

Lexie took a moment to weigh what she'd heard. Shane's loyalty to Brock Tolman was an unsettling surprise.

"So I take it you'd do anything for him," she said.

"Only within reason. I wouldn't break the law, if that's what you're implying. And I wouldn't do anything that might jeopardize my riding career. Brock knows that."

"Would you try to charm a woman into selling Brock her prize bull?"

He flinched. "Lady, you know right where to jab."

"You didn't answer my question. Would you?"

"Not if that woman was you. And I've already said as much to Brock."

"I'll accept that for now." Lexie took a deep breath and plunged ahead. "What about sabotage?"

"*Sabotage?*" His cocksure mask slipped out of place. "What are you talking about?"

She sat up, facing him. "Threats against the ranch. A note on my windshield. A gate opened in the night, and our best two-year-old bull dead. How's that for starters?"

He shook his head. "Lexie, I don't know what to say. This is the first I've heard of your trouble. But I had nothing to do with any of it—I swear to God."

"And what about Brock?"

"Why would he do something like that?"

"You can't be that naïve. If Brock can wear us down with dirty tricks, get our backs to the wall, we might be forced to sell him Whirlwind."

"That doesn't make sense. I know Brock. He can be ruthless when he wants something. But threatening notes and property damage—those things aren't his style."

"Aren't they?" Lexie demanded. "Oh, I know he never dirties his hands. But he has the means to hire people, maybe somebody from the res, who could sneak onto the property and disappear without a trace. I don't trust him. And I'm not sure I should trust you, either."

"I wouldn't blame you if you didn't." Shane swung his legs off the bed. "I'll be seeing Brock tomorrow. I'll let him know what's going on. I still can't believe he's involved, but he might know something."

"Or he might just lie through his teeth."

"That's a chance we'll have to take, isn't it?" He stood, found his boots on the floor, and carried them over to the chair.

Only as he sat and started to pull his boots on did she realize how far she'd pushed him. Maybe she'd gone too far. She wouldn't blame him if he walked out and left her to spend the rest of the night alone in this place.

"Are you leaving?" she asked, hoping she was wrong.

"Not until it's light outside—unless you want me to go now."

Lexie shook her head. "Don't go unless you need to. I know I haven't been a barrel of laughs. But I do appreciate your putting up with me—maybe even saving my life. You didn't have to do this."

"I know." He rose, walked back to the bed, and sat down on the edge, facing her. "But there's no way I would have left you to stay here alone."

"Thank you," she murmured, drawn by the warm intensity in his eyes. She felt as if she could float into their coppery depths.

Leaning toward her, he hooked her chin with his thumb and raised her face to his. Lexie could tell that he meant to kiss her and, against her better judgment, she wanted it to happen. A secret part of her had wanted it to happen from the first moment she'd laid eyes on him.

Her pulse surged as his lips settled on hers with gentle sureness and lingered in a long, easy kiss. She closed her eyes, letting her mouth soften, feeling the silkiness of his inner bottom lip, his warm breath on her face, the roughness of stubble against her skin. He smelled of expensive soap, fresh hay, man sweat, and the pungent odor of bulls—a blended aroma that was strangely arousing.

That he didn't touch her body or even use his tongue only heightened the kiss's dizzying impact. Heat coursed downward through her body, triggering subtle tugs and tightenings. By the time he eased away from her, Lexie was damp and breathless.

Speechless for the moment, she fell back, gazing up at him. His grin reminded her of a little boy who'd just stolen a handful of cookies and made a clean getaway. The rascal had known exactly what he was doing. He had played her again, and she had let him. Worse, she'd enjoyed every pulse-pounding second of it.

She opened her mouth to speak, but he touched a finger to her lips. "*Shhh*," he said. "We can pick up where we left off later. But only if you decide it's what you want. For now, give yourself time. Close your eyes and get some real sleep. You've got a big day coming up. It'll be here before you know it."

He was right, Lexie realized. She was tired—too tired to argue or even talk about what had just happened. With the big rodeo coming up tomorrow, she'd be wise to get some rest while she could.

"Don't worry, I'm right here." He had left her and walked back to the chair. Rolling onto her side, with her back toward him, Lexie closed her eyes and allowed herself to drift. The last thing she remembered was the distant wail of a police siren, fading away in the night.

The cacophony of morning traffic woke Lexie from a deep sleep. Light was pouring through the blinds into the room. Blinking and rubbing her eyes, she sat up.

Shane was nowhere to be seen. Had he gone out for coffee or simply left? Either way, for whatever reason, he had chosen not to wake her.

So where should she go from here? Shane had left that up to her. His kiss had had her almost begging for more. But there were two big, red flags against any kind of relationship with the man. First of all, he was working for Brock Tolman, and no matter what he told her, she couldn't afford to trust him. Second, he was a bull rider—and by his own admission, the dangerous sport was his life. After watching her brother die in the arena and seeing how Cory's accident had affected his wife and most likely his marriage, she had sworn that she would never go down that path.

There was only one right decision here. This evening, she would watch Shane ride Whirlwind in the arena. Whatever the outcome, she would congratulate him on a good ride. And then she would walk away, for good.

In daylight, the room looked even shabbier than it had the night before. Lexie got up, hurried to the bathroom, and rinsed off in the rusty shower before dressing in clean underwear, jeans, and a white western-style shirt from her duffel.

She had combed her hair, dabbed on a little makeup, and was organizing her bag when she heard a knock. That was probably Shane. But in this neighborhood, she'd be smart to ask before opening the door.

"Who's there?" she called out.

"Me." The voice was Aaron's. "Are you decent?"

"Come on in." She opened the door. He was clean-shaven and dressed in fresh clothes.

"Your friend knocked on my door about an hour ago." He gave her a disapproving look. "He told me he had business in town and couldn't stick around. But he made me promise that I wouldn't leave this place without you."

"Thanks," Lexie said. "This motel was a bad choice. Did you manage to sleep through the racket last night?"

"Racket? What racket? I didn't hear a thing." He sat down to wait while Lexie finished packing. "Not that it's any of my business, but I feel responsible for you. And that cowboy looked like a man who could turn a girl's head."

"Nothing happened, Aaron. He stayed in the room to keep me safe. That was all."

Aaron's forehead wrinkled in a frown. "That's what he said, too. I just wanted to make sure. I don't know what your sister would think about your spendin' the night with a strange fellow."

"She won't think anything if we don't tell her."

Aaron pondered her words for a moment. Then his weathered face lit in a mischievous grin. "What's my keeping mum worth to you?" he asked.

"How about breakfast—my treat, anywhere you want?"

"Sounds good. There's a cozy little diner just down the street. Let's go."

He picked up Lexie's duffel and followed her outside.

CHAPTER SEVEN

AFTER SHOWERING AND CHANGING IN THE TRAILER, SHANE took a cab to the Hotel Albuquerque, where Brock had arranged to meet him for breakfast. He wasn't looking forward to their conversation, but at least he could count on some good food.

He found Brock having coffee at an outdoor table on the patio. The boss was dressed for the rodeo in a light blue denim shirt, Wranglers, and custom-made boots that had probably cost more than their waitress made in six months. His silver-mounted turquoise bolo clip was authentic old pawn, a hand-made Navajo treasure from the early 1900s.

Shane pulled out a wrought-iron chair and sat down. He'd already weighed the question of how much to tell Brock about his night with Lexie in the motel. The answer: nothing.

"So how's it going?" Brock set down his coffee cup and passed Shane the menu. "Did you make arrangements to ride that bull?"

"I did. It wasn't hard. New bulls aren't in high demand. Too unpredictable."

"Do you think you can ride him?"

"I plan to try like hell. Somebody needs to end his buck-off streak. It might as well be me. I just hope he gives me a decent score." Shane stirred creamer into the coffee the waitress had brought him. The conversation stalled for a moment as she took their orders and left.

"And what about the fair Miss Champion?" Brock asked. "Any progress on that front?"

"None worth mentioning. She was parked next to the trailer last night. We . . . exchanged a few words. I invited her in for pizza, but she didn't stay long. The lady's not going to change her mind. That damned bull is like family to her."

"People have been known to sell out family members. It happens all the time." Brock sipped his refilled coffee. He liked it black and strong enough to strip paint.

"So when do I get to meet this wonder bull up close and personal?" Brock asked.

"I know where to find him. I could take you there after breakfast. But if Lexie's around, she might run you off with a pitchfork."

"I can deal with that. Maybe I can even convince her that I mean her and her family no harm."

"Good luck with that." While the waitress brought their plates, Shane relayed what Lexie had told him about the threats to the ranch and the loss of the two-year-old bull.

"And she thinks I'm behind it? Good Lord, I may have done some underhanded things in my life, but I'd never stoop that low!" Brock speared a piece of sausage with his fork.

"I told her it wasn't your style. But she didn't seem convinced." Shane ground pepper onto his eggs. "What did you do to her family, anyway? They all seem to hate your guts."

Brock shrugged. "Not much. It was years ago, when the

cattle ranches were losing their grazing permits on public land. One of the best parcels was still privately owned, and it was up for sale. A hundred ninety acres — grass, water . . . It was a cattleman's dream. Bert Champion wanted to buy it. He'd made an offer, put down a deposit with the owner, and was trying to work out financing with the bank. Buying that land would've meant mortgaging his ranch, but it would have kept him in the cattle business at a time when beef prices were going through the roof."

"Let me guess," Shane said. "You bought it out from under him."

"That's right. I went to the owner with cash in hand and an offer of ten percent higher than the asking price. He caved in and let me have it. Two years later I sold it for double what I'd paid. By then, Bert had been forced to sell off most of his herd. His family was living on beans and tortillas, trying to get their bull raising business off the ground. They've never forgiven me—not that I give a damn."

He tossed down the last of his coffee and pushed his half-finished breakfast plate aside. "Let's go look at a bull. You're driving."

Shane drove Brock's rented Cadillac Escalade to the rodeo grounds and parked it next to the trailer. Lexie's rig was a few spaces away, where she'd left it last night. There was no sign that Lexie had been there. He could only hope Aaron Frye had kept his promise to wait for her and see her safely back here.

Climbing out of the vehicle, he tossed Brock the keys. Brock would be here for the rest of the day—wheeling and dealing, meeting with other stock contractors over lunch, checking on his own bulls and going over the rider draws before the start of the competition. After the rodeo, he could drive himself back to the hotel.

With the sun climbing to late morning, they crossed the parking lot and entered the secure complex of pens and chutes that contained the bulls. It was a busy place this morning, with bulls being fed, watered, groomed, massaged with the latest electro-magnetic devices and, in general, pampered like Miss Universe contestants.

Gazing across the maze of steel-railed enclosures, Shane was able to spot a few genuine celebrities. Nearby was Fearless, black with a distinctive tan stripe down his back. He was currently number three in world title contention. And in the far corner was a red behemoth named Soup in a Group, weighing in at a full ton. In another pen behind him, was Cochise, a huge tan bull with horns that turned downward to frame his face. Animals like these were PBR royalty, the best among them valued in the hundreds of thousands of dollars.

As one of the top contenders, Shane might have been lucky enough to draw one of these bulls, who racked up high points for any cowboy who could stay on them. But Shane had chosen to ride Whirlwind with the less experienced bulls and riders. It was a gamble that might or might not pay off.

Brock nudged him impatiently. "Stop wasting time and show me that damned bull!"

"Over here." Shane led Brock through the maze to Whirlwind's pen. The silver-gray bull was in a bad mood, and Shane could understand why. He had a new neighbor in the next pen, a hulking, yellow bull with one downturned horn. Whirlwind was making it clear that he didn't like the newcomer. He was snorting, pawing the sawdust, and bellowing out challenges. The yellow bull, who had the look of an older veteran, was munching hay, ignoring the unruly youngster next door.

"Whirlwind is rank, I'll give him that." Brock was smiling. "I was hoping he might be even bigger, but he's got plenty of fight. I can't wait to see him buck."

"We'll try to keep you entertained." Riding Whirlwind had been Shane's own idea. Brock had taken to it right away, but Shane wouldn't be riding for Brock. Lexie would be watching from the chutes. He would be doing it for her, to show her what her bull could do with an expert rider.

That, or he was just another fool trying to impress a pretty woman.

"What are you doing? Get away from my bull!" Lexie came charging around the corner of the pens, angrier than a riled hornet. And she headed, not for Brock, but straight for Shane.

"How dare you bring that man here?" She spat fury, looking as if she wanted to draw blood. "You know how I feel about him! You know I wouldn't want him anywhere near Whirlwind!"

Without waiting for Shane to reply, Brock pushed his way between them. His height and bulk loomed over the defiant Lexie, but she didn't budge. Shane stepped to one side, prepared to interfere if he had to. Only then did he notice the Hot-Shot Lexie held in one hand. Shane swore under his breath. If she tried to use the low-voltage cattle prod on Brock, she could end up in jail on assault charges.

"I have every right to be here, Miss Champion," Brock said in a firm voice. "But I have no intention of harming your bull or interfering with you in any way. What I'm hoping is that you and I might come to an understanding— maybe even become friends."

"Friends!" The word exploded out of her. "After what

you did to my family, there's no way we'll ever be friends. And there's no way I'm letting you near Whirlwind!" Gripping the handle of the Hot-Shot, she brandished it in Brock's face.

"Really, Miss Champion." He took a reflexive step backward. "There's no need—"

"Just go!" she said. "Get out of here before I lose control and jab you with this thing. And take your two-faced errand boy with you."

"Lexie." Shane touched her shoulder. "I never meant to—"

She turned on him. "Don't say another word. You've already let me know whose side you're on. I know it's too late to stop you from riding Whirlwind tonight, but once it's over, I never want to see your face again!"

Lexie stood by Whirlwind's pen as the two men walked away. They'd departed politely enough, muttering excuses as they left, but the awareness that she'd made an emotional fool of herself stung like lye in a cut. Seeing Shane— Shane, who'd protected her through the night and set her on fire with his kiss—standing there, examining her bull with a man she hated, had pushed her past her limits. She'd grabbed the Hot-Shot and come charging in like a madwoman.

At least she hadn't zapped anybody. That would've meant real trouble. But she was still quivering with anger—mostly at herself. Once more, she'd played into Shane's hands. And once more, he'd betrayed her trust.

Damn!

She glanced at her watch. It was coming up on noon. Aaron had wandered off to get his own lunch and would probably end up playing blackjack at the casino on the south end of the fairgrounds. As long as he kept his cell phone on, and as long as he was here when she needed to load, unload, and drive, Lexie didn't mind. At least he wasn't trying to be her babysitter.

She could use some lunch herself. Breakfast had been light and early. But now her appetite had fled. She felt vaguely sick. If only she hadn't made such a spectacle of herself in front of Shane, Brock, and anyone else who happened to be watching.

Whirlwind was still out of sorts, snorting and slamming himself against the side of his pen, as if trying to get his neighbor's attention. The big yellow bull kept on eating, paying him no mind. Lexie reached between the rails and scratched the special spot behind Whirlwind's ear. "It's all right, big guy," she murmured. "Let him ignore you. Soon you'll get the chance to show the world what you're made of."

She could only hope it was true. Whirlwind was a young bull, unaccustomed to being without his companions. In an unfamiliar situation, he could become surly or distracted. He might even refuse to buck. It had never happened before, but today nothing would surprise her.

Maybe a walk would ease her dark mood. She'd been with Whirlwind most of the morning, fussing and worrying over him. It might be a good thing if she left him for a while. Maybe he'd even calm down. The complex was secure. Nothing was going to happen here.

Lexie forced herself to walk away from the pen. Tess was right, she reminded herself. Whirlwind wasn't her pet. He was property, bred to make money for the ranch. But she had raised him from babyhood; and while she had breath in her body, no one was going to sell him, especially to Brock Tolman.

She walked through the bucking chute area and out to the arena. Tingley Coliseum was a multipurpose indoor structure with a seating capacity of 11,000. At this hour it was a vast, empty cavern, dimly lit, with a few workers moving among the rows of seats. The shark cage, a pen-like structure, its top flat and its base planted in the earth, had been set up in the middle of the arena. From here, the press, the video crews, and a few elite guests could get a close-up view of the dangerous sport. The top of the shark cage also served as a stage and a safety island. Jets on its four corners spouted white steam to signal a successful ride.

Sponsor logos were everywhere—everything from western and outdoor gear to trucks to sports drinks. They blazed on the barriers that ringed the arena. There were logos on the gates and chute rails, on the shark cage, on walls, and even on people. Only the bulls were free of signage.

It was all about money. Lots of money.

Lexie sank into an aisle seat, letting the stillness of the place surround her—a place that, hours from now, would be exploding with noise. She closed her eyes and took deep breaths, willing her nerves to stop jangling. She'd have a long wait before the ride that would test Whirlwind's mettle and, possibly, determine the future of the ranch.

With Shane mounting her bull, anything could happen.

"Lexie? Is that you?" The deep baritone voice, familiar in a pleasant way, startled her. She turned in her seat to see a muscular man, dressed in the loose-fitting athletic gear of a bullfighter, striding down the aisle toward her.

"Casey!" Jumping to her feet, she ran to meet him, hesitated an instant, then flung herself into his open arms for a bear hug. "How did you find me?" she asked.

He let her go. "I saw your bull. Figured someone in your family must've brought him. I was hoping it might be you. When I asked around, somebody told me you'd gone in here."

His broad, handsome face wore a welcoming grin. Casey Boseman, Jack's best friend and Val's high school beau, was almost family. If Val had possessed the good sense to marry him instead of running off to Hollywood, he *would* be family. But it was too late to change the past.

"What are you doing in here by yourself?" he asked.

"Decompressing. It's a madhouse out there."

"It'll get worse. Be prepared. Have you had lunch?"

She shook her head.

"I know where to find some great barbecue. Come on, I'll treat you. We've got some catching up to do."

She let him usher her back into the blinding daylight. Casey had been crushed when Val left without warning. Later on, he'd married a woman he'd met at a party, but the marriage had lasted less than a year—in part, Lexie suspected, because he'd never gotten over his lost love.

On the night of Jack's death, Casey had been with him in the arena. He'd flung himself into the path of the bull, but hadn't been able to stop the beast from crushing his best friend. Every time he stepped onto the dirt, Lexie knew that the tragedy must be in the back of his mind. And every time he saved a rider from danger, he undoubtedly wished it could have been Jack.

The last time Lexie had seen him was at Jack's funeral, where he'd helped carry the casket. Casey had the kindest heart of anyone she knew—and it had been shattered twice, by members of her own family.

"I was sorry to hear about your dad, Lexie," he said as they left the arena complex and headed down the midway.

"Bert was a good man. I'd have come for the funeral, but I was working and couldn't get away."

"Val didn't come." Lexie knew what he was really asking. "She didn't even send flowers."

"You never found out what happened between them?"

"Dad never talked about it. But whatever it was, it must've been bitter. Val never came home again. Not even for his funeral."

"Now that he's gone, is there any chance that might change?" His voice held a faint note of hope.

"Val hasn't mentioned it—not that we hear from her that often. But the ranch can't compete with Hollywood. There's nothing for her in Arizona."

They walked in silence for a few minutes, both of them lost in thought. A couple of years ago Lexie, Tess, and Callie had driven into Tucson to see Val in a movie. She'd played the hero's receptionist, her only spoken line, "*Mr. Ames will see you now, sir.*"

Val had appeared in a few other bit parts and done some commercial work. She hadn't made it big in movieland. But she was still there, living her California life and waiting for her big break—a break that might never come. Meanwhile, knowing Val, the last thing she'd want would be to admit failure and come crawling home.

Lexie could only hope that Casey would understand.

"Here we are. What's your pleasure?" Casey had stopped at a food truck parked next to some picnic tables. Mouth-watering aromas drifted through the windows. Lexie ordered brisket with beans, coleslaw, and a Diet Coke before grabbing the shadiest table and waiting for Casey to bring their trays. When it arrived, the brisket sandwich tasted as good as it smelled.

"So tell me about your bull." Casey had taken his seat

across the table from her. He speared a forkful of potato salad and took a taste. "I've heard good things about him. Are they true?"

"I hope so. He's bucked off twenty-four good riders in the PRCA rodeos. But tonight will be a whole new test for him. I hope he's up to it. Will you be there?"

"Yup. I'll be right out there on the dirt with him. And I'll do my best to keep your boy from hurting anybody."

"He's not a mean bull," Lexie said. "In fact, he's a lamb when he's at home. But in unfamiliar surroundings, especially if he's angry or confused, Whirlwind can be a handful."

"Believe me, he won't be the first handful I've faced down." Casey took time for a bite of his pulled pork sandwich. "Who'll be riding him? Have you seen the results of the draw?"

"Shane Tully will be riding him. He arranged it ahead of the draw."

"Shane Tully?" Casey looked surprised. "That's interesting."

"Do you know him?"

"Only by reputation. He's a good cowboy. Decent man, too, from what I've heard. But he just made the top twenty. He could be drawing from the best bulls on the circuit. To keep his place, he'll need the score that a great bull could give him. Why would he take a chance on a rookie like Whirlwind?"

Lexie lowered her gaze to her plate. "He volunteered. Maybe you should ask him."

Casey chuckled. "I know that look. Something's going on here, Miss Lexie Champion. Would you care to tell me about it?"

Lexie looked up, meeting his kind eyes across the table.

Now that Jack was gone, Casey was the closest thing she had to a big brother. Outside of her family and Ruben, there was nobody she trusted more. And the need to unburden herself had become a pain that cried out for easing.

She gave Casey a half-hearted smile. "How much time have you got?" she asked.

He returned a grin. "I've got all afternoon if you need it, little sis," he said.

The bull riding event was scheduled to start at seven o'-clock, with the top riders and bulls getting into the action at eight. By six-thirty, with the stands already filling, the space beyond the chutes was a beehive of activity. The medical crew was already busy, taping and bracing injured riders who were determined to compete. The money and glory at stake were worth eight seconds of pain, no matter how excruciating. Riders were warming up in the locker rooms and halls. Some of them laughed and joked. Others prayed.

The air was electric. Even the bulls in the pens seemed to sense the excitement. They were restless, snorting and pushing at the gates as if anticipating what was to come. They'd been bred and trained for what they were about to do. Bucking was in their genes and in their blood.

Shane's ride on Whirlwind would be fourth in the lineup. He dressed in a quiet corner, doing his best to focus. Even thoughts of Lexie couldn't be allowed to break his concentration.

Under his Wranglers, he wore tight, supportive bike shorts in place of a cup. Over his jeans, he wore fringed leather chaps, to show off and protect his legs.

He took a moment to buckle on his spurs and tighten the

fit. The rowels were blunted, made for gripping the bull's tough, loose hide without hurting the animal. Over his blue western shirt went the solid, logo-covered vest to protect his ribs and vital organs. The vest, which had been invented after the great Lane Frost had died in the arena from a broken rib that pierced his heart, was required gear for every bull rider.

The heavy-duty helmet was not required. Shane was one of the riders who chose not to wear it. He opted instead for the traditional western hat, somewhat riskier than the helmet but more comfortable and stylish. Bull riding, after all, was show business.

Three more items remained—the mouthpiece, which Shane slipped into his pocket; his braided bull rope, custom-made for him by a craftsman on the Navajo reservation; and the thick leather glove used to grip the rope handle. Before the ride, the glove would be taped tightly around his wrist to keep it from slipping off. Shane couldn't wrap the tape one-handed, but he could always find another rider to assist him. There was no mean-spirited rivalry among bull riders. They cheered, helped, and supported each other, in and out of the arena.

With the glove tucked into his hip pocket and the rosin-coated bull rope slung over one shoulder, Shane was about to leave the locker room when Brock walked in, looking troubled. "Come with me," he said. "I need to talk to you—alone."

Brock led Shane down the corridor to an empty office, motioned him inside, and closed the door.

"This had damn well better be important," Shane said. "I need to focus on my ride."

"This is about your ride," Brock said. "I've been talking to Chip Harris. He's got his eye on Whirlwind."

This was news. Chip Harris was the biggest stock contractor in the PBR, famed for his championship-winning bulls. He bred superb buckers. He also liked to buy promising young bulls and develop their careers. If he wanted Whirlwind, he was in a position to make the Champions an offer too good to refuse.

"We've got to make sure Harris loses interest," Brock said. "He mustn't see what that bull can really do."

"So what are you getting at?" Shane didn't like where the conversation was headed.

"Don't let Whirlwind show his stuff. Let him dump you at the gate."

"Hell, I can't do that," Shane snapped.

"Sure, you can. All you have to do is let go. If it's extra cash you want for letting yourself get bucked off, that's no problem."

Shane felt his anger boiling, fueled by years of living on Brock's land and blindly taking orders. He owed Brock his loyalty—but not at the price of his integrity. Not at the price of his soul.

He had known there would be a breaking point. He had felt it coming. Now it was here.

"You're asking me to take a dive," he said. "I won't do it. I owe that bull, that woman, and myself my best effort. That's what I plan to give."

"And what about me?" The color deepened in Brock's face. "What the hell do you owe *me?*"

"Plenty, but not that. You can find yourself another flunky. Now, if you'll excuse me. I've got a bull to ride."

Shane headed for the door, then paused, sensing that Brock had more to say. He was right.

"We're done, you ungrateful bastard." Brock's voice was flat and cold. "I'll need you to drive the trailer and the two bulls back to the ranch. Once you get there, you can load your gear in your truck and clear out. I won't be here tonight. I'll be leaving my plane and taking a red-eye flight to Chicago for a meeting. When I get home Monday night, I expect you to be gone."

"Understood. I'll leave the key and the gate remote on the kitchen counter. So long, Brock." Without waiting for a response, Shane walked out and closed the door behind him.

He'd wondered how it would feel when he finally cut ties with the boss. Now he knew. It felt damned good, like putting down a heavy weight.

He strode back along the corridor, toward the chutes. He'd be fine, Shane told himself. He had savings in the bank, an old but reliable truck, and he shouldn't have any problem finding an apartment in Tucson. All he had to do was finish a few events in the money, and he'd be sitting pretty.

But first things first; and right now, as he'd told Brock, he had a bull to ride. Lexie's bull.

The score for a ride, based on a possible hundred points, was divided between the rider and the bull. If the rider was bucked off before the eight-second whistle, only the bull's performance would be scored. The rider would get zero.

What every rider wanted was to last eight seconds on a world-class bucker who would rack up the points. A combined score of over eighty points was a good ride. Over ninety points was a spectacular ride. The record stood somewhere in the mid-nineties.

For a rookie bull, Whirlwind had an impressive string of buck-offs. But in order to be noticed, what he needed was to score high with a good rider. That was what Shane hoped to accomplish tonight. He would give this ride his best—for Whirlwind, for Lexie, and for himself.

From beyond the stands, he could hear the strains of the national anthem. Shane felt his blood begin to race. It was showtime.

Waving down a friendly Brazilian rider, he got help wrapping his glove. On the far side of the chutes, he caught a glimpse of Lexie. She was standing on a rail, helping to fasten the flank strap on her bull. The strap, made of soft cotton, went around the bull's haunches—not over his genitals as many people believed. It wasn't painful, but the slight pressure was annoying enough to make the bull kick higher. Shane would add the bull rope himself, with a small bell attached to give it weight, just before he mounted.

Lexie had finished attaching the strap and had climbed down from the rails. For an instant, Shane was tempted to go and talk to her, to let her know that he'd broken with Brock. But that would have to wait. Right now there could be nothing on his mind but the ride.

There were three bucking chutes that opened onto the arena. Once the first one was empty, Whirlwind would be herded into it to await his turn. The silver-gray bull was already restless, banging his horns against the rails and back-kicking in the confined space, trying to dislodge the flank strap. A good sign. With luck, Whirlwind would be mad enough to buck like crazy.

Now all Shane needed to do was ride him for eight bone-jarring seconds. But before that would come the hardest part of all—the waiting.

The announcer's voice echoed in the hollow space above the crowd. Then the gate swung open and the first bull was out for a quick buck-off, barely two seconds into the ride.

The three bullfighters sprang into action and shooed the big animal back through the exit gate.

With the second bull being readied and mounted, Whirlwind was let into the bucking chute. By now, Lexie was nearby, hovering over her bull like a mother hen over her chick. Her eyes met Shane's as he climbed onto the rails with his bull rope in hand and mouthpiece in place. She swiftly looked away.

By the time the second bull had been ridden for seventy-seven points, Shane's rope had been threaded under and around Whirlwind's chest, using a hook to bring up the loose end. The tail of the rope had been threaded through the handle, waiting to be pulled and tightened just before the ride. Shane was braced on the rails, ready to mount, when word came down the line. There was a problem in the third chute. Whirlwind would be bucking next.

Shane lowered himself onto the bull's back. While a member of the crew pulled the rope tight, Shane rubbed it hard to make the rosin tacky and less likely to slip. As Whirlwind tossed his head and tried to slam the sides of the chute, the announcer's voice blared above the noise of the crowd.

"And now, ladies and gents, we have a change in the program. Coming out of Chute Number One is a rookie bull from the Alamo Canyon Ranch, ridden by Shane Tully, currently number nineteen in world standings. Let's give a big PBR welcome to . . . Whirlwind!"

Shane locked his gloved hand under the rope handle, palm up. He could feel the tension in the powerful body beneath him, feel the rippling muscles, the pent-up fury, on the very edge of explosion.

He nodded.

CHAPTER EIGHT

LEXIE FORGOT TO BREATHE AS THE GATE SWUNG OPEN. Whirlwind exploded into the arena with a twisting leap that looked as if he had invisible wings. He hit the ground with the force of a pile driver, raising dust clouds as he took off again, leaping, kicking, and spinning like a tornado.

Shane rode over his gripping hand, with his back erect and his free arm pumping the air with each jump. His legs, anchored by his spurs, gripped the massive body, his balance shifting with the rhythm of the bull's moves. Three seconds . . . four . . . Lexie was dry-mouthed. Was he going to end Whirlwind's buck-off streak?

Come on, Whirlwind, buck him off! She spoke the words in her mind, but her heart was with the rider as Whirlwind went into his blinding spin. Five seconds . . . six . . . Then it came—that subtle change in direction that had sent all the other cowboys flying. But Shane was ready for it. He shifted his weight to accommodate the change. Seven . . . eight. The whistle shattered the air. Shane released his hold on the rope, sprang clear—a perfect landing—and sprinted for safety.

The crowd broke into cheers as the three bullfighters

moved in. Still bucking, Whirlwind charged one, then another until a flick of the roper's lariat sent him trotting out the exit gate, leaving Shane's bull rope on the ground, where one of the bullfighters retrieved it.

Shane was walking out to meet the man when the judges' total went up on the board—90.1, a history-making score for a ride on a first-time bull.

Lexie didn't stay to watch Shane doff his hat and accept the applause of the crowd. When Whirlwind entered the narrow exit chute, she was waiting outside the rails to praise her bull and untie the flank strap, letting it fall from around his hindquarters. With the opening of another gate, he was freed to return to his pen.

Only then did Lexie allow her emotions to break through. Whirlwind's impressive buck-off streak had been broken by the man who'd almost broken her heart. But he'd done it in a blaze of glory. Brock Tolman must certainly be proud of his prodigy. He was probably congratulating Shane right now and plotting the next move to get their sneaky hands on Whirlwind.

A tear trickled down her cheek. She wiped it away with the back of her hand. Should she find Shane and congratulate him? Or should she just locate Aaron, load her bull, and head for the highway? She'd reserved Aaron's motel room for a second night, planning to sleep in the truck herself if they stayed, but right now she just wanted to leave.

"Excuse me. Miss Champion?"

Startled, Lexie turned to find a stocky, unassuming man in a battered Stetson standing behind her. He looked familiar, but she didn't realize who he was until he introduced himself.

"Chip Harris." He extended a hand. "I was told I might find you here."

Lexie's pulse skipped as she accepted his callused hand. Chip Harris was the biggest bucking stock contractor in the country, winner of multiple Stock Contractor of the Year awards and owner of half the contenders for Bull of the Year.

"It's an honor to meet you, Mr. Harris." Lexie's voice shook slightly.

"Call me Chip." He gave her a warm smile. "I just wanted to congratulate you on your bull's performance. He was pretty impressive out there."

"Thank you . . . Chip." It was slightly daunting to call the man by his first name. "I'm Lexie."

"I'll get right to the point," he said. "I wanted to talk to you before anybody else got down here. I'm very interested in buying Whirlwind. My offer's negotiable, but I'm prepared to beat anyone else's bid—including Brock Tolman's." He reached into his shirt pocket and took out a business card. "My starting offer's written on the back of this card. If you're interested, we can make a deal right now. Or you can take your time and let me know."

Feeling light-headed, Lexie took the card. The front side showed Chip Harris's name and contact information. She had a feeling that the figure written on the back represented more money than her family had ever seen. But there was only one way she could respond.

"I'm not even going to look at the back of this card," she said. "I can only tell you that Whirlwind is family. He represents the future of our ranch. We're not interested in selling him to anyone, not even to you."

Harris took his disappointment graciously. "Well, keep the card, and call me if you change your mind," he said. "But let me make you aware of something. Whirlwind's value will go up or down depending on his future performance.

I'm willing to take a chance on him because I can afford it. If you keep him, you'll be taking the same chance. He could become a superstar and make you a small fortune in stud fees. But if he gets injured or washes out, that's the luck of the draw."

"I understand, and I appreciate your advice," Lexie said, slipping the card into her pocket. "I'll call you if things change."

"That's all I'm asking." Harris touched the brim of his hat. "It's been a pleasure meeting you, Lexie."

Lexie made her way back toward the stands, her legs unsteady beneath her. She was sorely tempted to look at the back of the card. But seeing Harris's offer would only cloud her thinking. Chip Harris had a sterling reputation, both as a businessman and as a bull owner. If Whirlwind had to be sold, Harris would be the ideal buyer.

Not that Lexie would ever sell the precious bull. That was out of the question. But what would Tess say if she knew about the offer?

For now, it might be best not to tell her.

As she passed the hallway off the chutes, she spotted Shane. He'd taken off his vest and chaps and was just finishing an interview with a pretty, blond reporter from the sports network. Lexie's first impulse was to turn and go the other direction. But that would be the coward's way out. Sportsmanship demanded that she congratulate him on the ride. And she wouldn't mind needling him about Chip Harris's offer. With that offer as a backup, Brock would have no chance to own Whirlwind.

The reporter finished her interview, leaving Shane alone. Brock was nowhere in sight, which struck Lexie as odd. She'd expected him to be hovering around his star cowboy, demanding his share of the spotlight.

Before she could call out to Shane, he turned and saw her. Uncertainty flashed across his face. Then he managed a guarded smile. Beyond the chutes, out in the arena, the crowd was cheering another rider. But the air here, between the two of them, seemed strangely quiet.

"Hi, Lexie." He broke the silence. She cleared her throat.

"Hi. I just wanted to congratulate you. That was a great ride."

"Thanks. Whirlwind gave it to me. He was amazing."

"I was hoping he'd dump you in the dirt."

"I know you were. But a ninety-point ride will get your bull more press than a buck-off."

"And it won't hurt your press either." The sting of his betrayal, after that tender kiss, was still raw. "I imagine your boss is pretty proud of you. But I've got something for you to pass on to him. I've received another offer for Whirlwind—an offer from Chip Harris. I've no plans to sell our bull, but if I do, it'll be to him. So you can tell Brock—"

"Lexie—" He cut her off.

"I'm not finished. You can tell Brock I said he could go to—"

"Lexie, listen, damn it! I'm not going to tell Brock anything. I'm not working for him anymore."

"What?" Lexie stared at him.

"Brock ordered me to take a dive—literally—and fall off Whirlwind out of the gate, so Harris wouldn't get to see him buck. My answer was the one word Brock can't stand to hear. I told him no."

"So he fired you?"

"It was more like mutual agreement. I get to take the trailer and the two bulls back to the ranch. After that I'll be packing my truck and driving out the gate for good." He took off his hat and ran a hand through his sweat-dampened hair. "It was time. I feel like I can finally breathe."

"Well." Lexie was still trying to wrap her mind around his news. "Congratulations, I guess."

"Thanks. And there's one more thing I feel free to do," Shane said. "I'm hoping you'll join me for a late-night dinner after the competition—to celebrate your bull, my ride, and my freedom. Please say yes."

He looked as appealing as a puppy. Still, Lexie hesitated. One red flag was down—Shane wasn't with Brock anymore. But the other red flag was still flying. She'd vowed never to get involved with a bull rider. And something told her that sharing an intimate late-night dinner with this man would be putting her heart at risk.

Still, without being mean-spirited, she had no excuse to turn him down. Earlier she'd thought about leaving, but if Aaron had been drinking at the casino, she wouldn't want him on the road. She could always sleep in the truck. She'd done it before and managed fine. It might not be comfortable, but at least, with the doors locked, it would be safe.

"You're taking a long time to think about this," Shane said.

"Sorry," Lexie said. "I'm just trying to cover all the bases before I say yes."

"As long as it's yes, that's fine with me."

"Don't plan on any place fancy. These clothes are all I brought."

"Me, too, pretty much. You'll be fine." He grabbed her hand. "Hey, let's go sit down and watch some bull riding. We'll want to see if anybody beats my score—and Whirlwind's."

"You've got seats?"

"I've got seats. Come on."

She took a moment to call Aaron and tell him to be at the truck in the morning. Then she let Shane lead her to a pair of what had to be some of the most expensive seats in the house, right above the bucking chutes.

"To tell the truth, these are Brock's seats," he said, "but he's leaving town and won't be using them tonight. Guess I might as well enjoy the perks while I've still got them."

He seated Lexie on his right. Looking down the row, she saw Chip Harris. He gave her a smile and a nod. "So this is how the other half lives," she whispered to Shane.

He laughed, showing a dimple in his cheek. "Don't get used to it—not yet, at least. Just enjoy it while you can."

For the next hour, Lexie was treated to a front-row view of some of the greatest riders and bulls in the profession. When a Brazilian scored 92.1 on a burly animal named Big Black, she groaned, knowing that Whirlwind had been beaten out of first place. But seeing the great ride was a thrill.

The only dark moment came when a nineteen-year-old rider bucked off out of the gate and landed hard on his right side. Still bucking, the bull ran over him, striking him hard with its front hooves. After the bullfighters drove the huge red animal out through the gate, the young man was still lying on the ground, doubled over in pain.

As the medical staff rushed out to assist him, Lexie felt her heart contract. The memory of Jack's death flashed through her mind. She closed her mouth hard, stifling a cry as they bent over him. What if—? But no, seconds later he was on his feet, injured but alive.

As the medics supported him out of the arena, Lexie

could sense Shane watching her. Reaching over the arm of the seat, he covered her hand with his. He understood.

By the end of the event, Shane and Whirlwind had dropped to third place—after a 91.0 by the current world champion. But Lexie's bull had finished in the money. She wouldn't be going back to the ranch empty-handed. Tess would be happy.

Shane left his seat long enough to go down into the arena and congratulate the winner. The bullfighters stood together in front of the chutes, joining in the applause as the first-place rider received his check and trophy buckle on the shark cage. Turning to walk out, Casey caught Lexie's eye and gave her a thumbs-up.

By the time Shane returned to the seats, people were already leaving. "Come on," he said, reaching for Lexie's hand. "We need to pick up our prize money. Then we're out of here. I know a shortcut to a spot where we can get a cab."

"I'll need to look in on Whirlwind before we go," Lexie said.

"I know. That's the way we'll be going."

They picked up their checks at a table set up in the hall downstairs. Lexie glanced at her check and folded it into the hip pocket of her jeans. Ten thousand dollars, plus an additional payment for bringing her bull to the event. It wasn't a fortune, but it was better than nothing. Shane's check, she suspected, would be much larger.

They exited through the bull pen complex. Whirlwind had finished his chow and was relaxing in his pen. He appeared to have made peace with his neighbor. Lexie reached through the rails and scratched the spot behind his ear. The bull snorted softly and closed his eyes. "Good job, big guy," Lexie whispered. "Sleep tight. Tomorrow we'll be driving you home."

Shane chuckled as they walked through the parking lot to the street. "Good Lord, you really love that big, dumb brute, don't you?"

"I was there when he was born," Lexie said. "When he was two years old, I put the first dummy on his back and watched him buck it off. Yes, I love him, but he isn't a big, dumb brute. He's smart for a bull."

"What he is is very fortunate," Shane said. "Anybody—bull or man—who has a loyal, passionate person like you in their corner should thank their stars."

"My sister Tess says I treat Whirlwind too much like a pet. She's probably right. I tend to get very attached to things I love. People, too, I suppose."

"Then you're lucky. I don't recall being attached to any-thing—or to anybody." He gave her a sidelong glance as they walked. "So is there anybody else you're attached to—like maybe a boyfriend?"

Lexie shook her head. "Not really. I dated in college, but I always knew I'd go back to the ranch and raise bulls. Even when I was in school, I spent most weekends and holidays at home. I'd planned to graduate, but after Jack died, and with my father so ill, I knew that Tess couldn't carry the load of the ranch without me. I came home for good. I'm not sorry. I don't need a piece of paper to use what I learned in school."

It occurred to Lexie that she could ask Shane a similar question—whether he had a girlfriend somewhere. But something told her she already knew the answer. A man like Shane, who spent much of his time on the rodeo cir-cuit, would have a hard time managing a stable relation-ship, especially with the buckle bunnies—women who showed up to sleep with prize-winning cowboys—flocking to every event.

Shane flagged down a cab to take them to the restaurant he'd chosen. They sat in the dimly lit back seat, just close enough to touch. Lexie felt the tension and uncertainty of the competition melting away.

"I saw you doing an interview with that reporter," she said. "What kind of things did she ask you?"

"Oh, the usual—like how did it feel doing a ninety-point ride, and what I thought of the bull."

"What did you tell her—about Whirlwind?"

"I said he had incredible power and the smarts to go with it. And I said he could become one of the greatest bulls ever. How does that sound to you?"

"Wonderful, if it's true."

"It is. I wouldn't make a fool of myself by lying on national TV."

Lexie exhaled and settled back against the seat. He slipped an arm around her shoulders. The warm pressure felt good—maybe too good, but she had no will to move away. He was strong and solid, his skin smelling of clean, honest man sweat from tonight's ride.

She looked up at him, her gaze meeting his as the city lights flashed past through the cab window. He lowered his head for a lingering kiss, not pressing hard but holding the contact long enough to ignite a sensual tingling that rippled through her body to become a slow-burning flame. Feeling the barest flick of his tongue, she suppressed a moan.

Heaven save her, she was already in trouble.

As the cab pulled to a stop, he eased her away from him. His face wore a mischievous smile. "To be continued," he said. "Right now, I think we've arrived."

She waited while he paid the driver and walked around the cab to open her door. He'd brought her to a rustic, western-style steak house. As they approached the entrance, the savory aromas wafting through the open door and the sound of a live country band promised an enjoyable experience.

"I guess I should've asked," he said. "I hope you like good steak—really good steak, best I've ever had. If not, we can always go next door and get Chinese."

"Are you kidding? I love good steak, and I'm starved." Lexie let Shane guide her to their booth. It was surprising how comfortable she felt with him, now that Brock was out of the picture. But the issue of his being a bull rider was still a deal breaker. She would enjoy a pleasant date with him—if that's what this was—and that would be the end of it.

The booths and tables were arranged around an open area with a band and space for dancing. The country band—a guitar, a bass, a fiddle, and a male singer who looked like Brad Paisley and sounded like Willie Nelson—was good enough to keep the ambience lively. After the server brought their beers and took their orders, Shane reached across the table and caught Lexie's hand.

"How about a dance, pretty lady?" he asked playfully.

"I'm not much of a dancer," Lexie demurred. "I'd probably step all over your toes."

"My toes wouldn't mind a bit, as long as my arms were around you."

Lexie laughed. "Now that's what I call a great line. Okay, I'll try a dance, but don't say I didn't warn you."

The band had begun a slow, mellow number. At least she could manage that, Lexie told herself as he led her onto the dance floor. Several other couples were already swaying to the music. More were leaving their seats, drawn by the ease and romantic spell of a slow tune.

Lexie had never been a confident dancer, but held close,

in the circle of Shane's arms, she felt herself moving with him to the music. She closed her eyes, feeling the velvety roughness of his stubble against her cheek, the light friction of his jeans against her hips, his hand cradling the small of her back. She could feel herself warming, feel the blood singing in her veins, feel her heart thudding with the beat of the music.

"You're not stepping on my toes," he murmured in her ear.

"I know," she whispered. *I'm floating*, she thought. At least that's how it felt.

The music was ending. "Don't look now," he said, "but I think that's our waiter, headed for our table. We don't want our steaks to get cold."

They took their seats again. The steaks were tender and juicy, the baked potatoes crisp and fluffy, topped with cheese, sour cream, and bacon crumbles, the bread hot from the oven. Lexie was hungry, and so was Shane. They finished their meals and caught another ride back to the arena. Sitting quietly in the back of the cab, Lexie sensed that the moment of truth was at hand.

She'd mentioned to him earlier that she was planning to sleep in the truck cab. Shane hadn't tried to talk her out of it, but she wasn't naïve. In his world, any woman would be eager to share his bed, especially after an enjoyable evening and a great meal.

But was she ready to be part of that world? Could she spend the night with Shane, knowing that after the next rodeo, there would likely be another woman in her place?

Then again, if she turned away a man whose touch set her on fire, would she regret it for the rest of her life?

Shane had been quiet, too. As the cab let them out in the

parking lot and drove away, he turned to Lexie and gathered her in his arms. His kiss, searching, seeking, even demanding, made everything clear.

"I'll be damned if I'm going to let you sleep in that truck," he growled.

And just like that, the decision was made. She wanted him. All of him. Even if it was only for one night.

Leaving the lights off inside the luxurious trailer, he locked the door behind them. Last night, he'd offered to sleep on the sofa bed. Tonight, Lexie knew that wasn't going to happen. Two brief relationships since the night of that fateful, drunken college party had taught her what to expect. But when Shane took her in his arms, the rush of fierce desire that burned through her body left her breathless. Her arms caught his neck, fingers furrowing his hair as she pulled him down to her. Her mouth opened to his kiss, responding with tongue thrusts, tasting, and nibbling.

"I wanted you the first time I saw you," he murmured between kisses. "Now all I can think of is having you."

"Having me how?" she whispered, teasing.

"Like this, for starters." Clasping her rump with his hands, he lifted her against the rock-hard bulge beneath his jeans. Her legs wrapped his hips. Her head fell back as he pushed against her, the pressure sending heat swirls through her body. She moaned, shuddering against him once, then again, but knowing it wasn't enough. Her hands tugged at his clothes. "I think we're in the wrong room," she gasped.

"So do I. But I know how to fix that."

They left a trail of clothes all the way down the hall. By the time they reached the bed, Lexie was down to her bra and panties. Shane's jeans and the supportive bike shorts he wore for bull riding were down around his boots. He lowered her to the bed, then kicked them off before pausing to add protection.

Lying on her back, she looked up at him as he leaned over her. The outside security lights, filtered by the window curtains, cast his taught, muscular body into patterns of light and shadow. Here was a man with the physical strength and reckless courage to mount a nearly-2,000-pound bucking bull—a man who was about to make love to her.

He lowered himself to the bed. Lying beside her, he pulled down her bra straps and kissed her nipples, stroking and suckling as they hardened. The depths of her body pulsed with need, tightening and lightly throbbing. One hand slid down her belly to invade her lacy panties, stroking the moist, sensitive surfaces until she moaned and pushed against his fingers.

"What do you want, beautiful?" he whispered, nibbling at her ear. "Tell me."

"I want you inside me. Now. Please . . ." She breathed the words.

He chuckled softly. "That's what I wanted to hear."

The panties vanished somewhere under the covers as he moved over her, brushed a tender kiss on her lips, then thrust deep. Her breath eased out as he filled the needy hollow inside her. "Yes . . ." she whispered. "Oh, yes . . ."

She arched her hips to match his movements, every gliding push triggering exquisite shimmers in the depths of her body. Her legs cradled him as he rode her slowly, building to a wild, sensual rocket ride that burst like a sky full of fireworks, leaving them damp and spent in each other's arms.

Heaven.

* * *

Lexie woke to find Shane looking down at her. He lay next to her, his head propped on one elbow, his bare skin warm against hers, backlit by the pale dawn glow coming through the window. His hair was mussed, his mouth curved in a tender smile. "Wake up, sleepyhead," he said. "We need to be on our feet and looking sharp before this parking lot comes to life."

With a mutter of protest, she pulled him down for an easy kiss. They'd made love twice more in the night before finally tumbling into sleep. She felt gloriously lazy and utterly satisfied. But Shane was right. People would soon be coming to move their rigs and load their bulls. It wouldn't do for them to stumble out of the trailer looking as if they'd spent the night doing . . . what they'd been doing.

"I could stay right here all day," she murmured, yawning and stretching.

"I'm afraid that's not an option—unless you want to end up on the Tolman Ranch. I need to get this rig back, pack my gear, and hit the trail before the boss gets home. Come on." He flung back the covers and shoved himself off the foot of the bed. Without clothes, his body was all sculpted muscle—lean, hard, and emblazoned by scars from his injuries in the arena. He was beautiful, she thought, as she watched him walk down the hallway, where they'd both left a trail of clothes.

"What're you looking at?" He glanced back over his shoulder with an impish grin.

She laughed. "I'm admiring your butt. It's a hot one."

"Come on." He scooped up her clothes, except for the boots, and flung them onto the bed. "While you get decent, I'll put some coffee in the machine."

A few minutes later, with her clothes on, her face

splashed, and her hair finger-combed, she entered the kitchen to find him dressed and pouring coffee into two mugs.

"I'd fix you a real breakfast, but there's not enough time," he said. "Have a seat."

Lexie took a moment to pull on her boots, then sat on a stool at the bar and added creamer to her coffee. This was the awkward time, the *where do we go from here?* time. Since the answer would be *nowhere,* it was bound to be painful.

"You first." As before, Shane had an uncanny ability to read her.

She took a sip of coffee, forcing herself to meet his coppery eyes. "Last night was wonderful," she said. "But whatever we have stops right here. After watching my brother die in the arena, and seeing my friend's husband disabled for life, I've made a rule—a rule I broke last night."

"Let me guess. No bull riders." When she didn't reply, he continued. "I saw it coming, Lexie, but I don't have to like it. You're a one-in-a-million kind of woman and I wouldn't mind spending more time with you. But believe me, I understand."

"Thanks." She broke eye contact, staring down into her cup.

"Will you be taking Whirlwind to Pueblo next weekend?"

"It's on the schedule. I suppose so."

"I'll be there, too. We're bound to run into each other. If you've changed your mind by then, let me know. If not, we can just smile and say howdy. All right?"

"All right." She finished her coffee, set the mug on the bar, and stood. "Time to get moving, I guess. Aaron should be showing up soon."

He stood, too. "I'll be visiting Cory in rehab this week. If you want to give me your phone number, I'll pass on anything I learn about him. But that's up to you."

"Cory's my friend. I'll appreciate your letting me know." A notepad and pen lay on the counter. Lexie wrote down her number. He might be angling for a reason to call her, but her instincts told her otherwise. Shane had no need for subterfuge now. "I added my e-mail," she said, putting down the pen and walking toward the door. "We have Internet at the ranch, but the phone service is spotty at best."

"Thanks." He opened the door for her and held out his hand. "Friends?"

"Friends." She accepted the handshake. No kiss; not even a hug. He was only respecting her wishes, Lexie told herself. So why did she have the feeling she'd just been dumped?

"Be safe, Lexie," he said, releasing her hand.

"You, too." With the sun just coming up, Lexie walked out the door and down the steps. She didn't look back. She didn't want him to see that she was fighting tears.

CHAPTER NINE

THE SUN HUNG LOW ABOVE THE WESTERN HILLS AS LEXIE swung the rig off the highway and took the dirt road over the pass. Windblown clouds were racing up from the south, bringing another monsoon rain that would turn the road to slippery mud. But Lexie would be home before the storm struck. She could only hope that the trailer, with Ruben, Pedro, and the four bulls, had already arrived.

Aaron, who'd driven partway, was snoring in the back seat. She was grateful that he hadn't been much for conversation. Memories of last night in Shane's arms, along with a flood of doubts and uncertainties, would have made small talk a challenge.

She'd done the smart thing, walking away from the handsome bull rider, she told herself. So why didn't she feel good about her decision? Why did she feel as if she'd lost something rare and precious?

Coming over the pass and down the winding road, she could see the ranch below. To her relief, the big trailer was in the yard. Four bulls were in the paddock, although, from a distance, they appeared to be the same bulls Ruben had loaded for the trip.

Now she spotted Tess and Callie waiting on the front porch. Remembering Tess's evasiveness about what had gone wrong at the ranch, Lexie was anxious to hear the full story. She would have news for them, too, although she didn't plan to tell them about Shane—or the offer from Chip Harris.

She pulled the trailer into the yard and backed it up to the chute, where Ruben was waiting to unload Whirlwind. By now, Aaron was awake. Still drowsy, he stumbled out of the back seat to help.

As Lexie climbed down from the truck and strode toward the house, she slipped the two checks out of her hip pocket. With the ranch running so lean, Tess would be happy to get the money and to know that Whirlwind was living up to his potential.

Callie hurried off the porch to welcome her with a hug. "Thank goodness you're all right!" she exclaimed. "After what happened here, I was worried that—" She broke off as Tess caught her eye.

"What?" Lexie demanded. "What haven't you told me?"

"Sit down," Tess said. "It's a long story."

"I'll get you a cold beer," Callie offered, hurrying into the house.

"First take these." Lexie thrust the checks at her sister. "Whirlwind scored ninety points with the cowboy who rode him. That was good enough for third place."

Tess's expression didn't change as she took the checks. "Let's hope it's just the beginning. We're going to need the money. Oh—you'll want to hear this, too. Ruben took Whiplash to Flagstaff. The cowboy who drew him got a five-second ride and a high buck-off that broke his collarbone. Forty-four points for our boy, but no prize."

"That's a good start—though it's too bad about the rider.

Wait—Ruben took Whiplash? But he wasn't loaded when we left on Friday."

"I know. Sit down. I'll tell you everything."

Lexie sank into a chair, sipping the cold beer Callie had slipped into her hand. The monsoon storm was rolling in over the pass. Black clouds billowed high, blocking the sun. Thunder rumbled over the mountains.

Aaron struck out for home ahead of the rain. "You're invited for supper!" Callie called after him.

"I'll be back!" He gave her a wave.

"So how did Aaron work out?" Tess asked Lexie.

"Fine. He was there to help when I needed him. But he didn't have much interest in the bulls. He spent most of his time playing cards in the casino."

"And that was all right with you?"

Lexie shrugged. "I guess. He certainly wasn't a bother."

"And you feel all right taking him to Pueblo next weekend? It's a longer trip."

"I suppose so, if he wants to go. But we can talk about that later. Tell me what happened here."

Lexie listened as Tess told her about the blown tire on the switchback road, and the near loss of the rig, the bulls, and the lives of two men. Her hand tightened around the beer can, fingers crumpling the thin aluminum surface.

"But you could have died, Tess!" she exclaimed, horrified. "All three of you could have died, and the bulls, too!"

"Your sister was a hero," Callie said. "You should've seen her, galloping the horse up that road, pulling open the trailer doors to get the bulls out. That accident could've killed everyone involved."

"But it wasn't an accident," Tess said.

"What?" Callie stared at her. "And you didn't tell me?"

"I wanted to wait until I could tell Lexie, too," Tess said.

"Ruben showed me where the tire had been cut most of the way through, on the side. Someone had done it with a blade."

Lexie's stomach lurched as the whole situation came crashing in on her—the threatening note, the open gate, the loss of the young bull, and now somebody had tampered with the trailer. Somebody with access to the property.

This wasn't just a damaged tire. This was attempted murder.

Lightning split the clouds, accompanied by a deafening boom as the rain began to fall, first in stinging drops, then in gray waves that flowed over the house's tile roof and streamed down the gutters.

In the paddocks and pastures, cattle shook their hides and endured. Even the pampered bulls were outdoor animals. With no shelter except a few scattered mesquites, they weathered the storm, accepting it as a natural part of life. Rain drizzled off their long, blunted horns, sheeted down their massive sides, and puddled beneath their hooves to nourish the awakening grass.

In the cow pasture, spring calves clung to their mothers. A few bold ones, already showing promise, ventured out into the wet to buck and play. Over the fence, the untried yearlings and heifers were restless, displaying spurts of energy, then huddling against the storm.

It was still raining at suppertime. Aaron arrived on his Kubota ATV, pulling it up to the porch and shaking the water off his army surplus poncho before coming inside. The two boys and Ruben were eating with the family in the dining room tonight. Only Pedro, who'd gone home to his family, was absent.

Callie brought out the pot roast that had been simmering in the slow cooker. "My stars, doesn't that smell good!" Aaron exclaimed. The others responded with nods and murmurs. A heaviness, like the proverbial elephant in the room, seemed to hang over the group. By now everyone knew about the slashed tire and the tragedy that had been so narrowly averted. But nobody knew who could have been responsible, what to do next, or even what to say.

"Maybe we ought to call the sheriff." Lexie started the platter of meat and vegetables around the table.

"But what could the sheriff do now?" Tess countered. "Any evidence, like tracks or fingerprints, would be long gone, especially now, with the rain. Most likely, we'd have some pencil pusher come and fill out a report, and that would be the end of it. It's a shame you didn't keep that note, Lexie. At least it might be a clue."

"I know." Lexie sighed. She'd already beaten herself up over tossing the note. Tess didn't need to do it for her, especially since Tess's decision not to call the sheriff might have caused more clues to be wiped out.

"As I see it," Tess continued, "there are two possibilities. The person who slashed the tire—and possibly opened the gate—was either someone who knows the ranch, or at least the country, well enough to come and go without being seen, or . . ." She paused and glanced around the table. "It was one of us."

"Oh, honestly, Tess, that's enough!" Callie said. "There's no way anybody at this table could've done such awful things! We're like family here. If we can't trust each other, what's this world coming to?" She glanced around the table. "Let's talk about something else. Lexie, how did Whirlwind do in Albuquerque? I'd like to hear more about that."

"He did great." Lexie was glad to change the subject.

"Ninety points. Better for his record than a buck-off, or so I was told."

"And who did you say rode him?" Tess asked.

Lexie's cheeks warmed. She glanced down at her plate, then back at her sister. "I didn't say. It was Shane Tully."

Tess frowned. "Isn't he that cowboy who works for Brock Tolman?"

"Not anymore. He broke with Brock before the ride." Lexie could've said more, but she'd revealed enough.

"And you know this how?" Tess demanded.

"He told me. And in case you're wondering, Brock wasn't at the event. He was in Albuquerque, but he had to leave early."

"Interesting," Tess said.

Lexie speared a slice of beef and tried to focus on eating, but her appetite had fled. She knew what her sister was thinking. Brock Tolman was their number one suspect as the person behind the incidents at the ranch. And anyone with connections to Brock was under suspicion, too.

Even Shane.

By midnight the storm had moved on. The moon shone through drifting clouds, its golden image reflected in pools of rainwater. Crickets emerged to fill the darkness with their chirping songs. A lone coyote trotted across the yard and vanished behind the machine shed.

The house was dark and silent—except for the quiet opening of the kitchen door. The figure that emerged, keeping to the shadows alongside the house, made no sound.

The dogs, lying on the porch, raised their heads as Callie passed, but they didn't try to follow her as she skirted the yard and headed along the narrow road that led to the north property line, walking the grassy border to avoid leaving tracks in the mud.

Dressed in a dark rain jacket and rubber boots, she lengthened her stride until she rounded the curve in the road where the Kubota ATV was waiting. The driver climbed out and opened his arms.

"Damn it, woman," Aaron muttered as he pulled her close. "I thought you'd never get here."

Easing away from him, she went around the vehicle and climbed into the passenger seat. "We haven't got much time," she said. "I don't want to be missed."

"Hell, if you'd marry me, we'd have all the time we wanted. Now that Bert's gone—"

"You know better than that. The house and the ranch belonged to Bert's first wife. When Bert died, the property passed to their children, not to me. If we got married, you couldn't expect to move into the house. I'd have to move out and live with you."

"So?" He started the engine and turned the ATV around.

"Those girls are my family, Aaron. And that house is my home."

"Yup. And they could kick you out tomorrow if they took a notion to. Hell, if they ever found out you were carryin' on with me the whole time Bert was sick, they probably would."

She reached over and laid a hand on his knee. "I needed you. Bert was impossible. He treated me like dirt after he got sick. Being with you was the only thing that kept me sane."

"And now?"

"I'm here, aren't I?"

He chuckled as he turned into the yard and pulled up to his boxlike, prefabricated house. "You're here, all right, and

I know why. It's 'cause you *like* it. Never met a woman who liked it as much as you do."

"And you think that's the only reason I keep coming to your bed?" Callie shook her head. "I should've guessed that a man would see things that way."

"Something wrong with that? Hey, I like it, too."

"Don't you see, Aaron? I care about you. And I like to think you care about me, too. If this was just sex, I couldn't keep doing it."

He came around the vehicle, helped her out of her side, and gathered her into his arms. "'Course I do, honey. Hell, I'm the one who keeps askin' you to marry me. You're the one who keeps sayin' no. Now come on inside, and let's make each other happy. Okay?"

"Okay." She gave him a light kiss and allowed him to lead her into the house.

Two days later, after a restless night, Lexie woke before dawn, reached for her phone, and checked her texts and e-mails. Her spirits drooped as she failed to see anything from Shane—but then, after she'd made it clear that they had no future, what else could she have expected?

When he'd offered to let her know how Corey was doing, she'd secretly hoped that he was angling for a way to keep in touch with her. Whatever his motives, she'd jumped at the chance to give him her cell number and e-mail. Maybe she'd been too eager. Maybe it was time she faced the truth—as far as Shane was concerned, she was just another one-night stand.

Resisting the dark mood, she dressed in riding clothes, went out to the stable, and saddled her favorite horse, a buckskin mare named Sadie. An early-morning ride would raise her spirits, she told herself as she set out along the fence line. She could also make sure the cattle had weathered the storm—and hopefully that the mystery intruder hadn't struck again.

The dawn air was cool, the wet earth smelling of rain. *Petrichor.* Lexie remembered the word as she filled her lungs—the fresh, clean fragrance of earth after a storm.

Behind her, the ranch was stirring to life. Lights had come on in the bunkhouse and in Ruben's trailer. Tess and Callie had both been asleep when she'd left the house, but they would soon be waking to start the busy day. For now, Lexie would savor this peaceful, private time alone.

The eleven mature bulls were pastured closest to the house. As she rode along the fence, Lexie watched them with affection. They appeared to be in good spirits as they shook the wetness from their gleaming hides and nosed the ground for new grass.

Thunderbolt, the oldest, was a direct descendant of the great Oscar. Bert Champion had bought the retired black and tan bull, along with his half brother, to start his own line of buckers. Of the original bulls, Thunderbolt was the last one left alive. Crochety and arthritic, he was almost eighteen years old, ancient for a bull.

Whirlwind and Whiplash were the offspring of his old age. Full brothers, they'd been born a year apart, from a fiery cow that, sadly, had since died. When it came to breeding, it was the bulls that passed on their strength and agility. But the cows gave their sons the fighting spirit to buck. Experiments had proven that a bucking bull bred with a cow that lacked the bucking lineage would not produce bucking offspring. But a cow with the bucking bloodline, even when mated with a non-bucking bull, had a chance of producing a bucker.

Bert had kept immaculate records of which bulls were bred with which cows, doing everything possible to avoid inbreeding. The pedigrees were registered with the ABBI, a national organization that tracked the bloodlines of bucking bulls. Bert had shared his complex methods with Jack, but now that both father and son were gone, the girls were on their own—and it was time to breed the animals again.

Watching the bulls now, and seeing the old bull stumble, Lexie remembered a conversation she needed to have with Tess. Her college courses had taught her about breeding and genetics. She knew that the Alamo Canyon cows and bulls were too closely related to safely breed again. The ranch was in desperate need of new bloodlines.

Unfortunately, to purchase a bucking bull with great lineage, even injured or old, would be expensive—at least $20,000, likely more. So would paying a stud fee for a top bull. Getting the money would mean selling off some of their own stock or getting a bank loan. The cheaper alternative would be to buy semen from quality bulls and inseminate the cows they had now—proven mothers that would be hard to replace.

Tess, like her father, believed that natural breeding was the only way to go. She hated the whole idea of artificial insemination. She was bound to dig in her heels when Lexie suggested it.

And right now, the timing couldn't be worse. Between the recent deaths in the family, the money problems, and the threats to the ranch, Tess was stressed almost to the breaking point. But given the forty-week gestation period, if calves were to be born in the spring, the cows would need to be bred soon.

Before bringing the matter up, Lexie resolved, she would do some online research—check out available stock for sale and semen prices. If she could come up with a solid plan to take to her sister—and maybe get Ruben on her side— Tess might be willing to listen.

The aromas of coffee and frying bacon drifted to her on the breeze. Back in the house, breakfast would soon be ready. Lexie still needed to check on the cows and calves, the younger bulls, and the beef cattle, but now that she had a plan in mind, she was eager to start her research.

Nudging the mare to a trot, she made a circle around and above the pastures, a route that would give her a view of each group. Everything looked fine. No animals loose, stranded, or down, and no sign that the phantom intruder had been prowling on the property.

Skirting Aaron's place, she cut back along the narrow road that led to the ranch house. The earth was still muddy from the rain. Water, beginning to dry, glimmered in the hollows of yesterday's tracks. One distinctive set looked as if it had been made after the rain stopped. Lexie could see where Aaron's Kubota had come from the direction of his house, turned around and gone back, then done it again a second time. Strange—but not hard to explain. Maybe he'd heard something in the night and gone out to investigate. Or maybe he'd dropped something on the way home and gone back after the rain to look for it.

By the time she'd returned to the yard and put the mare away, Lexie had forgotten about the tracks. She finished her late breakfast alone, helped Callie clean up, and then headed for the desktop computer in the ranch office to begin her research. Tess had driven to Ajo for a dentist appointment and some other errands, so she'd be gone for several hours. Lexie would have the place to herself.

Logging onto the computer, she resisted the urge to check her e-mail, which would only frustrate her and waste time. Instead, she brought up Google and did a search for bucking bull semen. The results were jaw-dropping.

She'd heard bull semen referred to as "liquid gold." She was just beginning to understand why.

Bucking bull semen was stored and sold in plastic straws, which were kept frozen in liquid nitrogen until ready for use. A single ejaculation from a healthy bull could fill as many as thirty straws. The value of a single straw depended on the bull and could range from a few hundred dollars for a proven bucker, to more than a thousand for a top bull and several thousand for a world champion like Bushwacker.

Inseminating even a few of the best cows, with the help of a vet, would be expensive, and there was always the risk that the process would fail. But in order to compete with other breeders, the ranch needed new, high-quality bloodlines. This would be the cheapest way to get them—cheaper than buying a new bull or paying stud fees for breeding.

Now all Lexie had to do was convince Tess that it was the best way to go.

By the time she'd exhausted her research, it was noon. She could hear Callie in the kitchen, the radio tuned to her favorite country music station, as she made sandwiches for Ruben and the boys. Lexie would make her own sandwich later, if she was hungry. Right now, a mail notice had popped up in the corner of the screen. Probably just a sale ad or donation request, she told herself. Still, her pulse quickened as she clicked on the notice and found herself looking at an e-mail from Shane.

Hi, Lexie,
Here's hoping you made it home before the storm. I promised to give you an update on Corey. Here it is. I haven't been to see him yet because I was moving out

of Brock's place. But I did give him a call at the rehab facility. Sorry the news isn't better. He sounded pretty bad—still dealing with the reality that he won't likely ever walk again, let alone ride bulls. And Rianne hasn't been to see him since he left the hospital and went into rehab. He can't reach her by phone, and he's getting worried. As you might know, his parents are gone. She and the baby are all the family he has. Could you possibly check on her and let me know— maybe give her a call or even go see her folks if you know them? I plan to visit Corey first thing tomorrow. It would help if I could have some news for him.
Hoping to see you and Whirlwind in Pueblo.
Shane

Lexie reread the message. Whatever she'd been expecting, this wasn't it. Their wild night in Albuquerque, and whatever was or wasn't to follow, was overridden by concern for his friend. Of course, she would help. She was worried, too. She sent a quick, noncommittal reply.

I'm on it. Stay tuned.

She'd tried to phone Rianne on the way home from Albuquerque but had gotten nothing but voice mail. Now she tried again, hoping for a decent signal. She heard the phone ring on the other end, but again, there was no answer.

The easiest way to check on her friend would be to call Tess in Ajo. If she was still in town, she could stop by the family home and ask about Rianne.

She was about to call her sister's cell when Tess pulled

into the yard, driving the pickup with a load of groceries in the front and other supplies in the back.

Lexie hurried outside to help her unload. "You're home early," she said.

"The dentist had to cancel and couldn't get word to me." Tess climbed out of the truck, her arms loaded with grocery bags. "So I just picked up everything we needed and came home."

"Well, your timing's good." Lexie told her sister what had happened with Rianne. "I need to drive the truck back to Ajo. I should be home before dark."

"Fine. You'll need to get gas before you start back. Make sure you've got the credit card." Tess carried the bags inside.

Lexie helped unload the supplies, including the two dozen twenty-pound bags of Total Bull feed that Tess had picked up at the freight office. After stacking them in the shed, she climbed into the truck and set out on the hour-long drive to the isolated town that served as a lifeline for the ranch.

Decades ago, Ajo, pronounced *ah-ho,* had been a copper boom town. The boxlike company houses, laid out on formal streets that radiated from a central plaza, were still there, as was the huge open pit on the outskirts and the long row of tailings that stretched as far as the eye could see. After the mine closed, the town had almost died. Now it was thriving again as a retirement community and artist's colony.

Lexie hadn't been to the home of her childhood friend in several years, but she had no trouble finding the small, neat, stucco house with desert landscaping in the front yard.

But a dark premonition crept over her as she parked the truck and walked through the front gate. It was as if she were about to learn something she didn't want to know.

What would she say to Rianne and her parents? She'd already decided not to tell them she was here on behalf of Corey. Just a friend coming to see the baby—that would be her excuse. Too bad she hadn't brought a gift to back it up.

It was Rianne's mother who answered the door. She'd aged since Lexie had last seen her. Today she looked especially strained. Her eyes were red, as if from recent weeping. Behind her, in the living room, her husband was reading the newspaper in the same La-Z-Boy recliner that Lexie remembered from the old days. He looked up, then returned to his paper.

"Hello, Mrs. Hurtzler," Lexie said. "I was in the neighborhood and I thought I'd stop by to see Rianne and the baby. Are they here?"

Ella Hurtzler stepped back from the door. "Come in, Lexie. It's good to see you. Have a seat. Would you like a soda?"

"Thank you, but no," Lexie said, perching on the edge of an overstuffed chair. "Is something wrong? Where's Rianne?"

"She told me you came to the hospital. She said you were kind."

"I tried to be. She was very distraught—and still in shock, I'm sure. But I thought she was going to stay with you. Isn't she here?"

Mrs. Hurtzler plucked at her collar as she shook her head. "Rianne left two days ago. She took the baby and went to live with her sister in California."

Shocked speechless, Lexie stared at her.

"I tried to talk her out of it," the woman said. "But she

insisted she couldn't be a good mother and take care of a disabled husband at the same time. She had to choose between Corey and little Rowdy. She chose her baby."

"But why now? Why so soon? Corey's still in rehab."

"The lawyer she talked with told her that the sooner she files for divorce, the less chance she'll have of being stuck with his expenses."

"Didn't he have insurance through the PRCA?"

"Yes, but not enough for this. Not enough for a lifetime." Mrs. Hurtzler sighed. "We love Corey, and we're heartbroken about what happened. But Rianne's our daughter. We have to stand by her. I'd give you her new address, but she doesn't want anybody trying to find her and change her mind."

Still numb with disbelief, Lexie said good-bye to Rianne's parents, filled the truck's gas tank, and took the road out of town. She remembered Rianne weeping desperately in her arms, wondering how she was going to manage with a baby and an injured husband. This was her answer—she wouldn't manage. Or maybe she was too scared to try.

It was hard not to judge her. But Lexie had never walked in her friend's shoes. Faced with the same decision, what would she do?

Lexie understood that the baby's needs had to come first. But what a heartless decision—and Rianne had made it without even telling her husband. Now Corey had lost the use of his legs, his career, and his family.

And it would fall to Shane to break the news.

Sick at heart, she drove home, shut herself in the office, and composed a long e-mail to Shane, telling him everything she'd learned. She'd left him the choice of how much and when to tell Corey, even offering to help if he needed her. There were no words for how terrible she felt. She could only hope he'd read between the lines and understand.

Brock Tolman rode Haroun, his prize Arabian stallion, into the barn, dismounted, and turned him over to the groom. An hour spent riding around the ranch usually helped lift his black spells. This time it hadn't helped. If anything, his mood had darkened.

Leaving the stable, he strode up to the house. He'd fully expected to find an apologetic Shane waiting for him when he returned from his business trip. But the ungrateful wretch had taken him at his word. Shane was gone, with his truck and all his gear, and he hadn't come back. Hell, he hadn't even called.

Brock's ill-fated marriage had given him no children, and he had no plans to marry again. The scrawny, fatherless teen he'd taken in ten years ago had been the closest he'd ever come to having a son. He'd even dreamed of a future in which Shane became a world-champion bull rider, raised a family on the ranch, and one day took over.

Basura, as the Mexicans would say. Garbage. He should have known he couldn't count on the damn fool ingrate to stick around. In the end, as he should have learned by now, there was nobody he could count on but himself.

The old man who managed the house was waiting on the porch when Brock came up the steps, still in a foul mood. "Scotch," he growled, sinking into a chair. "Just bring the damned bottle and a glass."

While he sipped the whiskey, he let his gaze wander over the bulls in the pasture. By now, most likely, Chip Harris would have made an offer on Whirlwind. But as long as the deal hadn't been signed and the money paid, Brock wasn't ready to give up. He was already making plans to put the financial pressure on the Alamo Canyon Ranch—a sweet piece of property that he wouldn't mind owning. For starters, he was negotiating to buy the neighboring hay-field parcel from the investment company. And if Aaron Frye wanted to keep his job managing the property, he'd be smart to sell Brock his small parcel, too. That done, Brock would start squeezing the Champion sisters until they had no choice except to sell Whirlwind—and maybe the ranch—to him.

There were just two women—three, counting Bert's widow. How hard would it be to convince them that he was doing them a favor?

CHAPTER TEN

THE SUN ROSE OVER THE AJO MOUNTAINS, ITS LIGHT flowing like slow water over the yellow hills of the Tohono O'odham reservation and up over the rocky bank of land that marked the boundary of the Alamo Canyon Ranch.

Riding fence along the upper pasture, Lexie felt the heat as the sky brightened to the glossy hue of polished turquoise. The rains had moved on, leaving days of muggy heat that parched the ground and sapped the energy from humans and animals alike.

Two days had passed since her visit to Rianne's parents and her e-mail to Shane. She'd heard nothing back, not even an acknowledgment that he'd gotten her message. She was trying not to worry, but that was a losing battle. She'd lain awake most of last night, wondering why she hadn't heard from him. Was he just putting her off, or had something gone wrong?

A collared lizard, sunning on a rock, flicked its tail and vanished as Lexie approached. She paused a moment, resting the mare and taking a moment to look out over the ranch. From here she could see the house and outbuildings, the pastures, and the road to Aaron's property in the near distance. The two boys were working in the pasture with the younger bulls, giving them water and unloading feed from the four-wheeler ATV. All peaceful, she told herself, or so it appeared.

To the south, the road to the pass zigzagged up the long, steep slope. A moving vehicle had just emerged over the pass. Shading her eyes against the glare, Lexie saw that it was an older, dark blue pickup. She couldn't see the driver, but it had to be a stranger. No one she knew owned a truck like that one.

Turning back the way she'd come, she trotted the mare back along the fence line. The truck was coming down the road now, moving a little too fast. She had yet to identify the driver.

Nudging the mare, she reached the yard and dismounted as the blue pickup pulled in and stopped. The driver's side door opened. Shane climbed out.

Lexie couldn't help staring at him. His unshaven face wore a haunted expression, eyes bloodshot and framed by shadows.

"What is it?" She dropped the reins and hurried toward him.

"I need to tell you something, Lexie." The words came out low and raw. "Where can we talk?"

The sight of him and the tone of his voice terrified Lexie. But for his sake, she willed herself to stay calm. "I need to put the mare away. Come to the stable with me. We'll have the place to ourselves right now."

He walked beside her as she led the mare to the stable. His mouth was a thin, hard line, as if he were biting back emotion. Inside the cool shadows of the stable, she dropped the reins and turned toward him. "Tell me," she said. "What would make you drive all this way?"

"I came to tell you in person. I didn't want you to get this in an e-mail or hear it on the news." He took a ragged breath. "It's Corey. He's dead."

Lexie felt her legs wilt beneath her, as if someone with a bat had bludgeoned her knees from behind. She forced herself to speak. "How?"

He steadied her, his hands bracing her shoulders. "Pills, mostly Vicodin they think, although there'll be an autopsy. He must've been saving them—or got his hands on some." His voice broke. He swallowed and continued. "If I'd known what he was thinking, I'd have been right there and never left his side."

"Was this after you told him about Rianne leaving?"

"I never got the chance to tell him. He was gone when I walked in and found him. The divorce papers were on the bed."

"Oh, Shane!" Her arms went around him. Trembling, they held each other, giving and getting what little comfort they could. Behind them, the mare snorted. Shane released Lexie with a broken sigh. "Let me put her away for you," he said. "It'll give me something to do while we talk."

"Thanks." Lexie opened the gate to an empty box stall where the mare was to go. Shane led her inside.

Unfastening the saddle, he lifted it off the mare's back and laid it over the side of the stall. He did the same with the bridle. "Somebody on the medical staff called the police. They left it to me to notify his family. I finally found the number of his wife's parents on his phone and called them. They said they'd let Rianne know and help her with arrangements. The divorce papers weren't signed, so the marriage was still legal. But if it was suicide, I don't know if his life insurance will pay out."

"Nobody can be sure, can they?"

"Not until the autopsy." He took a towel that hung over the gate of the stall and began rubbing down the mare. As he worked, he fell into silence. His back was toward her, but the quivering of his shoulders told Lexie that he was overcome by shock and grief.

Impulsively she stepped close behind him and wrapped him in her arms from the back. He exhaled jerkily, on the edge of tears. "Damn it, if Corey was going to die, why couldn't it have been in the arena? That was what he'd have wanted. He would've died a hero—an example for his boy to remember—" He broke off as if realizing what he'd just said and who was listening. "I'm sorry, Lexie. After what you must've gone through—"

"It's all right. I know what you meant." Her arms tightened around him. Breaking her clasp, he turned around and caught her close. His mouth covered hers in a long, hungry kiss.

Thoughts spun and swirled in Lexie's head, like leaves blown on an autumn wind. She'd made firm rules against what was happening. But suddenly the rules didn't matter anymore—didn't even exist. All she wanted was to be close to this man.

Ending the kiss, she looked up at him. "Why did you really come?"

"Because I needed you," he said. "Because I knew I couldn't get through another day without holding you in my arms. Life can be so short, Lexie, and I've already wasted too much of mine. I don't know where we're going or what's going to happen, but if you're not willing to stick around and find out, let me know now, and I'll leave."

Her only reply was another kiss, even longer and deeper than the last one. Whatever was to come, Lexie wanted him. If this was love, she was in it all the way.

The sound of the ATV pulling up in the yard broke them apart. As Lexie spiraled back to reality, the drifting aromas of coffee and bacon reached them from the house.

"Come on," she said, tugging at his hand. "As long as you're here, you might as well stay for breakfast and meet the gang."

How long had it been since he'd sat down to a real family breakfast? Not since he was a kid in foster care, Shane reflected. Even then, he'd usually had to make do with cold cereal or toaster waffles. And he'd never felt like he belonged at the table. But breakfast with Lexie's ranch family was different. The spirit of caring was as real as the platters of delicious food on the long dining room table.

Warmed by the welcome they'd given him, he filled his plate with bacon, eggs, sausage, and a couple of pancakes. The two hired boys, who'd mentioned that they usually ate in the kitchen, were seated across from him. They'd recognized him at once. Starstruck, they peppered him with questions about bull riding.

"For heaven's sake, boys, let the man eat," the woman named Callie scolded them. Lexie's widowed stepmother was voluptuous and earthy, with twinkling blue eyes and a ready smile. When Shane had complimented her on her cooking, she'd replied with a laugh and a playful wink.

Lexie sat next to him. She hadn't shared the news about Corey—maybe because it would have cast a pall over the gathering, or perhaps because she was still dealing with her own emotions. But even under these strained circumstances, Shane enjoyed sitting next to her, feeling the subtle, warm tingle when his arm brushed hers.

The Native American foreman sat on the far side of her.

He was quietly eating, but Shane sensed that his ears and sharp, black eyes missed nothing that was going on.

Only Lexie's sister Tess, seated at the foot of the table, seemed guarded. She was a striking woman, lean and dark, with chiseled features and stunning gray eyes that held a well of sadness in their depths. As the head of the family, she seemed as fiercely protective as a hawk—especially toward Lexie.

Shane could imagine why. After the losses she and the family had suffered, the last thing she'd want was to see her vulnerable young sister taking up with a bull rider. Winning Tess's approval—if it came to that—was going to take time and effort.

The foreman got up, excused himself, and motioned for the boys to follow him. They bolted down the rest of their breakfasts before trailing him outside. Callie began clearing away their plates, but Tess remained seated, her eyes fixed on Shane. Sensing that she wanted to talk, he stayed in his place.

"So, I understand that you used to work for Brock Tolman," she said.

"Used to. That's right." Shane had nothing to hide. "We parted ways last weekend when I wouldn't take a fall off Whirlwind. He fired me, and I left his ranch—for good. It was time."

Tess leaned back in her chair slightly, studying him with narrowed eyes. "What does he want from us? The bull? The ranch?"

"He wants whatever he can get," Shane said.

"And what will he do to get it?"

"Brock's a determined man." Shane took a sip of his coffee, feeling as if he were under a microscope. "But I've never known him to do anything he could go to jail for, or do physical harm to anyone, human or animal. I think you can feel safe on that account."

"Safe? Do you have any idea what's been happening here?"

"I know about the open gate and the dead bull."

"There's more. We almost lost a rig, with four bulls and two men, because somebody slashed a tire. Did you know about that?"

Shane shook his head, glancing at Lexie.

"I haven't had time to tell you," Lexie said. "But if the rig had rolled . . ." She shook her head. "Ruben and his son-in-law would likely have died, along with four good bulls, and Tess, too, because she was there, trying to save them."

"I know what you must be thinking, Tess," Shane said. "But things like property damage and murder for hire aren't Brock's way. I've seen him operate. He'll offer you a fair price, and if you turn him down, he'll use the banks and his lawyers to squeeze you until you've got no choice. That's the Brock Tolman method."

"In other words, he's capable of blackmail."

"Only legal blackmail. But if you're going up against him, be prepared for some nasty surprises."

Tess pushed back her chair and stood. "Thank you," she said. "It helps to know what I could be dealing with. Now, if you'll excuse me, I've got office work to do."

Shane stood also. "I need to be going, too. Thanks for breakfast. Walk me to the truck, Lexie?"

"Sure." Lexie was already out of her chair. "Oh, wait. Callie made some oatmeal cookies yesterday. I'll get you a few to take along." She dashed into the kitchen, the door swinging shut behind her.

Tess was on her way out of the room, but she paused and

turned back to Shane with a stern look. "One more thing," she said. "If you hurt my sister, I'll be coming for you, and there'll be hell to pay. Understand?"

Shane had expected something like this from her. "I do," he said. "And believe me, I wouldn't hurt Lexie for the world."

"Here you are." Lexie came out of the kitchen with a half-dozen cookies sealed in a zip lock bag. They walked out onto the front porch before speaking. "I like your family," he said. "You're lucky to have them."

"I'll remind myself of that when Tess is driving me crazy," she said. "I'll tell her about Corey tonight, when she's not so distracted. Do you know when the funeral will be? I want to be there for Rianne. She's still my friend. With the guilt she must be feeling, she's going to need some support."

Shane wasn't sure he could be that nonjudgmental. But that kind of compassion made Lexie who she was. It was part of why he was falling in love with her. "The date hasn't been set. But I imagine it'll be in Ajo, sometime next week, after the body's released. If you want, we could go together."

"I'd like that. Let me know when you hear," she said. "Are you still going to be in Pueblo this weekend?"

"I'm planning on it. I'll be competing both Saturday and Sunday, if I don't get bucked off the first night." They'd reached his truck, which was parked with the driver's side door away from the house. Opening it, he pulled her close for a quick kiss. "I'm hoping for more than that 'howdy' we talked about."

She kissed him back. "I'll keep that in mind."

* * *

Lexie watched him drive away. His words and his kiss had made it clear that he wanted them to spend more nights together. The thought of being with Shane again, his hardness filling the need inside her, sent a shimmer of heat through her body. A tiny moan quivered in her throat.

Her gaze followed the truck as it zigzagged up the road and vanished over the pass. *Keep him safe.* The silent prayer came unbidden to her mind. What if something were to happen to him—like Jack? Like Corey, or other rodeo cowboys she'd known about?

Bull riders faced danger every time they climbed on a bucker. But the leading cause of death in the rodeo profession wasn't the arena. It was highway accidents, driving from event to event—driving long, late, and tired.

Keep him safe. There were so many dangers, so many things that could go wrong. But she already knew that; and if fate willed it, she still wanted to share a life with Shane Tully.

But Shane would never give up the arena, not even if she begged him—not even if she made threats and demands. Pulling him away from the sport he loved would only drive a wedge between them. Did she have the courage to accept that? Days ago, she might have said no. Now she had no alternative except to try. She loved him too much to walk away.

Hopefully, she would be with Shane in Pueblo this weekend. But right now she had other concerns. She had yet to approach Tess with her idea of buying bull semen for their cows. She'd hoped to get Ruben on her side first, but she'd had no chance to talk to the foreman alone. With time growing short, and Tess in the office this morning, now could be her best chance.

In her bedroom, she gathered up the printed copies of her research and took them back up the hall. The office door was closed, which meant Tess didn't want to be disturbed. But Lexie couldn't let that stop her. It was now or never, she told herself as she rapped on the door and, without waiting for an answer, opened it and walked in.

"Tess, we need to talk," she said.

Tess looked up from a desk spread with bills and receipts. "If it's about your boyfriend, he seems all right. But the last thing we need around here is another bull rider. Why can't you hook up with some nice tax accountant? We could use one of those."

"This isn't about Shane," Lexie said. "I'm here about something else." She pulled up a straight-backed chair and sat down. "Are you aware that it's getting past time to breed our cows?"

"I am, and I've got it covered."

"Covered how? I've looked at Dad's records. There's no way we can use our bulls without inbreeding. We need new bloodlines."

"I know." Tess paused to enter an item on the computer. "I said I've got it covered. It's part of my job."

"Well, I took genetics and breeding classes in college, and I've been doing research online. Take a look at this." She spread the pages she'd printed in front of her sister. "If we go with artificial insemination, we can buy semen from some really great bulls. The calves from our cows could ensure the future of this ranch."

Tess pushed the pages away with scarcely a glance. "Forget it, Lexie. Good semen is expensive, and there's no guarantee that the process will work. If it fails, there goes the money. Besides, natural breeding is healthier for the cows."

Lexie bit back her frustration. She should have expected this. "You say you've got it covered. So what's the plan?"

"You know the Jensen Ranch—the one east of Phoenix? They raise beef cattle and a few bucking bulls."

"I know who they are. But their bulls aren't first-class. They do small-town and high school rodeos, mostly."

"Well, I've been in touch with them, and I've arranged a trade," Tess said. "They'll truck one of their better bulls here to our ranch and take him back once he's done his job. In return, they'll get one of our yearling bulls—their pick. Our cows will be taken care of, and it won't cost us a cent."

By the time her sister finished, Lexie was livid. "It's not just about money, Tess. They'll be taking the best of our yearlings. I already know which calf they'll want. And we don't even know whether the bull will be any good." She shoved the papers back in front of her sister. "Just look at this list. Right here—for a few hundred dollars we can get a straw from a bull with lineage going back to Little Yellow Jacket. And here's another one—a bull from a granddaughter of Bodacious. These are fabulous bloodlines, Tess. Even one straw, with the right cow, could give us a line of world-class bulls."

"All that money for one little straw—to take care of just one cow." Tess shook her head. "We'd have to pay a vet to do the job right, and even then the pregnancy might not take. It isn't going to happen, Lexie. I've already made the arrangements. The Jensen bull will be arriving in the next few days."

"And if his calves don't turn out to be any good?"

"Then we'll sell them. At least that'll leave us with some money."

"Money! That's all that matters to you!" Lexie stood up so abruptly that the chair crashed over. "I'm thinking of the future—where the ranch will be in five years, in ten—"

"If we can't pay our bills, we won't have a ranch," Tess said. "Now leave me alone and let me get back to work."

Lexie stormed out of the office, slamming the door behind her. How could Tess be so shortsighted? Of course, the ranch needed money to survive. But using a mediocre bull for stud was a BandAid solution. To be successful as stock contractors, they were going to need a great line of bulls—or at least one truly great bucker and a way to make the most of breeding him.

Still seething, she strode outside and crossed the yard to the bull pasture. For a long moment she stood watching the bulls. There was old Thunderbolt, getting more feeble by the day; and Renegade, who, through no fault of his own, had triggered Corey's tragedy. There were the good, solid bulls—the brindle, the massive white, and the others. There was Whiplash, young and barely tested but full of fight. And there was Whirlwind, her silver bull, the dominant one. She could see him standing like a monarch on a grassy rise, pawing the earth and lowing a challenge to all comers.

He was her best hope. Maybe her only hope.

"It's up to you, big guy," she said as if the bull could understand her. "We're all depending on you to win for us. So get out there this weekend and buck your heart out."

In a comfortable hotel room, overlooking Pueblo's Riverwalk, Lexie and Shane lay snuggled on the king-sized bed, watching bull videos on his laptop. It wasn't for enter-tainment. Shane's score of 88.8 in Saturday's first round had qualified him for the finals on Sunday. He would be riding one of the high-ranking bulls—but since he didn't yet know which one, he needed to study all the possibilities.

Sunday would be a big day for Whirlwind, too. The silver-gray bull had been set to buck on Saturday, but he'd been moved up to fill in for another bull that had been in-jured in transport. Shane had been ruled out as his rider, but the draw had yet to be posted. In tomorrow's finals, Whirlwind could be bucking one of the top bull riders in the world.

Lexie was excited for her man. She was even more ex-cited for her bull. Even after making delicious, passionate love with Shane, she was too keyed up to close her eyes. That was one reason why they were streaming bull videos at one-thirty in the morning.

"Here's what you look for in a great bull." Shane had loaded a video of Sweet Pro's Bruiser, a regal tan and brown bull with three world titles. "His leaps are in a class by themselves. But watch this trick. First the front end goes up. Then he just flows into this massive rear kick, twisting his hindquarters. When the rider has to lean back to stay balanced, that butt twist scoops him right off."

"Did you ever ride him?" Lexie asked.

"Nope. But I've watched him. He isn't in town, or I might have a chance." Shane yawned. "Bulls have a lot of tricks. And the older they are, the smarter they get. They can tell where a rider's weight is, which hand he's using, and what kind of move will throw him off."

Shane yawned again. "Some bulls do the same thing

every time out. They're the kind a rider likes to draw. With others, you never know what they're going to do. Something tells me Whirlwind will be one of those."

"I hope so." Lexie snuggled closer, took the laptop out of his hands, and switched it off. "Get some sleep. You're the one who needs it. I'll be fine."

He kissed her, rolled over, and was snoring in minutes. Lexie lay next to him, feeling his warmth and listening to him breathe. *Heaven,* she thought. Life couldn't get much better than this.

So far, a good luck spell had hung over this trip to Pueblo. Again, she'd brought Aaron along to help her drive and load. This time she'd been prepared for his disappearing act. She'd given him enough cash for a room and meals and let him make his own plans as long as he kept in touch and showed up to leave before dawn on Monday. The arrangement suited them both. With Aaron out of the way, Lexie was free to be with Shane.

Not that Shane was free to be with her. Tomorrow she would be on her own as he prepped for what could be the most important ride of his career—working out in the state-of-the-art training facility at Pueblo's PBR headquarters, studying the bull he'd drawn, and focusing entirely on the ride. Lexie understood this. Jack's need to focus had been much the same. Once the ride was over and Shane had had a chance to unwind, he'd be all hers again.

That was her last thought as she finally drifted into sleep.

The next morning, when she opened her eyes, he was already gone. Giving herself time to come fully awake, she lay back on the pillows, watching the daylight steal across the ceiling. If what she and Shane had found turned out to be for a lifetime, she would have to accept sharing him with this other love of his.

She was prepared to do that, and more. But her heart would be in her throat every time he climbed into the bucking chute.

The hours of the day seemed to crawl. Lexie had arranged to meet Casey for an early lunch. Seeing her sister's old flame always gave her spirits a lift.

They'd chosen a bistro with outdoor tables on the River-walk. Casey had shown up in jeans and a T-shirt that showed off his powerful chest. He'd insisted on treating her to French onion soup and croissant sandwiches. The food was tasty, but Lexie's anxiety had stolen her appetite. She ate out of politeness, forcing every bite.

"I've heard some buzz about your bull." Casey hadn't asked about Val today. Maybe because he already knew what the answer would be.

"What have you heard about Whirlwind?" Lexie sipped her Diet Coke.

"After that ninety-point ride in Albuquerque, the question folks are asking is, was it a flash in the pan or has he really got what it takes? The riders I talked to were anxious to try him."

"So who won?" Lexie asked. "Who drew him?"

"None other than Carlos Machado."

Lexie gasped. The Brazilian was a former world champion, in close contention for another title this year. He was currently in position number three—and he was taking a big chance. In a high-stakes sport where ranking was everything, a single great ride—or a buck-off—could make all the difference.

What if Whirlwind didn't measure up?

Lexie stopped eating and shook her head. "I'm sorry. My stomach's in knots. I won't relax till the ride's over."

"I understand." Casey helped himself to a chip on her plate. "You've got a lot of hope riding on that bull."

"More than you know," Lexie said. "Did you happen to notice which bull Shane drew?"

"Sorry, I forgot to check," Casey said. "Anyway, I thought you'd written the guy off."

"We gave it a second chance—and it seems to be working." Lexie's face warmed.

"So I see. You're glowing. If it's the real thing, I wish you all the happiness—and all the luck—in the world."

Lexie gave him a smile. "Happiness I can manage. Luck—I'm going to need all I can get."

She dismissed the brief, unforeseen chill that passed through her as she spoke. Nothing was going to happen on this beautiful day. Everything in her small, happy world was going to be fine.

Early Sunday morning, when Tess went out to check on the bulls, she saw that old Thunderbolt had died. He lay on his side in the middle of the pasture, the other bulls keeping their distance, as if frightened by something they didn't understand.

The death was sad but not unexpected. Tess had known that the old bull's days were numbered. But with Ruben, Aaron, and Lexie gone, the timing wasn't the best. She would have to depend on the two boys to get the backhoe running and dig a grave in the pasture. If they couldn't start the cursed machine, which hadn't worked in months, it would mean long hours of shoveling.

Entering the pasture through the gate, she walked over to the body. Only then did she notice the swollen belly and the froth of white foam around the bull's mouth. Her heart slammed. Thunderbolt hadn't just dropped from old age. It appeared that he'd been poisoned.

As the sky paled to dawn, she struggled to make sense of the situation. Cattle on the range sometimes ate poisonous plants. But there were no poisonous plants in the pasture, and the other bulls seemed fine. What would Thunderbolt have eaten that the others didn't?

Steeling herself, she leaned close to the dead bull's mouth and breathed in the smell of the white foam. She straightened, stifling the urge to gag. Was it her imagination, or had her nose detected a faint metallic odor?

It was some kind of chemical poison. It had to be.

Aside from the grass in the pasture, the only other thing the bulls ate was the Total Bull supplemental feed, which came in sealed twenty-pound bags. The most recent supply, which Tess had picked up a few days ago at the freight office, was stacked in the feed shed.

The bulls were fed in the fenced paddock, with the food in black rubber tubs that were set out ahead of time, one for each bull. But if the feed had been poisoned, even by accident, why had only one bull been affected?

The two boys had come out of the bunkhouse to start their chores, which included feeding the bulls. Tess could hear their groans of dismay even before she turned and left the pasture to meet them.

In a few words, she told them what had happened. "Don't worry, you're not in trouble," she said. "But I need to know exactly what happened the last time you fed the bulls. Did you open a new bag of feed?"

"We did," Ryder said. "But there was another bag that was almost empty. There was just enough feed in it for one tub. So we used that one first. Then we opened the new bag and filled the rest of the tubs."

Things were beginning to make sense. "What did you do with the first bag—the empty one?" Tess asked.

"It's in that trash barrel by the shed," Chet said. "Hang on. I'll go get it."

He was back in a moment with the empty, crumpled bag. When Tess opened the top and took a cautious sniff, the odor of the residue that lingered in the bottom of the bag was unmistakable. Zinc phosphide, the deadliest ingredient in rat poison.

She could picture it in her head—the tubs of feed set out in the paddock, the bulls coming in through the gate, each one going at random to a tub. Any of the bulls could have gotten the poison. It was pure chance that the unlucky animal had been old Thunderbolt—a good bull who'd deserved a gentler death.

The fury that welled up in Tess was almost blinding. Someone with no conscience was out to destroy her beloved ranch, and she'd had enough. Whatever she had to do, she would find out who was behind these atrocities and stop them, once and for all.

CHAPTER ELEVEN

WHIRLWIND WAS IN THE CHUTE, SNORTING, BANGING, AND so keen to buck that Lexie had needed help attaching the flank strap. She stood back now, letting the handlers do their job as Carlos Machado climbed onto the rails above him, preparing to mount.

Machado was currently the highest ranked among the Brazilians who'd come north to ride with the PBR. Raised on the vast South American cattle ranches, they were seasoned cowboys, darkly handsome, sleek and agile as panthers. Out of the arena, they tended to be polite and soft-spoken. Most wore crucifixes and prayed before each ride.

Lexie forgot to breathe as Machado lowered himself onto Whirlwind's silvery back and settled into place. After the rope had been rubbed and pulled tight, he wrapped his glove, checked his position, and nodded.

Whirlwind flew out of the open gate. At the top of his bounding leaps, he arched like a cat, coming down with a body twist at the bottom. Once . . . twice . . . then a shift in direction, like the subtle click of a gear, and a drop into a sudden spin. Machado wasn't ready for the surprise. With two seconds left on the clock, he lost his hold and was pitched off onto his side. He scrambled for safety as the bullfighters closed in to herd the bull into the exit.

Lexie was jumping, cheering wildly. Whirlwind had just bucked off the number three rider in the PBR. The bull's score: forty-five points.

Casey caught Lexie's eye and gave her a grin. She returned a thumbs-up before hurrying to the inside chute to unfasten her bull's flank strap and release him back to the pen.

"Good boy! You did us all proud!" She scratched his ear, opened the narrow gate, and watched him trot back to the pens.

"I see you still haven't sold him." The deep voice, coming from the shadows behind her, made Lexie's nerves clench. She forced herself to turn around and confront Brock Tolman.

"If you're still wanting to buy my bull, Chip Harris is in line ahead of you," she said. "But that doesn't matter, because Whirlwind isn't for sale."

He loomed over her, a confident smile on his face. "How much did Harris offer you? I'll beat his price by twenty percent. Hell, make it thirty percent."

"Didn't you hear me? Whirlwind isn't for sale. Not at any price—and especially not to you. So get out of my face and stay away from my bull—and our ranch!" Lexie turned away and strode off before he could reply.

As she headed for the stands, she could hear him laughing. "Tell Shane I said hello," he called after her. "Tell him I said he's welcome to come back anytime."

You don't own him anymore!

Lexie was tempted to fling the words at him. But she'd only be wasting her breath. All she really wanted was to get to her seat so she could watch Shane ride.

She hadn't seen Shane all day, but she'd known better than to look for him. Riding a bull involved as much mental focus as physical strength and balance. He didn't need a woman distracting him from that focus.

She hadn't seen any posted results of the draw, either, although she'd looked for a list on her way to the bucking chutes. But since Shane's ninety-point ride on Whirlwind had boosted him in the rankings, he was bound to be in the draw for the most challenging bulls. The one he'd drawn would be a surprise to Lexie. She could only cross her fingers and hope for another great ride—or at least a safe one.

Lexie's seat along the side gave her a view of the bucking chutes. Her pulse quickened as Shane walked out onto the raised platform and climbed down above the number three chute. Below him, through the barricade of legs and bodies that surrounded the chute, she glimpsed a flash of yellow hide—a huge bull, but not one she could readily name. She would have to wait for the announcement.

As Shane lowered himself onto the bull's back and began the last-minute adjustments in the rope, the announcer's voice blared, echoing against the roof of the arena. "Now for the last ride of the night. Coming out of chute number three, we have Shane Tully, ranked number fifteen, riding Train Wreck."

Train Wreck!

Lexie's throat closed off tight, stifling a scream. *Train wreck was the bull whose stomping hooves had killed Jack.*

Since Jack had fallen under the bull, Lexie knew that Train Wreck hadn't been blamed. He'd been kept on the PRCA circuit, where Lexie had lost track of him. Now here he was, carrying memories that slammed into her like the flood from a dam burst. When had the bull been moved to the PBR circuit?

Shane had seen Jack die. He would have known about Train Wreck's past. Why would he have agreed to ride him?

The questions went unanswered as the gate swung open.

Shane felt the raw power of bunching muscles as Train Wreck burst out of the chute. He'd agreed to ride the huge, rank bull in the hope of purging Lexie's nightmares, conquering the demon that haunted her. Maybe it hadn't been the best idea. But he wasn't thinking about that now. He couldn't think about anything but staying on the bull and getting a good score.

Train Wreck was a kicker. He turned like a carousel, with those massive hindquarters going up so high that his body was almost vertical, then plunging down with the bone-jarring force of an 1,800-pound boulder dropping to Earth. Shane gripped the tough hide with his spurs, keeping his free arm high as he struggled to match the bull's weight shifts with his own. The seconds crawled past. He was barely aware of them until he heard the blast of the eight-second whistle and the sound of cheering.

With Train Wreck still bucking like fury, he lowered his arm, freed his gloved hand from the rope handle, and pushed off, springing to the right. The dismount would have been perfect if his spur hadn't tangled in the rope.

Weighted by the metal bell, the rope dropped off the bull. But the split-second delay pulled Shane off-balance, causing him to land on his side. With the bullfighters closing in, Train Wreck suddenly changed directions. As Shane rolled, trying to protect his face and chest, the rear hooves came crashing down onto his body.

He heard a scream inside his head—then nothing.

As the roper herded the bull through the gate, the bullfighters and medical staff swarmed over Shane's inert body. Lexie fought her way through the departing crowd, pushing and shoving, pleading to be let through. By the time she made it down to the chutes, Shane was gone. The fading wail of a siren told her he was on his way to the hospital.

Trembling and alone at the edge of the arena, she stood in the spot where he'd gone down. She could see the slight hollow where his body had lain, the prints where Train Wreck's hooves had gouged the dirt, and the sneaker tracks of the bullfighters and medics.

First Jack, then Corey, and now Shane.

She wanted to scream, cry, and fling herself onto the ground. But that wouldn't do any good. Right now what she needed was to get to Shane. But how? She was surrounded by strangers. She didn't know the way to the hospital. Even if she did, the cabs would be busy, and she'd left the truck key in her duffel, in the hotel room.

"Come on." A powerful hand seized her arm from behind. "I've got a car. I'll get you to the hospital."

For an instant, Lexie thought she'd imagined the deep voice. But as she turned and looked up, she realized that Brock Tolman was propelling her toward the exit.

Keeping a grip on her, he bulldozed his way through the crowd and out the rear doors to the VIP parking lot. The long, black Cadillac was waiting for them. Brock must've called ahead, she realized as an attendant opened the passenger door. She slid onto the leather seat, her legs collapsing beneath her.

"Buckle in." The motor roared to life as Brock turned the key in the ignition. Lexie buckled her safety harness as the big car squealed away from the curb.

Brock's mouth was a thin, hard line. She should at least thank him, Lexie thought. She'd never said anything to the man that wasn't hostile. But that didn't matter now. All that mattered was Shane.

"How much do you know?" she asked.

"Not much more than you do." Brock floored the gas pedal, barreling through a traffic light as it changed from yellow to red. "He was unconscious when they carried him out to the ambulance. We'll know more when we get to the hospital."

"Thank you," Lexie said.

He didn't reply. Guided by the car's GPS, they sped through a blur of city streets.

Parkview Medical Center was a vast complex of connected red-brick buildings. Signs along the road pointed the way to the emergency room.

Brock pulled up to the entrance, braking with a squeal of tires. "Go on in," he said to Lexie. "Find out as much as you can. I'll park and meet you inside."

Lexie dashed out of the car. Her legs were rubbery, but she ran anyway, half stumbling through the automatic double doors. A sense of unreality hung over her, as if she still expected to wake from the nightmare her life, and Shane's, had become. But she knew better. This wasn't a dream or a movie. This was real.

A corridor opened into a dreary-looking waiting room with tan walls and fake neon leather seats, arranged in rows. Vending machines and magazine racks lined one wall. A set of heavy double doors closed off the treatment rooms. There were people sitting, some thumbing nervously through tattered magazines as they waited.

Lexie was headed for the reception counter when a familiar figure stepped into sight.

"Casey!" She flung herself into his arms. He was still in his bullfighting gear. As he held her, she could feel the rigid protective vest underneath his shirt. He must've ridden in the ambulance with Shane. Otherwise he might have spotted her in the arena.

She drew back and looked up at him. His expression was so grim that he looked like a different person from the affable man she knew. She fumbled with words for questions she was too scared to ask. Never mind, he knew what she wanted to know.

"Shane is awake, Lexie," he said. "But he has a concussion, and he took a real pounding from that bull. His spine—"

"No—" Her thoughts flew back to another night, another hospital, another broken man and another frantic woman. Now it was Shane's turn, and hers. Could she be stronger than Rianne?

But who was she to judge? Rianne had been strong enough to make a choice and walk away. Even now, Lexie knew that, whatever had happened, she could never walk away from Shane.

"Will they let me see him?" she asked.

Casey shook his head. "You could ask. But when I had to leave him, he was still in shock. They had him on an IV drip and were trying to get his vitals stabilized. Once they do that, they'll know more."

"I'll wait, for as long as it takes."

"How long will that be? Is he conscious? Is he even

alive?" Brock strode into the waiting room, demanding answers. Lexie turned to face him. "Talk to Casey here. He knows more than I do."

While the two men talked, she sank onto a chair, struggling to unscramble her thoughts. She'd left Whirlwind in his pen at the arena. She couldn't just abandon him. Forcing herself to concentrate, she found her phone in her purse and called Aaron's number. The phone rang once, twice. *Please, please pick up . . .*

"Hullo?"

At the sound of Aaron's voice, Lexie breathed a sigh of relief. In a few words, she told him what had happened. "I need you to get back to the arena and check on Whirlwind," she said. "You can stay in Shane's hotel room tonight—I'll call the hotel and make sure they'll let you in. The key to the rig is in my duffel. Pack my things and take them when you go to load the bull in the morning. You'll probably need to drive him home alone, so make sure you're rested. I'll call Tess and let her know what's going on. All right?"

"Sure." Aaron was nothing if not laid-back. "Don't worry about your bull. I'll take care of him. But how will you get home?"

"I'll figure that out when I know more." Lexie ended the call. She was concerned about Whirlwind, but all she could do was trust Aaron to do his job. Right now her place was with Shane.

"I couldn't help overhearing that," Casey said. "Are you planning to spend the night in the hospital?"

Lexie nodded. "I'm not leaving Shane. If he needs me, I want to be here."

"Well, he's not going to need his truck," Casey said. "He left the keys in the locker room. I could get them and bring it here for you. Then you'd have something to drive."

"How are you going to manage that? You're stranded, too, aren't you?"

"Don't worry. I've got it figured out," Cascy said. "I don't plan on staying the night, but I won't go home without making sure you're okay."

"Thanks." Her gaze flickered toward Brock, who was still talking to the nurse. She lowered her voice. "It's a long story, but I really don't want to owe him any more favors."

"Understood, little sis. I'm on it. But I'll need to borrow your phone. Mine's in my locker."

He took her phone and walked a few paces down the hall. Minutes later he came back and handed her the phone. "I'll be taking a cab back to the arena. From there, I'll find a way to get you the truck." He clasped her shoulder for a moment. "Hang in there, girl. You're tough, and so is he."

He walked back outside to wait for the cab. Casey said she was tough. But was she tough enough? The next hours, days, and weeks would tell.

The nurse at the counter was on the phone. She hung up and spoke a few words to Brock. He nodded and turned back to Lexie. "We can see him for a few minutes. I'd like to go first. That way, you can stay longer if you want. I have the room number."

A nameless fear shot through Lexie as she stood. Whatever the new reality was, she was about to meet it.

Brock gave her a questioning look as she followed him into the hallway. "I'll wait outside the door," she said. "That way, I can go in as soon as you leave."

"Whatever you like." He lengthened his stride as if determined to leave her behind. Seconds later he disappeared through an open doorway. As the door closed behind him, Lexie leaned against the wall, her heart pounding. This wasn't about her fear or her nerves or her strength. It was about the man she loved—the man lying shattered on the other side of that door.

Shane lay in a drug-blurred haze. He knew where he was and what had happened to him. But he didn't know how badly he was injured. Part of him didn't want to know.

He tried moving his head to one side, but his neck was in a brace. He blinked his eyes, flexed his fingers, and made fists of his hands. So far so good. But what about his legs? His feet? He tried wiggling his toes. Was anything happening? He couldn't tell.

The lower part of his body was encased in some kind of brace. Was that what kept him from moving? But he would deal with that later. His head hurt like hell. And now someone had come into the room. A heavy step. A face leaning over him.

"Shane, can you hear me?" The voice brought everything into focus. It was Brock.

He muttered a yes. "How bad . . . ?" He struggled with the question.

"Bad enough. They won't know till they run some tests. Do you remember what happened?"

"Yeah . . . damn bull was right on me. Couldn't get away. Did I win?"

"You came in second. Ninety-one points. Fifty thousand dollars. Not bad. But I'm planning to buy that damned bull and put a bullet through his brain."

"No . . . don't do it. Wasn't his fault. I just got in his way. Promise me."

Brock exhaled. "All right. But what I really came here to say was, you won't have to worry about money or a place to recover. We can set up a therapy room, hire somebody full-time if you want."

"I'll think about it." Shane could feel the clouds in his brain clearing. His new reality was going to take some getting used to. But one thing was certain. If he went back to Brock's, he'd never leave.

"Have you seen Lexie?" he asked.

"She's right outside, waiting for me to go so she can come in."

Anguish burned its way through Shane's body, as if he'd swallowed acid. Lexie couldn't be part of this. She deserved better. She deserved a life. "Damn fool woman," he muttered. "Tell her I said to walk away and don't look back."

"I could try. But you know she won't listen. If that's what you want, you'll have to tell her yourself."

Shane took a deep breath, knowing what had to be faced. "I'm not going to walk again, am I?" he said.

"Wait for the tests. And give yourself some time. Nobody knows yet."

"*I* know. I can't even feel my damned toes."

"It's too soon to jump to conclusions, Shane. There's always hope."

"Hope is horse shit. Why should I lie to myself?" Shane was losing patience. "Go on. Get out of here and take Lexie with you. I don't need your platitudes, and I don't need anybody's god-damned sympathy."

"Lexie is your problem, not mine. I'll be in touch." Brock turned and walked out of the room, shutting the door with too much force.

Shane lay staring up at the ceiling. Knowing Lexie, she would walk in here like a saint, ready to offer all her love and support. But how could he ask her to stay with him? He was a washed-up bull jockey with nothing to give her.

Hell, he didn't even know whether he'd be able to make love to a woman.

Rianne had done the smart thing, taking her baby and walking away. But he wasn't about to off himself like Corey had. He was too angry for that.

Brock stepped into the hall, closing the door so abruptly that Lexie was startled. "How is he?" she asked.

"Scared, I think. Good luck." Brock's expression was a rigid mask as he turned to walk away. Then he paused. "If you need a ride—"

"No. I'll be staying."

He nodded. Lexie watched him walk down the hall and disappear from sight. Then, steeling her resolve, she opened the door and walked into the small treatment room.

Shane lay flat on his back, on a high, narrow bed with rails. His neck was in a brace. A white flannel blanket hid whatever was supporting his back and legs. Only his hands and arms were free. A saline drip, probably laced with painkillers, was attached to a needle on the back of his hand. Other lines led to a blinking, beeping monitor above the bed. A nose clip supplied extra oxygen to his lungs.

She leaned over him. His face was drained of color. Only his coppery eyes held signs of life. They blazed up at her. Proud eyes. Defiant eyes.

"You look like hell, Shane Tully," she said.

A corner of his mouth twitched slightly. "That's the most honest thing I've heard since I got here."

"Did you know that you took second place?"

"Brock told me. I guess they'll hold my check."

"I can pick it up and deposit it if you want." Lexie felt an odd sense of déjà vu, like being in a play that she'd seen performed with different actors. "We can celebrate after you get out of here."

"Lexie—"

"No arguing," she said. "One way or another you *will* get out of here. And we'll get on with our lives. I'm not Rianne. I'm not going anywhere."

"And I'm not Corey. I'm too damn ornery to die. But you need to move on. Last night I was in a position to offer you the world, Lexie. And that was what I wanted to do. Now . . ." A grimace of pain crossed his face and passed. "For all I know, I could end up camping on the sidewalk like those poor, disabled war vets. I can do that. I can survive. But I've got to do it on my own."

"Brock would help you. I know he would. He may not be my favorite person, but I've seen how much he cares about you."

"No. I'm done with Brock. I won't be owned, and I won't take his charity—or yours, if that's what you're offering."

"I'm not offering charity. Whatever happens won't be easy. But I'm here, Shane. I love you."

She'd never said those words to him before. She knew that they were true. But clearly, they weren't the words he wanted to hear.

He swore under his breath. "Don't be a fool. Rianne had a wedding ring and a baby, and she still walked away. You don't have either one. You're free. You can have any life you want—find a good man, a whole man who'll give you everything you deserve."

The words cut deep, as they'd been meant to. Lexie's rising frustration spilled over. Her voice took on a chill. "I'm aware that I have options," she said. "I could leave, and I might. But right now I'm here. I'll be here today, and

I'll be here tomorrow. No promises about the rest. If you want to play by those rules, fine. That's what we'll do."

Fighting tears, she turned and walked out of the room.

In the hallway, she almost collided with a middle-aged nurse carrying a clipboard. "Sorry." Lexie stepped aside.

The woman was Latina, with kind, brown eyes. "I was about to get his information so we can admit him," she said. "Are you family?"

Lexie shook her head. "I was hoping to become family. Now I don't know. But right now I'm all he has."

"I understand. Times like this can be hard. Do you know his birthdate, address, and insurance information?"

"You'll have to ask him. But he's awake and talking. You say you're admitting him?"

"That's right. Now that his vitals are stable—a good sign—we'll be moving him to a room in the neurology wing. We've got an MRI scheduled tomorrow. After we know more, we can talk about what to do next."

"How soon will he be in his room?" Lexie asked.

"Probably in about an hour. You'll be able to visit him there. Meanwhile, you look like you could use a break. There's a coffee machine in the waiting room, but the coffee's better in the cafeteria. Just follow the signs."

After thanking her, Lexie headed for the cafeteria. Then she remembered that Casey would be coming to bring her the truck and the keys. She would need to stay in the waiting room, where he could find her.

After filling an insulated cup from the coffee machine, she settled in a quiet corner to wait, sip the scalding liquid, and sort out her churning thoughts.

Right now, the only thing certain was uncertainty. Lexie had always liked having life settled and planned. Now she would have to let that go. She would have to take Shane's condition and their relationship one day at a time. She loved him—that much she knew. But what if his pride wouldn't allow her to stay? For now, that, too, would have to be taken day by day, or even hour by hour, with no expectations. Could she do that? If not, she might be better off walking away and leaving Shane's welfare to Brock.

She had just finished the coffee when Casey walked into the waiting room. As she rose to meet him, he gave her a half smile and held up the keys. "Come out with me—I'll show you where it's parked," he said.

The night air was fresh and cool. Lexie filled her lungs as she walked with Casey to the space where the dark blue pickup was parked.

"Any change?" he asked.

"He's awake and talking. They'll be moving him to a regular room tonight. But he's angry and proud, pretty much insisting he doesn't need anybody, not even me."

"That's understandable. He's a man, little sis. When I got the keys, I cleaned out his locker. His things are in the truck, but you'll want to take his wallet and his phone inside."

"Thanks." Lexie pocketed the phone and cradled the worn leather wallet between her hands, feeling the shape and texture of it.

"Oh, and I checked on your bull," Casey said. "He's fine. Your man, Aaron, was there. He says not to worry. If he doesn't hear from you, he'll be loading and leaving at first light. He gave me your duffel. It's in the truck."

"Thanks again, Casey—for everything." Lexie hugged him.

"Gotta go—my ride is here." He turned and headed for

a Jeep that had pulled up to the curb. Pausing, he looked back at her. "Call me if you need anything—I mean it, girl."

She blew him a kiss and watched the Jeep drive away. It was too soon for Shane to be settled in his room. She'd have time to call Tess, if she could get a signal. And it wouldn't hurt to find something to eat. She didn't have much appetite, but she'd be smart to get some nourishment while she could.

Sitting on a bench outside the entrance, she made the call. No answer, but she did get her sister's voice mail and left a brief message. It wouldn't hurt to back it up with an e-mail. She could do that inside.

In the cafeteria, she forced down a grilled cheese sandwich and more coffee. At the table, she composed an e-mail on her phone, telling Tess what had happened.

> . . . Aaron will be driving the bull home in the
> morning. I have Shane's truck. I don't know how soon
> you'll see me. That depends on what happens with
> Shane. But I'll keep in touch.

She paused, thinking of Corey's funeral and how she and Shane had talked about going together before their world collapsed. She wouldn't be going now. She could only hope that, for the family's sake, the divorce papers would be buried and forgotten, that Rianne would be portrayed as a faithful wife, and that Corey would be remembered as a hero.

More than an hour had passed since she'd spoken with the nurse. Hopefully Shane would be in his room by now. She could at least find out.

At the hospital's main desk she learned that he'd been moved. She followed the directions to the neurology wing, took the elevator to the third floor, and walked down the hall to Shane's room. A nurse, a young man in scrubs this time, had just stepped out the door.

"Is it all right for me to go in?" Lexie asked. "I was planning to stay if it's allowed."

His gaze flickered to her ringless hand. Maybe he'd assumed she was Shane's wife. "It's fine," he said. "But we gave him something to help him sleep. He probably won't know you're there."

"That's fine, as long as he can get some rest. I can push the call button if he needs anything."

"Okay, then." The nurse nodded. "There's coffee at the nurses' station. You can help yourself if you want it. And there's a chair you can pull next to the bed. I've got to tell you, I'm a fan of his. I've seen him ride. He was one of the best."

Was. The word wasn't lost on Lexie. "Is there anything else I should know?" she asked.

"You might keep an eye on the monitor, in case anything changes, like his oxygen level or his blood pressure."

"I know about that. I'll make sure he's stable."

"We'll be right outside if he needs anything." The nurse turned away and hurried back down the hall to answer a blinking call light.

Lexie walked into the room. The lights were dim, but she could see Shane lying flat in the bed, still wearing the neck brace. She glanced at the glowing monitor screen above his head. Everything appeared normal—reassurance that there were no internal injuries except to his back. He would live—but his quality of life hung in the balance.

She found the chair—overstuffed and upholstered in fake brown leather. As she moved it next to the bed, she discovered that the back reclined partway. She could doze in it if she needed to. Before sitting down, she leaned over the bed. Shane's eyes were closed, his breathing regular.

"I'm here, Shane," she whispered.

His eyelids fluttered open for an instant, then closed again. "Lexie . . ." he murmured, ending her name in a breath.

As she sank into the chair, she found his free hand. Her fingers slid into his cool palm. He clasped them, his strong grip holding her tight.

She laid her head beside him, holding his hand, listening to him breathe and knowing that, whatever happened, whatever he might say to her in his anger and frustration, she would be here for him.

CHAPTER TWELVE

Tess and Callie sat on the porch, their lawn chairs pushed back into the narrow ribbon of afternoon shade. Callie, who'd grown up in Louisiana, had made a pitcher of sweet tea. It wasn't Tess's favorite, but at least, with plenty of ice, it was cold.

The bulls, Whirlwind among them, lazed in the pasture, where a mound of fresh earth marked old Thunderbolt's grave. Aaron had arrived the night before, bringing Whirlwind and a check for the prize money the bull had won. His score had come in third, behind two nationally ranked bulls, so the check hadn't been impressive. But the ride had been featured on the PBR Web site, and he'd been touted as the rookie bull to watch.

Ruben would be taking four of the other bulls to Wickenburg this coming weekend. But there were no nearby PBR events scheduled, so Whirlwind would get a rest—which was fortunate, since there was no telling when Lexie would be here to take him again. Nonetheless, the silvergray bull needed to buck. He needed the points and the exposure if he was to make the November finals in Las Vegas—with the chance to earn big money.

But that was a worry for another day. Right now Tess had more pressing concerns on her mind.

"I can't believe this!" Her hand crumpled the letter that Aaron had picked up for her at the post office in Ajo that morning—the letter informing her that the hayfields on the property next to Aaron's were under new ownership, and the ranch would no longer be able to buy hay at a discounted price.

The letter was from a new property investment company. The owner's name wasn't mentioned, but Tess knew who it was. Brock Tolman was doing just what Shane had predicted—he was squeezing the ranch, little by little, slowly backing them into a corner.

"What are you going to do?" Callie asked.

Tess shook her head. The discount on hay—because it didn't have to be loaded and hauled— had been a boon to the ranch over the years. Hay at the market price would cost twice as much. "For now, we don't have much choice," she said. "But my plan is to plant a couple of our pastures in hay. By next summer we should have our own crop."

Brave talk. Planting hay would involve seed, a watering system, and harvesting equipment to cut and bale the hay, unless they could rent the machines that Aaron used. Maybe it would be cheaper to just bite the bullet and buy the hay.

Damn Brock Tolman to hell!

"Do you think Aaron will still have a job?" Callie asked.

"I don't see why not," Tess replied. "Somebody needs to take care of the hayfields, and he's right there. Maybe the bastards will even give him a raise."

As if the words could summon him, Aaron appeared around the bend in the road, driving the Kubota. He parked in the yard and came up onto the porch. "I'll take some of that tea," he said. "It's hotter than hell out there."

Callie refilled her own empty glass with tea. He took it and sank into a chair. "Hear any more from Lexie? When will she be back?"

"I don't know." Tess remembered the few brief lines her sister had written.

The MRI showed major damage to Shane's lower back. Surgery tomorrow will brace the spine, but the spinal nerve is beyond repair. He's still struggling to accept that he won't have the use of his legs. I'll be here as long as he needs me, or until he goes to rehab.

Tess sighed. Lexie's absence left the ranch seriously shorthanded. But Lexie was in love, and as sorely as her sister was needed here, Tess knew better than to demand that she make a choice.

"So who's going to take the bull to the PBR?" Aaron asked.

"I don't know." Tess knew he was offering, but she remembered Lexie saying how he'd gone off on his own as soon as Whirlwind was unloaded. She needed someone who'd be there full-time for the bull. Ruben was busy with their PRCA contracts, and the boys were too young and inexperienced to go alone.

"Our next PBR event is almost two weeks away," she said. "It's in Window Rock. If Lexie isn't back by then, I'll take Whirlwind myself."

Aaron leaned back and propped his feet on an empty chair. His gaze wandered over the bulls in the pasture. "I can't believe that ornery old bull is just a heap of dirt," he said. "How did it happen? Did you just find him dead?"

"It happened while you and Lexie were gone. Didn't I tell you? Somebody poisoned his food."

"What?" Aaron's feet swung to the ground as he sat up. "How'd you figure that?"

"From the way he looked. And from the smell. It was rat poison, in a bag of Total Bull that was almost empty. I kept the bag for the police. The inside smells of zinc phosphide—that's heavy-duty rat poison. The other bulls got food from a fresh bag."

"Have you called the police?"

"Not yet. I'm hoping to figure out who did it before I call them. Otherwise, they'll just file a report and forget it."

"Who the hell would do a thing like that?" Aaron exploded. "Maybe you ought to take a closer look at those boys. Aren't they the ones who put the food out?"

"Yes, but I can't imagine it was them. They brought me the bag when I asked, and then they had to dig the grave. It was a miserable job. It took them all day. Why would they bring that on themselves? And why would they poison the feed if they knew they could be the first ones blamed?"

"And it was only the old bull? The others were all right?"

"There was only enough in the bag for one serving of feed. Anyone of the bulls could've gotten it."

"Wait a minute," Callie spoke up. "If there was only one serving left in the bag, the rest of the food had already been eaten. And it was fine. So the poison couldn't have been there more than a day or so."

"That's the explanation that makes the most sense," Tess said. "There could be others—like the bag came from somewhere else. But the thing that matters most is not letting anything like this happen again. That means stopping the person who's responsible."

"Well, if it isn't the boys, it's got to be somebody sneaking in from the res—somebody with a grudge against the ranch, or maybe against your dad. There's nothing to gain by what they're doing. It's just plain old meanness."

Tess sighed. "I'll have Ruben check again. But he insists that it's not any of his people."

"Well, it's not any of us—and it sure as hell isn't me. I wasn't even here." Aaron handed Callie his empty glass and reached down to scratch one of the dogs.

"What do you think of this, Aaron?" Changing the subject, Tess handed him the letter from the investment company. He gave it a quick scan, holding it at arm's length to focus his eyes on the small print before handing it back to her.

"It jibes with the letter I got," he said. "The new outfit wants to buy my property. They offered a fair price and a guarantee that would let me stay in the house and keep my job for at least five years—but only if I want to."

Tess forced her face to freeze in a calm expression. She could just imagine Brock Tolman's mind working. Buy the hayfields, buy Aaron's property, and the next domino to topple would be the Alamo Canyon Ranch.

"So, are you going to accept the offer?" she asked Aaron.

"I'm thinking on it. The money would keep me in style for the rest of my life. And it's not like I have any kids to leave the place to, like my old man left it to me." He shrugged. "Why not?"

Yes, why not? Tess asked herself. Aaron had grown up in this mountain valley. His parents had been neighbors to her own, much wealthier grandparents. Aaron and her mother, Isabel, had been childhood playmates. He'd never known a life anywhere else. With money from the sale of his property, he could travel, move away, do whatever he wanted. All he had to do was sell out to the evil empire of Brock Tolman.

"Is that what you came to tell us, Aaron?" she asked.

"You've been good neighbors, the closest thing I've got to family. I didn't want to spring this on you after it was a done deal."

"It sounds like you've already made up your mind," Tess said.

"Pretty much." He rose from his chair. "So I guess I'll be headed home. I've got dry hayfields to water."

"I hope you'll make the right decision, Aaron." Callie's tone sounded oddly formal.

"Thanks. And thanks for the tea, Callie." Without another word, he was off the porch and starting the Kubota.

"Well, how about that?" Callie said as they watched him drive away. "Nothing stays the same anymore, does it? First Lexie, and now Aaron. And the boys will be gone when school starts. We're running out of people."

Tess sank back into the chair. "We can always hire new help. But I need Lexie. I worry that she'll go off somewhere with Shane and leave me to run this ranch without her."

"I have an idea," Callie said. "If you want to keep Lexie on the ranch, there's one way to do that—hire Shane and let him live with us."

"But—" Tess's first reaction was to protest. "He won't be able to walk, let alone ride. What can he do?"

"Think about it. How much time do you spend in that office? Shane knows the ranching business, he knows everything about bulls, and he's smart. You saw that when he was here. He could take over the day-to-day management and free you and Lexie to work the bulls or take them to events."

"But would he do it? Wouldn't he see it as charity?"

"Not if we really needed him—and we do. Besides, I just thought of something else. Before your dad got sick, he was talking about holding classes for young bull riders. Shane could teach—and he has the name recognition to draw students. The kids could live in the bunkhouse for a few weeks at a time and be around the bulls. They'd love it."

Tess had to admit the idea was appealing—and it would provide a solid reason to hire Shane. Another benefit—he could furnish insight into dealing with Brock. But would he agree to do it?

"We probably shouldn't rush things," Callie said. "Shane's still in the hospital. We don't know how long his recovery will take or what kind of condition he'll be in afterward—physically or mentally."

"Lexie will have to be the judge of that," Tess said. "And the timing will be up to her. I'll e-mail her tonight and let her know what we're thinking. She can decide when to tell Shane." Tess stood, picked up the iced tea pitcher, and opened the screen door to go inside. "Thanks for the ideas, Callie. I'm feeling a little better about the situation now."

Callie didn't reply. When Tess looked back at her, she was gazing up the road in the direction Aaron had taken.

Shane was having a restless night. Not that he was in much pain—that was the one advantage of having no nerve connections from his lower back on down. What was keeping him awake tonight was the uncertainty of what lay ahead.

He'd lost track of his time in the hospital, but it couldn't have been more than a few days. At least the doctors were pleased with his progress. Today they'd informed him that he'd soon be going to the rehab facility he'd requested— the one in Tucson where Corey had been sent. The place had an excellent reputation for working with spinal injuries like his.

"With your upper-body strength, you should do well," his doctor had told him. "You'll be transferring and getting around in your wheelchair in no time."

Sure. Hell. What about learning to piss by myself and putting on my own pants? What about driving a car, riding a horse, and making a living? What about loving my woman?

The thought of what it would take to become independent was like facing a mountain he had to climb with his bare hands.

He was scared—scared to death. But he wasn't about to share his fears with Lexie. It was for her sake that he'd put on a brave face and tried to behave as if everything would be all right—even though nothing could be farther from the truth. He would never walk again, probably never get married or have a family. And he would never ride another bull.

Turning his head, he could see her sleeping in the recliner next to his bed. She'd spent all her nights here and much of her days, always cheerful, always positive, never allowing him to slip into the morass of self-pity.

In the faint light, she looked exhausted. When he went to rehab she would be forced to go home. That was where she needed to be. She needed to rest and get back to her life—a life without him.

Her eyelids fluttered open. She gave him a tired smile. "Hi," she said. "Do you need anything?"

"No, just can't sleep. I can't stop thinking about what comes next, after rehab."

"It'll work out," she said. "It might take time, but you'll do fine. You'll see."

"I wish I could be that sure." He'd meant the comment to be sarcastic, but it hadn't come out that way. He couldn't use sarcasm, not with her. "Brock's invited me to come back and live on the ranch. I'd have the best of everything—no money worries, my own personal trainer, probably my own vehicle with hand controls. You name it."

A stricken look flashed across her face. "Is that what you want?"

"I've given it some thought. It would be the easy choice. But with Brock, I wouldn't amount to much more than a house pet. What I really want is to be useful, to make my own living and my own choices. I want to be my own man, Lexie. Is that such an impossible wish?"

"No." She sat up straight. "Not at all. You've already got another offer—from my sister."

Shane listened while she explained Tess's idea—that he would live on the Alamo Canyon Ranch, take over some of the office work, supervise workers, and possibly teach young bull riders. The plan would involve some real challenges, but it would be better than moving back with Brock.

"You've seen our house," Lexie said. "It's all on one level—no steps anywhere. And we could build a ramp onto the front porch. You could have Jack's old room. It has its own bathroom with a shower, and his workout equipment is still there. It wouldn't be charity, Shane. We need you. Tess has more responsibility than she can handle, and we can't offer classes without you to teach them."

And what about us? Shane thought. If he moved to the Alamo Canyon Ranch, would he and Lexie be a couple?

Would they be expected to marry? He loved her, but what if he couldn't function as a whole man?

It was too soon to ask that question.

Lexie seemed to sense his hesitation. "Just think about it," she said. "You don't need to decide right away."

"Thanks," he said. "It's not a bad idea. But I can't make plans till I know how I'll do in rehab. I won't come to you as an invalid who needs to be bathed and diapered. I need to be able to take care of myself. Does that make sense?"

She sighed and lay back in the recliner. "Yes, of course it does. I just want you to know that whatever happens, there'll be a place for you, where you'll be welcomed and needed."

He reached over, found her hand, and squeezed it. This beautiful woman deserved so much more than what he could offer her. Maybe once she got home, away from him, she would come to her senses and realize that.

For now, all he could do was let her go and focus on his own recovery. The future would have to wait.

Tess rose at dawn, already thinking of the busy day ahead. In the afternoon, the people from the Jensen Ranch would be showing up with their bull. The cows and heifers would need to be ready for them, herded into a pasture with plenty of feed, water, and a secure fence.

She pulled on her clothes, brushed her teeth, and splashed her face. Hopefully the Jensen bull would be a good one. If he turned out to be a dud, she might wish she'd listened to Lexie's argument for buying semen. But it was too late to change plans. Maybe next year things would be different.

After unloading the bull, Alma Jensen would be keen to pick out a choice yearling. If he had an eye for bucking stock, Tess already knew which one he was likely to choose. The feisty young bull, still unnamed, was the last full brother of Whirlwind and Whiplash. Tess was tempted to hide him, but that would be a violation of her principles and her father's. She would keep herself honest and hope for the best.

After a restless night, she still felt groggy. But a cup of Callie's strong coffee would clear her head. Usually she could smell it brewing as she came down the hall. This morning the aroma was absent. When she reached the kitchen, she found it empty and dark.

Tess turned on the light and started the coffee maker. Callie must've overslept. Any second now, she'd come bustling into the kitchen, apologizing as she took over the coffee and started breakfast.

Minutes passed, and Callie didn't appear. Maybe she was sick. Setting her coffee mug on the counter, Tess went back down the hall. The door to Callie's bedroom was closed. Tess knocked cautiously. When there was no answer, she opened the door.

The bed was unmade, the covers looking as if they'd been pulled up over the pillows to make a lump, like someone sleeping. But Callie was nowhere to be seen.

Tess checked the bathroom and found it empty. Concern mounting, she hurried out to the front porch. She was scanning the yard and the pastures when Ruben came around the house.

"I can't find Callie," she said. "Have you seen her?"

The foreman shook his head. "Not since yesterday. You look worried."

"I am. With all the crazy things going on around here, anything could have happened. Check the barn and the sheds. Ask the boys to help. I'm going back inside to look again."

In the house, she checked all the rooms. Then she returned to Callie's bedroom for a more careful search. Her plain blue nightgown lay half-stuffed beneath a pillow. The white blouse and denim slacks she'd worn yesterday should have been in the laundry basket, but they were missing, along with her bra and underwear. So were the brown loafers she liked to wear in the yard. Wherever Callie was, it appeared that she'd gotten out of bed, dressed, and left on her own. But she hadn't taken her purse, which hung on the closet doorknob, or her phone, which lay on the nightstand, plugged into the charger.

Dread raised goose bumps along Tess's arms and up her spine. She left the bedroom and made one more check of the kitchen before striding outside again.

Ruben was waiting on the porch, a grim expression on his stoic face.

"I can't find her." Tears of frustration burned Tess's eyes. "I can't find her anywhere."

"Look." He turned and pointed in the direction of the ranch's north boundary, where it joined Aaron's land. There, above the deep arroyo where the young bull had fallen earlier, black wings flocked and circled against the morning sky.

No. It couldn't be Callie. It just couldn't be. But Tess's instincts told her otherwise.

"Come on," Ruben said. "We can take the ATV."

Moments later, with the foreman driving the open, four-wheeled vehicle, the two of them were roaring up the narrow dirt road toward the arroyo. The black wings circled higher as they stopped a few yards from the rocky edge and climbed out.

Sick with dread, Tess forced herself to walk forward and look down. What she saw was even more shocking than she'd imagined.

Callie's body lay sprawled and broken on the rocks below. Lying next to her lifeless hand was an open box of rat poison.

CHAPTER THIRTEEN

"LORD, I NEVER WOULD'VE FIGURED CALLIE FOR THE ONE doing that deviltry." Aaron stood next to Tess, behind the yellow crime scene tape, watching the recovery team hoist the stretcher bearing Callie's body.

Still in shock, Tess forced herself to reply. "I still can't believe it. She was like a mother to our family. We loved her, and I thought she loved us. Why would she do those awful things?"

Aaron thrust his hands into his pockets and squinted into the cloudless sky, where a single vulture still soared and circled. "I know a few things," he said. "Callie never let on to you folks, but she was pissed about Bert's will. All those years of raising his family and nursing him through cancer, and all he left her was a few thousand in cash. The rest— the whole kit and kaboodle—went to his kids. Can't say as I blame her for lashing out."

"But Callie understood—at least I thought she did— that the ranch belonged to our mother's family, and it was to be passed down to her descendants. It was part of the agreement Dad signed with our grandfather when he married her."

"Well, Callie may have understood it, but she didn't have to like it." Aaron fell silent as the stretcher came up over the rim of the wash, with the body on it—an impersonal, lumpy shape, already zipped into a black bag.

Tess had called 9-1-1 after finding the body. The sheriff and his deputies had arrived from Ajo an hour later in their white crime scene van. They'd taped off the area, taken photos, bagged the rat poison, and interviewed everyone at the scene before bringing the remains up. Tess had sent Ruben and the two boys off to finish the chores. Only Aaron had stayed.

Your family owes me. Tess remembered the words on the note Lexie had thrown away. They fit with what Aaron had just told her. But Callie couldn't have put the note on Lexie's windshield. She'd been at home all day.

Of course, there were other ways. She could've paid someone else to do it. Still, for Tess, it was impossible to believe that a sweet, loving woman like Callie could be responsible for the awful things that had happened on the ranch. But the evidence argued otherwise.

"How do you suppose it happened?" Tess asked, thinking out loud.

"Her falling, you mean?" Aaron watched as the body was loaded into the back of the van. "I'm guessing she decided to throw the poison into the arroyo—maybe got too close to the edge in the dark. That's about the only thing that makes sense—unless she jumped."

"Either way, it's hard to believe."

With their work done, the crime scene team was ready to leave. The sheriff, a middle-aged man with the weary look of someone who'd seen it all, walked over for a few last words with Tess.

"The medical examiner's report will take a few days—

longer if the state lab gets involved," he said. "I'll let you know what we find out. Will you be wanting the body when it's released?"

"Yes. I'll make arrangements," Tess said. "Whatever the real story is, she was family. Is it possible to keep this out of the news? I really don't want reporters and camera crews up here."

"I can't control the folks who listen in on the dispatches," the sheriff said. "But until we know more, I'll try to keep things quiet. Call me if you find anything else that might help."

Tess thanked him, took his card, and watched the van drive away. Then, leaving Aaron, she headed back down the road to the house.

Memories swept over her as she walked—Callie making birthday cakes, cutting paper dolls, and reading stories to her sisters; Callie listening to her teenage troubles and hugging her tight when she got the news about Mitch; Callie by their father's bedside, holding his hand as he died. Warm, laughing, loving Callie.

This couldn't be real.

But there was no getting around the truth. When it came to the acts of destruction on the ranch, Callie had motive, means, and plenty of opportunity. Even so, Tess couldn't shake the feeling that something wasn't right.

She reached the house and crossed the porch—the porch where she and Callie would no longer sit in the lawn chairs with a cold drink while they watched the sunset and talked over the events of the day. She passed into the kitchen where the coffee sat cold on the counter, and no one had even started breakfast—not that anybody, except maybe the boys, would have much appetite.

Standing at the back door, looking out over Callie's

lovingly watered garden, Tess sucked in her tears and prepared to call her sisters.

When Lexie got the call from Tess, she was in the hospital parking lot, clearing Shane's personal belongings out of his truck. Except for the pistol and ammo clip in the glove box, the other odds and ends, like his spare keys, sunglasses, and faded baseball cap, along with his boots, clothes, and the things Casey had taken from his locker, would go with him when he went to rehab tomorrow morning. After he left, she would be driving the truck back to the ranch.

Yesterday she'd bought a nylon zipper bag and filled it with several sets of sweatpants, shirts, tees, socks, and underwear, along with a pair of sneakers for Shane to wear in rehab. Seeing to these small needs was becoming routine. It even gave her pleasure. Tomorrow, when they went their separate ways, she would miss being there for him. But she knew that Shane needed to move ahead with the next chapter in his life, and she needed to let him—even if it meant losing him.

She was locking the truck when her phone rang. The connection was a bad one, cutting out Tess's too-calm voice. Only when Tess ended the call and switched to texting did Lexie get the essence of the message.

Callie is dead. Come home.
Coming.

Lexie sent the single word before the news sank in, doubling her over like a body blow. Callie dead? How could that be? She wasn't sick. She wasn't old. It couldn't be true.

Lexie barely remembered her own mother. From her early childhood, it had been Callie who'd tucked her in at night, Callie who'd brushed her hair, read her stories, driven her to the bus stop, and helped her with her homework. Callie who'd done everything a mother would do except give birth to her.

"*No!*" She wanted to scream the word at the top of her lungs. First Jack, then her father, then Shane's terrible injury, and now this.

Fighting tears, she carried the bag of Shane's things up to his hospital room. She didn't want to burden him by falling apart, but he'd always been able to read her.

"Tell me," he said.

Sinking onto the chair when her legs failed to hold her, she told him what little she knew. Toward the end she broke down. Leaning over the edge of the bed, she pressed her face against his shoulder. Her body quivered with sobs.

"God, I'm sorry, Lexie." He stroked her hair. "You already had too much to deal with. Now this. I wish I had some way to help."

"It's not just me . . ." Lexie spoke between sobs. "Tess didn't say how Callie died. I have the feeling it was something awful."

"You need to go home," he said. "You need to go now."

"What about you?" She raised her head. "What about the transfer to Tucson?"

"I'll be fine. Brock's arranged for helicopter transport. I didn't ask for his help, but this will save me a long day of lying in the ambulance on bumpy roads. I couldn't say no."

"That's great." Lexie forced the words. Brock again—and she could only imagine what helicopter transport from Pueblo to Tucson would cost. The man was fighting her for control of Shane's future, with a whole arsenal of weapons she would never possess. All she could offer Shane was her love and a lifetime of challenges.

But she had to let him be the one to choose.

She pulled away from him, stood, and placed the things she'd brought for him on the chair. "These are to go with you," she said. "Make sure—"

"I'll be fine, Lexie. Your sister needs you. Just stop mothering me and go."

"All right, I'm going." Stung, she gathered up her purse and forced herself to say what needed to be said. "One last thing. You're right about my mothering you. And I'm not going to do it anymore. You need some space while you get strong and figure out your life. While you're in rehab, I'm going to give you that space. If you don't see me or hear from me, you'll know why."

"Lexie—"

"No more. We've both said enough." She leaned over the bed and gave him a quick kiss, then turned and walked out of the room.

Struggling against waves of emotion, Lexie took the elevator to the hospital lobby and strode outside to the truck. For now, Shane would have to fight his own battles. It was time for her to go home and face whatever awaited her there.

The Jensens, father and son, showed up with their bull that afternoon. Named Gadianton after a Book of Mormon villain, he was old and surly with a bad hip. But Alma Jensen claimed he'd been a great bucker in his time and could still satisfy the ladies.

"We'll see. I'm holding back my end of the bargain until I know for sure." Tess had taken the grief and shock of Callie's death and locked it into a black box while she dealt with other things, like this bull. It was a skill she'd mastered with far too much experience.

"Go ahead," she said. "Back up to the pasture gate and turn him loose. Let's see how he does."

Jensen's son backed the trailer up to the open gate. When the big, black bull stumbled on the way down the ramp, Tess's heart sank. But once he caught the scent of the cows, who'd been herded away from the gate by the two boys on horseback, he came to full attention. His head went down and forward. His upper lip curled. Lowing his intent, he trotted toward the cows. Soon enough, it became clear that, although the old boy had a hitch in his gait, he knew how to make babies.

So far so good. Tess could only hope she'd made the right choice. Spring calving would tell the tale. "All right," she said, dreading the next step. "Let's go look at the yearlings."

The yearling bulls and heifers had been herded into the paddock. Alma Jensen sat on the fence, looking them over for a good twenty minutes. The more time he spent, the more Tess's spirits drooped. The man was a good judge of animals. He wouldn't just pick the biggest or the flashiest and call it good. He would choose the best one—the brother of Whirlwind and Whiplash.

And that was exactly what Jensen did.

Tess cursed her own sense of honor as the young bull was loaded into the trailer. To hell with doing the right thing. She should have hidden him in the stable or with the beef cattle. Lexie had predicted what would happen—and she'd been right.

The only good thing that could come of this would be the hope of getting some quality calves out of old Gadianton.

As the trailer disappeared over the pass, Tess reopened the black box that held the awful circumstances of Callie's death. She'd been able to get word to Lexie, telling her as little as possible. But there was no answer on Val's phone. She hated delivering tragic news by text, but that might be her only chance to reach her unpredictable sister—unless Val had lost her phone again or changed her number. If that was the case, she was out of luck.

Sooner or later, the authorities would release Callie's remains. Then what was to be done? Tess didn't want to make plans without her sisters. Whatever vengeance Callie might have carried out in the past few weeks, she had been a mother to them all.

A surge of grief raised a lump in her throat. Tess willed it away. Mourning would have to wait. Right now, there were bills to be paid, decisions to be made, and supper to cook for Ruben and the boys. She didn't even know what was in the fridge, but she would find out. With Callie around, there'd always been something good to eat on the table.

Always . . .

Squaring her shoulders, Tess mounted the porch and walked into the house.

It was after midnight when Lexie drove Shane's truck the last few miles over the pass. As she descended the switchback road, she could see the shadowy outlines of the house and outbuildings below. The porch light shone through the darkness like a single star, guiding her home.

A coyote—a flash of gray in the headlights—streaked across the road in front of her. Lexie braked hard, the tires crunching gravel. As the animal dashed off into the scrub, she took a moment to breathe before shifting down and starting again at a crawl—the only safe speed at this hour. She was exhausted—not only from the long hours of driving, but from the constant turmoil playing like a loop in her head.

Leaving Shane, without knowing whether they'd have a future together, had been wrenching. Now she was returning to a home that would be forever changed—braced to hear truths that she didn't want to know.

But this wasn't about her, she reminded herself. Tess would be grieving, too—probably struggling to be strong and carry on as she always seemed to. But Lexie couldn't let her sister deal with this tragedy alone. Whatever had to be faced, they would face it together.

As she drove into the yard and climbed out of the truck with her duffel, the front door opened, spilling light onto the front porch. Tess stood in the open doorway. Wrapped in Jack's old flannel bathrobe, she hurried across the porch and down the steps. Tess had never been physically affectionate, but as she wrapped her sister in her arms, Lexie could feel her desperate need to give and receive comfort. "Thank you for getting here so quickly," she said. "Come on inside. I'll tell you everything."

In the glare of the kitchen light, Tess's face showed the strain she'd been under. She looked haggard and pale, with pools of shadow below her eyes. Her hair was tangled, as if she'd tried to sleep and ended up tossing and turning.

Lexie sipped the chamomile tea Tess had made for her. The cup grew cold in her hands as she listened to her sister's account of all that happened on the ranch since she'd left to take Whirlwind to the PBR in Pueblo—the poisoned bull feed and the death of old Thunderbolt; the search for Callie and the discovery of her body with the poison nearby.

Too shocked to cry, Lexie stared across the table at Tess.

"So she was the one—the note, the opened gate, the slashed tire, all of it? I can't believe—I won't. Callie would never do those things."

Tess shook her head. "I don't want to believe it either. But the evidence says otherwise. She had the poison when she fell. She even had a motive. According to Aaron, she was angry about Dad's will. And the note—"

"I know what it said. And yes, it fits. But Callie didn't have a mean bone in her body. She would never have done those things. There has to be another explanation."

"Well, if that's true, I hope the police can find it." Tess rose, massaging the small of her back with one hand. "Meanwhile we need to decide on funeral and burial arrangements."

"Have you talked to Val?" Lexie asked.

"I've tried her a half-dozen times and left messages for her to call back. So far, no luck. You know Val. If we don't hear, all we can do is move ahead without her."

"Val loved Callie. I can't help thinking she'd want to be here."

"Then why in blazes hasn't she called?" Fatigue and frustration laced Tess's voice. "Get some rest while you can. You're going to need it."

"You, too. Promise me." Lexie stood and carried the two cups to the sink.

"Did you tell Shane about my offer?"

"I did. He seemed interested, but he said it was too soon to decide. I'll tell you more in the morning."

"And morning will be here before we know it." With a weary sigh, Tess turned away and headed down the hall to her bedroom.

Lexie turned off the kitchen light and made her way to her own room. Before sitting down with Tess, she'd tossed her duffel on the bed. Everything inside needed to go into the wash. Unpacking could wait until morning.

A plastic laundry basket, stacked with clean, folded clothes, sat next to the bureau. Callie's work. As Lexie lifted out a fresh nightgown, stripped off her underwear, and pulled the soft, fragrant cotton over her head, the loss hit her. Tears she'd been holding back for long hours came in a flood. Crawling into bed, she pulled up the covers, buried her face in the pillow to muffle her sobs, and let the world cave in on her.

The barking dogs woke Lexie from an exhausted but fitful sleep. Still muzzy, she lay still a moment. Then, turning, she glanced at the bedside clock. The glowing digits said 4:10 A.M., too early for anyone to be out doing chores.

The aging border collies were still barking. Maybe the coyote she'd seen earlier had ventured into the yard. But no—she knew those dogs. She knew the threatening tone of their barks when they sensed an intruder. But that wasn't what she was hearing now. It sounded more as if the dogs were excited.

What on earth?

Lexie flung herself out of bed. In the dim hallway, she almost bumped into Tess. Her sister was wrapped in a bathrobe and armed with a pistol. "Stay behind me," she said.

"But the dogs—"

"Keep still. This could be anything—or anybody."

Better safe than sorry, Lexie told herself as she moved behind Tess and followed her across the dark living room to the locked door. Someone outside was rattling the latch. From the other side came a voice, husky but unmistakably female, the words muffled by the thick wood.

"Damn it, unlock this door and let me in!"

"Oh, good grief!" Tess lowered the gun and flung open the door. A figure in a rakish fedora stood on the porch, fighting off the licking, wagging, ecstatic welcome of the dogs.

"For crying out loud, get these damned mutts off me!" There could be no mistaking that gravelly Lauren Bacall voice.

Val was home.

While Val fled to the bathroom and Tess started an early breakfast, Lexie pulled on sweats and sneakers and went out to bring Val's luggage in from the car. To her surprise, she found the back seat and trunk of the vintage red Cadillac convertible crammed with boxes, bags, and an assortment of suitcases. This could only mean one thing. Val hadn't just arrived for a short visit. It appeared that she'd come home to stay.

Bursting with questions she knew better than to ask, Lexie began carrying items inside and stacking them in the living room. Where they'd go from there would be up to Val and Tess. It felt almost like the old days, being the little sister again—not that she'd ever liked it much.

Lexie had been in her early teens when Val had left for California. Since then, it was as if her sister were living on some distant, glittering planet—acting in movies, dating co-stars and producers, attending premieres and parties dressed in glamorous designer clothes. Lexie had never envied that life or wanted it for herself. But over the years, Val had become like a mythical goddess or a fairy-tale queen, living in a make-believe world. Now, suddenly, she had become real.

"Lexie!" Val came rushing back into the living room to clasp Lexie from behind and spin her around. "Let me look at you! My God, you're a grown woman! And you're gorgeous!"

Val, with her mother's petite stature, was a halfhead shorter than her sisters. Dressed in jeans and a black sweater, her hat gone, she looked thin and tired. But she was still beautiful with her stunning green eyes, porcelain skin, and fiery mane of auburn hair.

"It's . . . good to see you, Val." Lexie was still at a loss for words. "Breakfast!" Tess called from the kitchen. "I'm guessing you'd rather sleep than eat, Val. But we need to talk now, so come on in and sit down."

"I could do with a bite or two." Val walked into the kitchen, with Lexie following. Tess had made coffee and toast, and was adding cheese to some scrambled eggs.

Taking a seat at the small table, Val glanced around the kitchen. "Where's Callie?" she asked.

The spatula that Tess was holding dropped from her hand and clattered onto the floor. She stared at her sister in horror. "You didn't get my messages? You don't know?"

"My phone got stolen last week. What—?" The color drained from Val's face as the implication sank home. "What's happened? Tell me."

While Lexie pulled the cast-iron pan off the burner to save the eggs, then poured the coffee, buttered the toast, and scooped the eggs onto a plate, Tess told Val the whole story. By the time she'd finished, Val was slumped in her chair, looking as if she'd been flogged. Her thin shoulders shook with unvoiced sobs.

"I didn't . . . know," she muttered, the words breaking apart. "I loved Callie. I had . . . no idea."

"You're saying that, after all these years, you just decided to come home?" Tess demanded.

"I need a minute." Val took a few sips of coffee, then set her mug down with a ragged sigh. "You'll find out sooner or later, so I might as well come clean now. I've spent the past nine weeks in rehab for alcohol and opioid addiction. The doctors told me that if I didn't get away from the Hollywood scene, I'd be right back where I was and probably end up dead. So yes, I just decided to come home. Any questions?"

"Only one." Tess's expression remained frozen, like a mask. "Are you clean?"

"As clean as a friggin' tin whistle, and determined to stay that way, hopefully with your help." Val pushed her chair away from the table and stood. "You'll forgive me if I've lost my appetite. I'm going to my room now. We can talk more about Callie after I've had some sleep. For the record, I can't believe she'd do the things you say she did. And I won't rest until I know the truth."

"That's fine," Tess said. "But your room's full of storage boxes. The bed's made up in Jack's old room. You can crash there for now. If you want your room back, you're welcome to clear it out."

"Thanks . . . I think." Val left the kitchen, grabbed a small bag from the stack in the living room, and headed down the hall and into the bedroom that had been her brother's. Seconds later the door closed behind her.

By now it was almost five o'clock—time to start the day for Tess, Lexie, and the rest of the ranch crew.

"I'll clean up here and cook something for a real breakfast," Lexie offered. "You can go get dressed and head outside if that's where you need to be."

Tess glanced down as if she'd forgotten that she was

still in her pajamas and robe. "Thanks. But first there's something I need to do."

She walked down the hall and into the master bedroom, which hadn't been touched since Callie's disappearance. Moments later, Lexie heard the toilet flushing again and again. Intrigued, she followed the sound to the master bath. She found Tess emptying bottles of prescription pills into the toilet and flushing them down.

"Dad's leftover pain meds," she explained to a surprised Lexie. "I thought they might come in handy in case somebody fell off a horse or got stomped by a bull. But we can't risk letting Val find these. Have you got anything else we should get rid of?"

Lexie shook her head. "What about the beer in the fridge?"

"Leave it for now. We'll see how it goes." Tess checked the cabinet one last time and closed the door.

"You don't seem happy to have Val back," Lexie said. "You're not even pretending to be glad to see her."

Tess sighed. "Val's got a lot to answer for. She ran off without even saying good-bye and left me to carry her share of the ranch load. It wasn't too bad until Dad got sick and couldn't work. And then when Jack died . . ." She shook her head. "Val was off living her glamorous movie star life. She didn't even care enough to come home for the funeral. Why should I be overjoyed to see her, especially since she might need babysitting to keep her clean and sober?"

"She's our sister, Tess."

"I know. But she's got a lot to prove." Tess left to get dressed for the day.

Lexie stood for a long moment in the room her father had shared with his two wives, the room Callie had kept after his death. The bed was still unmade. Callie's clothes still hung in the closet.

Somebody, she realized, would need to strip the bed, launder the bedclothes, and box up Callie's personal things—a heartbreaking task that would likely fall to her. Maybe she would ask Val to help. It would give them a chance to get reacquainted, maybe even take the first steps toward becoming close. Unlike Tess, Lexie was ready to welcome Val with open arms.

But first things first. In her own room, she dressed in work clothes for the day. Again and again, her thoughts flew back to Shane. Today he'd be transferring to the rehab facility in Tucson, where he would learn to function in his new, limited world. Tears welled as she imagined him struggling to move his body, dragging the dead weight of his unresponsive legs. Lord, he was so proud—so passionate about the sport that had been his life. And the only thing she could do to help him was stay away while he tried, failed, and tried again.

In the kitchen she fried bacon and scrambled eggs and made pancakes from a mix she found in the back of the cupboard. Callie had made everything from scratch, and everything she'd cooked had been wonderful. But Lexie had never gotten past the basics of cooking. Not that she planned to make this her permanent job—but for now, somebody had to do it.

Tess, Ruben and, a little later, the boys, trickled in and out of the kitchen, shoveling down their food without saying much, although Tess and Ruben did exchange a few words about the stud bull in the paddock with the cows. The big, ugly animal seemed to be doing his job, but Lexie hadn't given up on the idea of buying semen. And she was still sore about allowing Tess to trade away their best yearling.

She sighed as she piled more pancakes on the platter and set it on the table. Maybe next year, if she proved herself, her suggestions would carry more weight.

Through all of this, Val's door remained closed. It was still closed when Lexie finished cleaning up in the kitchen and walked back down the hall to start clearing out Callie's bedroom. By now the morning was getting on. But Val had spent most of the night driving, Lexie reminded herself. Or maybe Hollywood was a place where people were accustomed to sleeping late.

But what if something was wrong? Lexie stood in the hallway, gazing at the closed door. What if Val was sick, or what if she'd taken pills to make her sleep and swallowed too many?

She'd give it another half hour, Lexie resolved. If Val wasn't stirring by then, she would open the door and check on her.

Steeling her emotions, she flung open the door to the master bedroom and started on the bed. As she pulled away the rumpled sheets, the scent of Callie's perfume rose from the fabric. *Shalimar*. There was a bottle of it on the dresser. Lexie gathered the sheets into a ball and buried her face in them, overcome by memories of Callie hugging her, that fragrance rising from between the warm cushions of her breasts.

"You look like you could use some help."

The husky voice startled Lexie. She looked around to find Val standing in the doorway, wearing black jeans and a forest green silk tee that matched her eyes. She still looked tired, but she was freshly showered, her curls still damp. No makeup—but Val had never needed any.

"Yes, thanks, I could use some help," Lexie said. "In fact, I was hoping you'd show up. There should be some empty boxes in your old room. If you'll get some, we can start packing her . . . things." She spoke past the lump in her throat.

While Lexie finished stripping the bed down to the mattress, Val went for boxes. When she returned, they started on the bureau drawers. Neither of them spoke about Callie. The grief was still too raw.

"I can't believe how beautifully you've grown up, Lexie." Val folded a cotton nightgown before laying it in a box. "You must be fighting off the boys."

"Not really." She'd tell Val about Shane later, Lexie decided. "I've been busy helping Tess on the ranch and taking one of our bulls, Whirlwind, to PBR events. He's good. The best bull we've ever had. And his younger brother, Whiplash, could turn out to be even better."

Val was silent for a moment, as if her thoughts had flitted away to some secret place. Then she smiled and spoke. "The PBR, you say? Wow, that's great. That's where the big money is these days."

"And money is what this ranch needs. Just ask Tess." Lexie took a deep breath. "I've run into Casey a few times. He still treats me like his little sister—and he still asks me about you. Wait till I tell him you're back."

A look akin to panic flashed across Val's beautiful face. She shook her head. "No, Lexie. Whatever you do, you can't tell him I'm here. Casey and I were finished a long time ago. And the girl I used to be—the girl who loved him—doesn't exist anymore."

CHAPTER FOURTEEN

Cursing silently through clenched teeth, Shane worked his way along the parallel bars. The muscles in his arms and shoulders, which did the work of supporting his weight and moving him ahead, bulged and throbbed. His upper-body strength had been formidable before the disaster that he'd come to call the wreck. Now the slave drivers who were his therapists were doing their damnedest to turn him into the Incredible Half-Hulk. The regimen at this sports rehab facility, one of the best in the country, would make military boot camp look like a tea party. Shane had only been here nine days, but it already felt like forever.

Below his hips, his useless legs dangled and dragged. Shane had come to hate those legs, hate them for their weakness and for all the things they could no longer do. He was angry most of the time—but it was rage that fueled his determination to get stronger.

"Had enough?" Meg, a tiny, snub-nosed blonde, six months pregnant, was the toughest member of his therapy team. When it came to anger motivation, she knew just where to prod. "You must be getting tired by now, cowboy." Her tone was deliberately teasing. "I wouldn't blame you if you wanted to give up and take a break. There's a cold Gatorade waiting for you in the fridge. You've earned it. How about it?"

Shane suppressed the urge to tell her what she could do with the cold Gatorade. When he made it to the end of the bars, he turned around and started back. He would show the little tormentor just how much he could do. Sweat was running down his face, but if he lifted a hand off the bars to wipe it away, he would fall. "I'm fine," he muttered. "I'll tell you when I'm ready to quit."

"Whatever." She walked away, disappearing into the hallway. Shane had made it to the other end of the bars and was about to turn around and go again when Meg returned.

"Sorry to disturb you while you're having so much fun," she said. "But you have a visitor in the lobby. I told him you'd be right out."

Him. Shane felt a twinge of disappointment. So it wasn't Lexie, which meant that it was likely Brock. Meg wheeled his chair over to the bars. He used his arms and upper-body strength to swing himself onto the seat—one of the new tricks he'd learned. His hands, already tough from bull riding, pushed the large side wheels forward, propelling him down the hall, through the automatic doors, and into the lobby.

Brock rose and walked forward to meet him. "You're looking good," he said.

"Tell that to my legs," Shane growled.

Brock returned to his nearby chair and handed Shane the cold can of Bud Light he'd smuggled in. "Your trainer says you've made amazing progress. She's never worked with a patient as strong as you are."

Shane popped the tab on the beer and took a long swig. "That woman's in the wrong profession. She needs whips and chains. But hey, I went to the bathroom by myself for the first time today. That's a real accomplishment."

Brock nodded. "Have you met the other patients here?"

"Barely. I'm not here to be sociable. I'm here to get out and get on with my life."

"And does that life include a pretty blond lady stock contractor?"

Shane finished the beer and crushed the can in his fist. "That was the plan before the wreck. But I'd never ask a woman to take me on like this." Shane's gesture swept his lower body. He weighed the idea of mentioning the job offer from the Alamo Canyon Ranch, then decided against it. No sense raising Brock's hackles until he'd made up his mind for sure.

"Then you're still open to living on my ranch." It wasn't a question. Brock didn't ask many of those.

"Why would you want me?" Shane asked. "I can't ride bulls. I might not even be able to sit a horse. I don't have any special job skills. Being a cowboy is all I know. What use would I be, except to take up space and cost you money?"

"Don't sell yourself short," Brock said. "You're smart, and you know plenty about ranching, especially bull ranching. What's even more important, I can trust you—that's rare in my business."

"Your business?" Shane felt a prickle along his nerves— a premonition that he was about to hear something he'd never heard before.

"Let me lay my cards on the table," Brock said, leaning closer. "My one try at marriage was enough to convince me that I'm not a family man. I'll never have the patience for a wife and kids. That leaves me with nobody to carry on the legacy of the Tolman Ranch.

"What I'm proposing is that you come back and let me teach you everything I know—not only about ranching but about my business—the investments, the properties, all of it. You're the closest thing I've ever had to a son. If you meet my expectations, when the time is right, I'll draw up the papers and designate you as my legal heir."

Shane's throat had gone dry. After knowing Brock for a decade, he'd assumed that he understood the man. But he'd never expected anything like this.

"Well, what do you say?" Brock demanded, impatient as always.

Shane groped for words. "It's . . . a very generous offer. Not just generous, but unbelievable. I appreciate all you've done for me, Brock. But this is a huge decision. I won't accept unless I can be sure that I won't let you down. For that I need time—time to heal and time to think."

Brock studied him for a long moment before he rose to his feet. "Understood. I know my offer isn't one to be taken lightly. Take all the time you need. I'll be in touch." He extended a hand. Shane accepted the handshake and watched as Brock turned away and walked outside to his vehicle.

What Brock had just offered him was beyond belief—a future of untold material wealth and power. Only a fool would turn him down. But the owner of the Tolman Ranch never did anything without a self-serving purpose. Shane understood that if he said yes, Brock would demand unconditional obedience, and that would include acting against his principles—acting ruthlessly if Brock required him to.

Even so, Shane was tempted. Who would he ever be without his legs? Not a champion bull rider. Not a man who could stand alone and hold a place in the world. What if signing his life over to Brock was his only chance for a solid future?

But he wasn't blind to the consequences. A deal with Brock Tolman would be a devil's bargain—everything a man could want for the price of three things—his conscience, his freedom, and Lexie's love.

With Lexie and Ruben both hauling bulls, it had fallen to Tess to drive into Ajo for supplies. Val had taken over cooking lunch and dinner, though she refused to get up early for breakfast. She'd given Tess a long list that included delicacies like bok choy, shiitake mushrooms, hoisin sauce, and a wine with a name Tess couldn't pronounce, let alone find on the shelves of Ajo's single, large grocery store, which specialized in basics like Ritz Crackers, canned beans, and frozen pizza.

Tess had taken one look at the list, stuffed it into her purse, and bought the usual items. Val would just have to make do.

She was walking out to the truck, pushing a loaded cart, when her cell phone jangled. Fumbling with her free hand, she pulled it out of her purse and took the call.

"Tess?" It was the sheriff calling. "We must have a clear signal today. I can hear you fine."

"You can hear me because I'm in town," Tess said. "What's happening? Have you heard from the medical examiner?"

"I have a report from the autopsy and the crime lab. Since you're in town, why don't you stop by my office?"

"Sure. Let me load my groceries, and I'll be right there."

The sheriff's office was only a few minutes away. Tess's spirits darkened as she drove. Callie's death had haunted her for the past ten days, but with so many other concerns, she'd done her best to put the tragedy aside. Now she was about to learn what the investigation had found. But with so many unanswered questions, she sensed that no conclusion would give her peace. All she felt sure of was that Callie shouldn't have died the way she did.

The receptionist was at lunch, but the door to the sheriff's office was open. He rose to greet Tess as she walked in. "Sit down. I've got everything right here." He motioned to a folder on his desk. "This might not be the way they do things in the big city, but I know what a blow this death has been to your family. I'm willing to share everything we've learned."

"Thank you. I appreciate that." Tess sat on the edge of a folding metal chair, facing the desk. Her palms felt sweaty. She wiped them on the sides of her jeans.

The sheriff cleared his throat and opened the folder, holding it in a way that kept the pages from her view. There were bound to be photographs. If she asked to see them, would he show her? Or would she be better off without burning those images into her memory?

"The coroner believes your stepmother's death was accidental," the sheriff said. "There were no obvious signs of foul play—no sign that a weapon was used or that another person was on the scene. And there was no indication of rape—no bruising, tearing, or semen. But we have yet to make a final determination."

Tess held her tongue, but she was screaming inside. There had to be an answer—a reason why Callie had been found lying dead at the bottom of the deep, dry arroyo. And clearly, that answer wasn't here.

"The cause of death was blunt force trauma to the back of the head, likely from striking the rocks at the bottom of the arroyo. She would have died instantly." The sheriff appeared to be reading, skipping the less relevant parts of the text. "There was a trace of alcohol in her blood, but not enough to make her drunk."

"Callie liked having a cold beer in the evening."

"That would explain it. However—" He looked up from the pages. His eyes, peering from under bushy brows, fixed on Tess. "However, a few elements were found that can't be readily explained. We're hoping you might be able to shed some light on them, to help close the case."

"I'll try." Tess's pulse was a drumbeat in her ears.

"First, and I hope this won't embarrass you, your stepmother was found fully dressed, except that she wasn't wearing a bra. I know a lot of women go braless, but in her case . . ." He trailed off. Tess understood. Callie was a size 38DDD. She needed the support of a bra to be comfortable.

"I've never known her to go without a bra," Tess said. "Maybe she had to get dressed in a hurry. I've no other explanation."

"Next, I understand she wasn't a smoker."

"That's right. She hated the smell. No one was allowed to smoke in the house. Why?"

"Traces of cigarette smoke were found in her hair and on her clothes. You say she didn't smoke. But she must've been around someone who was smoking."

"I can't explain that," Tess said. After speaking, she remembered that the hired boys smoked in and around the bunkhouse. But she wouldn't bring that up yet. Not until she knew more.

"Another thing," the sheriff said. "When her shoes were examined in the lab, one of them was smeared with something that turned out to be rancid bacon fat and mold. Could she have picked that up in the house?"

Tess shook her head. "Callie kept that kitchen spotless. Nothing would've been allowed to go rancid or moldy."

"What about the bunkhouse?"

"The boys have a microwave for snacks and a camper-sized fridge. But they don't really cook. They take their meals in the kitchen. What about the box of rat poison? Was it tested for fingerprints?"

"Hers were on it. Nobody else's. I'm inclined to think she was trying to get rid of it when she fell—the fact that she had it suggests that her death wasn't a suicide." He closed the folder. "You understand that we're a small county with limited resources. The doctor who acts as coroner is a general practitioner and quite elderly. His main job was to determine the cause of death, which was readily apparent. If you want a more thorough examination, including a tox screen, we could send the body to the state lab."

"Don't bother." Tess had heard all she could stand. "Finding out more won't bring Callie back." She stood. "Do you have anything else to tell me?"

The sheriff rose with her. "Only that the body's been signed off for release. Have you made any arrangements?"

Tess rummaged through her purse and came up with a card from the funeral home. "These people will pick it up when you call them. I've arranged to have Callie cremated. We'll have a small, family service and bury her ashes next to my dad."

"Regardless of—?"

"Yes, regardless." Tess forced a smile. "Whatever she did or didn't do, she was family for a lot of years."

Driving home, Tess turned the radio up full blast to drown out the clamor in her mind. She didn't want to think, didn't want to ask any more questions. Callie was gone, and the more Tess learned about the circumstances of her death, the more it hurt, deep down inside where anguish lived.

Close the door, she told herself. *Mourn her, bury her*

remains, and move on. Nothing she'd learned today would bring Callie back or ease the pain of the people who'd loved her. Callie's death had been a tragic accident—that was what she would tell anyone who asked.

The resolution eased her mood some. She even tried singing along with the radio to raise her spirits. But something was troubling her—some unnamed thing gnawing around the edge of her awareness, a small detail she'd forgotten until now. Tess gasped as she realized what it was.

If Callie had stumbled forward, or even jumped, she would have landed facedown. But she'd landed on her back. Her body had been lying face up when Tess and Ruben discovered it.

There could be a number of explanations for that. But was there a chance that Callie's body, dead or unconscious, had been carried to the arroyo and dropped over the edge?

Was there a murderer lurking around the ranch?

Lexie shifted down, pulled Shane's truck onto the highway, and headed south toward Tucson. Behind her, the sun was rising over the pass. Its light sent shadows streaking across the desert. On the low-growing clumps of brittlebush, leaves damp with dew gleamed like drops of polished turquoise.

Cactuses that had blossomed that spring were laden with fruit now. Birds flocked and chattered, feeding on the bounty. On the reservation, the women would be harvesting juicy red saguaro fruit, knocking it to the ground with long poles and making it into jam. Every year, Ruben gifted the ranch with a few precious jars. It was tart, earthy, and delicious.

Lexie rolled down the windows to let the morning

breeze blow through the cab. When she'd left Shane to come home, she'd promised to give him space while he was in rehab. But after almost three weeks, she felt that she'd waited long enough. It was time to see him and to hear what he'd decided about his future.

Knowing what Brock Tolman had the power to offer him, she was braced to say good-bye.

She sped up to pass a lumbering cattle truck on an open stretch of the two-lane road. She'd kept busy while she and Shane were apart. Whirlwind had bucked at two different PBR events, in Mesquite and Window Rock, throwing off good riders both times. Because he'd started in midseason, he was still low in cumulative points. But his high scores were getting him noticed. Next year, if he kept performing well, he could be among the top bulls.

She'd driven to both events alone. With the sale of his property about to happen, Aaron was less inclined to want extra work. And by now, Whirlwind had settled into the routine. He would trot up the ramp and into the trailer with little urging, almost as if he looked forward to the trip.

She hadn't seen Brock Tolman at either event. But Casey had been at the one in Mesquite. Lexie had given him a quick greeting and hurried away. If he were to ask her about Val, she would have to lie—and she would hate herself for it.

A few days ago, Lexie and her sisters, with Ruben and Aaron, had buried the urn containing Callie's ashes in the family graveyard beyond the upper pasture. The family had never been religious, but Ruben had offered a ritual prayer in his native language and purified the earth with burning sage. Then the little group had trudged down the hill and gone their separate ways, too sad to commemorate the funeral with food and drink. Even Aaron, who'd been close to tears, had turned away and walked back to his own house without a word.

Only at the end of the day, as the sisters shared cold beef sandwiches for supper, had Tess mentioned her suspicions about Callie's death. "There's no way of knowing for sure," she'd said. "But we all loved Callie, and she loved us. Even if we can't prove it, I'd like to go forward thinking that she could have been innocent."

Nothing more had come of the idea. There was some speculation that Callie had caught the unknown intruder in the act of doing more harm, and that he'd killed her, which made sense to Lexie. But there'd been no more secret sabotage on the ranch, which suggested that it had been Callie all along.

But what if Callie was innocent? What if she'd actually been murdered and framed?

Your family owes me, the cryptic note had said. In a way, that did fit Callie. But the things that had been done—the dead animals and the slashed tire that had almost killed two men and four bulls—were not like gentle Callie at all.

Lexie pushed the thought aside. She was entering Tucson now, driving past the trailer parks and strip malls, and into the picturesque downtown historic district. She'd never been to the Santa Cruz Sports Rehabilitation Center, but she'd Googled directions online. With some trial and error, she found it—a low, pueblo-style building surrounded by trees, in a high-end business neighborhood.

Her heart crept into her throat as she parked and climbed out of the truck. She hadn't called ahead to let Shane know she was coming. In fact, she hadn't called him at all. She'd wanted to give him space—but maybe she'd given him too much. Maybe he'd already made plans that didn't include her. It was even possible that he'd already left.

Braced to make a fool of herself, she squared her shoulders, lifted her chin, and strode through the front door, into the reception area.

"May I help you?" The dark-haired girl behind the desk was pretty enough to be a model.

Lexie cleared her throat. "I understand Shane Tully is a patient here. Is he available?"

"I believe he's in the weight room. Give me your name, and I'll let him know you're here."

The receptionist took Lexie's name and pressed a button on the intercom system.

"Shane, a Miss Champion is here to see you."

The reply was muffled but Lexie recognized Shane's deep baritone.

"He'll be just a few minutes," the girl said. "If you'd like to have a seat—"

"I'll stand, thanks." She left the desk and walked to the window, which was screened by tropical plants. Part of her wanted to make an excuse, run out the front door, and never look back. Anything would hurt less than how she would feel if Shane didn't want to go home with her.

At the swish of the automatic door, she turned. Shane was coming out of the hallway, using the large wheels of his chair to speed along the floor. He looked fit and healthy. His hair was longer than she remembered, and his face sported a short, well-trimmed beard. His shoulder muscles bulged beneath the fresh blue tee he wore with the gray sweatpants and sneakers she'd bought him. His motionless legs rested on the chair's foot supports.

"Hello, Lexie," he said.

"Hello, Shane." Her voice betrayed her nervousness. "We need to talk."

"Yes, we do. I've been wondering if you'd even show up."

"I have your truck." As soon as she said the words, Lexie realized how inane they must sound. As if that were her reason for coming.

The girl at the desk was watching them. Maybe she had a crush on Shane. Lexie wouldn't blame her if she did. Maybe he had a crush on her, too. But this was no time for petty jealousy.

"There's a patio out back," Shane said. "We can talk there. Come on."

She followed him back down the hallway to the rear of the building. Shane kept the chair flowing along smoothly and expertly. It occurred to Lexie that she could give him a push, but she knew better than to offer. Clearly, he wanted to show her what he could do on his own.

The patio was small but charming, with benches surrounding a Spanish-style fountain. Flowers bloomed in painted clay pots, and a stuccoed wall, overgrown with bougainvillea, provided seclusion. Lexie sank onto the edge of a bench. Shane swung his chair around to face her. For a moment they sat in awkward silence. Then he spoke.

"You can keep the truck, Lexie. I'll even sign the title over to you. I'll never drive it again."

She shook her head, fighting tears. "You know that isn't the reason I'm here, don't you?"

"I suspected it wasn't. Are you here to tell me you've come to your senses?"

"Shane—"

"Because if you have come to your senses," he continued, "there's no need to worry. Brock has offered me a place. I'll be fine."

"You know better than that," she said, pushing past the sting of his words. "You told me you needed time. That's what I've given you. The offer of a job on our ranch is still open. Have you thought about it?"

"More than you can imagine."

"And?" When he didn't reply, she plunged ahead. "I know we can't compete with Brock. Have you already accepted his offer? Is that what you're trying to tell me?"

He reached out and took her hand, cradling it against his leathery palm. Lexie braced for the news she'd feared.

"Actually, I haven't accepted anything yet. I know what Brock could give me, but I also understand the price I'd have to pay for it. The job on the Alamo Canyon Ranch would give me a challenge—a chance to grow and to be of use. I'd say yes right now, but there's one thing you need to understand."

She waited, letting her eyes ask the question. Her hand felt strangely cold in his.

"You and I—we can't just go back and pick up where we left off, Lexie. I'm an old-fashioned kind of guy. I need to be able to take care of my woman—to protect her and provide for her. Right now, I can barely take care of myself.

"I don't know if I can ever be a husband to you or give you a family. And unless I can be a man, in every sense of the word, I won't go half measures. I won't saddle you with what I've become, not even if you're willing. Do you understand what I'm saying?"

"Yes." Lexie could feel the crack widening in her heart, but she forced herself to say the words. "No expectations. No pressure. We'd be like good friends. Nothing more."

"Can you accept that, as I've had to?"

She nodded, pressing her lips together.

"If you can do that, then I'd like to take your ranch job on a trial basis. I have one week of rehab left. Then I'll be out of here. All right?"

"Yes. All right."

"It's not too late to change your mind."

"I won't change my mind. You'll be welcome—and needed. I'll get your room ready and come for you in a week." Lexie forced herself to smile. "It'll work out. You'll see."

His expression told her he had misgivings, but at least he was willing to try. As for the rest . . . she should have known it would be like this. Shane was a proud man. For now, all she could do was respect his wishes. But it wouldn't be easy—not when the need to be in his arms was already tearing her apart.

She made it out to the parking lot before she crumbled and broke. Falling in love with Shane had been a dream come true. But fate had had other plans for them. She thought of Tess and Mitch, of Val and Casey. It was as if her family was cursed. But now it was her turn to grow up and play the hand that life had dealt her.

The AC had gone out on Shane's truck. She drove with the windows down, the radio blaring, and the hot desert wind drying her tears.

Later that week, Alma Jensen came to collect his bull. Tess had kept an eye on the cows, taking note of the ones that showed signs of having been bred. By now, most of them had been taken care of, and Gadianton was looking ragged. The lame old bull had done his job. But Tess wouldn't know for sure until a few months from now, when the cows should begin to look pregnant.

She waited by the paddock gate as the truck and trailer crawled down the winding road. Inside the house, Lexie and Val were moving storage boxes out of Val's childhood room and into the master bedroom where Callie had slept. When the job was done, Val would have her room back, and Jack's old room could be set up for Shane, who'd be arriving in a few days. Musical bedrooms. Tess was well out of it.

Having Shane here would be an adjustment for the family. Tess could only hope that her instincts were right. If things worked out between Shane and Lexie, he could be a real asset to the ranch. If not . . . Never mind. She would take things as they came. Right now the Jensen rig was pulling into the yard.

As the rancher backed the trailer up to the loading ramp and climbed out of the cab, Tess remembered how she'd let him take that choice yearling in exchange for Gadianton's services. She seethed at the memory—not angry so much at Jensen but at herself for allowing it to happen.

The cows had been moved to fresh pasture, leaving the bull alone in the paddock. Ruben, on horseback, stood by with a rope, in case extra help was needed getting him into the trailer. But the loading turned out to be no problem. Gadianton lumbered up the ramp, as if relieved to be going home.

"How did the old boy do?" Jensen asked as he bolted the trailer door.

"Well enough," Tess said. "We'll know for sure in a few months, but I can't fault him for lack of effort. Say, how is that yearling doing? What are your plans for him?"

Jensen looked sheepish. "Well," he drawled, "the thing

is, I haven't got that little bull anymore. I'd planned to raise and buck him, but out of the blue, I got an offer to buy him—for so much money that it made my head spin. I couldn't say no."

"So you sold him?" The premonition that crept over Tess made the hair bristle on the back of her neck.

"That's right." Jensen checked the bolt and walked around to climb back into the cab. "I sold him to that big stock contractor out of Tucson—Brock Tolman."

CHAPTER FIFTEEN

VAL'S OLD BEDROOM WAS PILED HIGH WITH CARDBOARD boxes. The newer, more recent ones were folded in on top, the flaps tucked to hold them in place. Others, older, had been sealed shut with silver duct tape. For a time, as Lexie barely remembered, the taped boxes had been stored in a spare room of the bunkhouse. But later, after Val had left home and the space was needed for other purposes, they'd been moved into Val's empty room, where they'd stayed until now.

Lexie hefted one of the taped boxes in her arms, carried it down the hall to the master bedroom and added it to the stack along the wall. The job was tedious, and she was getting tired. But if this was the price of getting Val out of Jack's room, so it could be readied for Shane, she would gladly pay it.

The afternoon was hot, even inside the thick adobe walls of the house. Beneath her cotton shirt, Lexie's body was sticky with perspiration. As she paused to wipe her face with the back of her hand, Val appeared in the doorway with two chilled cans of Diet Coke. "Here." She held out one to Lexie. "You look like you could use a break."

Lexie popped the tab and took a deep swallow. "Thanks. I notice you've taken a few breaks yourself," she said.

"I've done my share of the work." Val perched on the foot of the stripped mattress. Even in ragged jeans and a faded tee, her face bare of makeup and her hair twisted up in a clip, she managed to look like a movie star.

"You could have taken this room," Lexie said. "It's bigger, with its own bathroom and a double closet. And we wouldn't have to move all these boxes."

A lock of Val's fiery hair tumbled over her face as she shook her head. "Everybody who's slept in this room has died before their time. I think it might be cursed."

"Jack died before his time. You slept in there."

"That's different. It was temporary." Val's gaze roamed the shadowy room, coming to rest on the growing pile of duct-taped boxes. "I can't believe nobody's opened these."

Lexie shrugged. "I figure they're sealed for a reason. Kind of like Pandora's box."

"You know what's in them, don't you?"

"Yes. Our mother's clothes and things that Dad boxed away after she died."

"That's not the whole story. But you don't remember, do you?"

"Not really. I was barely old enough to walk."

"And Tess never told you what happened?"

"I never asked." But Lexie sensed that she was about to hear a story, whether she wanted to or not. Val had a way of stirring things up, even things that were better left alone.

"Our mother died on her thirtieth birthday," Val said. "Our father, who worshipped her, had given her this beautiful palomino horse. She was riding it for the first time when it shied at a rattler and threw her. She struck her head and died. Dad took the horse out and shot it. I remember how we cried, Jack and Tess and I, not just for our mother but for the horse."

"And that was when Dad boxed her things?"

"No." Val took a deep swig of her Coke and crushed the can in her fist. "He left all of her things in the closet and in the drawers, even her makeup on the dresser and her slippers under the bed. Then he married Callie and brought her home. I think you can see the problem."

Lexie nodded, pulled into the story in spite of her misgivings.

"Callie wanted to throw everything out, or at least donate the clothes and shoes," Val said. "But Dad would have none of that. They had some rip-roaring fights over it. But finally he agreed to let her box up everything and store it away."

"So it was Callie who packed these boxes?"

"That's right. And she used plenty of tape to seal away the memory of her new husband's first wife."

Val sighed. "Our mother had lovely things . . . silk slips, nightgowns trimmed with lace, and negligees to match. Even her underwear was beautiful. I used to sneak into this room just to touch it, and to smell her perfume. *Arpège*. It was heavenly. Even after she died, I used to come in and smell it—before Callie packed everything away."

Mischief twinkled in Val's emerald eyes. "Haven't you ever wondered about what was in those boxes?"

"Maybe a little. But I knew I'd get caught and be in trouble if I looked, so I never did."

"You're a big girl. You won't be in trouble now." Val picked up a pair of Callie's sewing scissors that had been left on the empty bureau. "Here." She held them out to Lexie. "Go for it. Pick a box and cut it open."

"I really don't think—"

"Aw, come on. I want to see you do it."

"This isn't getting your room cleared out, Val."

"It won't take a minute to open a box and look inside. I triple-dog dare you!"

"Oh, all right, if it'll make you happy!" Lexie took the scissors, grabbed the nearest box, and began cutting away the tough layers of tape. Val had always been the instigator in the family. At least some things never changed.

Val watched, an impish grin on her face, as the last of the tape parted and Lexie raised the flaps. "Well, what's inside?" she asked.

"Shoes. Lots of shoes. Take a look for yourself." Lexie passed the box to her sister.

Laughing, Val began lifting out the pretty little size four slippers, pumps, and sandals. The shoes weren't sorted into pairs. It appeared they'd been tossed at random into the cardboard box, most likely by an angry hand.

"Look at these! Most of them are still in style!" Val began pairing the shoes and arranging them in a line along the floor. "Too bad nobody in the family has tiny feet like hers, not even me."

"Put them away, Val," Lexie said. "We've got work to do."

"In a minute." Val pulled more shoes out of the box. "I remember some of these. I used to sneak into the closet and try them on when she wasn't around. Of course, I was little then, and—Whoa! What's this?"

She lifted out what looked like a fancy candy box, decorated in gold swirls and tied with a blue ribbon, wrapped and knotted to hold the lid closed. Lifting it to her ear, she gave it a shake. "What do you suppose is inside? It certainly isn't shoes."

"Oh, no, you don't!" Lexie began gathering up the shoes and tossing them back into the cardboard box. "No more distractions, Val Champion. We need to finish this job so we can get you settled in your old room. Besides, you don't want Tess to come back inside and catch us playing around. She's been in a bad mood all afternoon."

As if the words were prophetic, the slamming of the front door reverberated through the house. Tess had been in a funk since Alma Jensen had told her about selling the prized yearling bull to Brock Tolman. Tess's decision to borrow the Jensen bull had gone just as Lexie had predicted, but she knew better than to mention that. Maybe next year, before breeding time, Tess would listen to her ideas.

Val stood and tucked a stray lock of hair behind one ear. "All right, I get the message. It's back to work. But I'm hanging on to this." She slipped the candy box out of sight, into an empty bureau drawer. "I want to see what's inside."

They finished moving the boxes in time to cook a pot of spaghetti for supper. Ruben and the two boys were invited, as well as Aaron, who had the tools and supplies needed to help Lexie set up the room for Shane. Tomorrow they'd be installing several grab bars and a frame on both sides of the toilet, as well as laying a ramp up to the front porch. Shane would be bringing other devices with him. But even with help, Lexie knew that his adjustment would take patience and courage—on her part as well as his.

The mood around the supper table was subdued. The only conversation centered around the plans for the weekend. Ruben and Pedro would be taking four bulls to a rodeo in Bisbee. Tess had offered to drive Whirlwind to a competition in Gallup, freeing Lexie to pick up Shane and get him settled.

At times like this, everyone missed Callie. Her love of good food and good company had made meals happy occasions. Now supper was just food, the spaghetti sauce too bland, the pasta overcooked, and the garlic bread store-bought. The worst of it was, it didn't matter anymore. Eat and get on with whatever came next. That was the order of things these days. Without Callie, even sitting on the porch and watching the moon come up had lost its magic.

Lexie cleared the table, loaded the dishwasher, and went to her room. By the time she'd showered and laid out her clothes for tomorrow, she was ready for sleep. She lay in the darkness, listening to the sounds of Val rummaging in her room across the hall, moving furniture and putting things away. It was nice having Val home, she thought. Tess had always been the boss, unwilling to let go of her duties and have fun. Val was more like a real sister, more like a girlfriend. With that thought, Lexie drifted into sleep.

She was deep into dreams when she felt hands on her shoulders, shaking her awake. "Lexie!" It was Val. "Wake up! You've got to see this!"

"Huh . . .?" Startled, Lexie opened her eyes and sat up. "What time is it?" she asked, still groggy.

"It doesn't matter." Val, dressed in the baggy tee and leggings she used for pajamas, thrust the open candy box before her. "Look at what I found in this box!"

"This had better be good, Val." Lexie swung her feet to the floor and turned on the bedside lamp.

"Trust me, it is." Val sat down beside her and laid the box on Lexie's lap. "Take a look."

The box held old photographs, some in black and white, some in faded Kodachrome that had turned to a sepia color. There were about a dozen of them. They appeared to be arranged in chronological order—but maybe Val had done that. Lexie's pulse raced as she held the stack in her hand and viewed the images one by one.

The first picture showed two children dressed for the first day of school. They were standing on the front porch of the house, the pretty little girl looking nervous, the boy, older and much taller, with a mop of dark blond hair, appearing to comfort her. The girl reminded Lexie of Val in her old school photos. But this wasn't Val. And girls didn't wear those little ruffled dresses to school anymore.

"That's our mother, isn't it?" Lexie asked. "But who's the boy? As far as I know, she didn't have a brother."

Val gave her a mysterious smile. "Keep looking," she said.

The second photo showed the same girl and boy, a little older, her in a swing, him pushing. In the next picture they were riding horses with the ranch house in the background. By now the boy was beginning to look vaguely familiar, but Lexie still couldn't place him—he certainly wasn't her dark-haired father.

There were more photos, then the classic prom picture— strapless formal, ill-fitting tux, in front of a big crepe paper heart. Lexie stared at it, the boy's maturing features finally recognizable.

"Oh, my God," she whispered. "That's Aaron, isn't it!"

"I was wondering when you'd catch on," Val said. "Go on, keep looking."

The last two photos told the story—the young man in the uniform of the U.S. Army. The beautiful girl poised to kiss him good-bye, a modest diamond engagement ring on her finger. The last photo was a formal portrait of a soldier—the sort of picture a girl would keep next to her bed while she waited for him to come home.

There were letters tied in a bundle—too personal and too painful to read—and, in the bottom of the box, wrapped in a lace-edged handkerchief, a small gold ring with a tiny, twinkling star of a diamond.

"I can't believe it!" Lexie replaced the contents in the box and fell back onto the bed, gazing up at the ceiling fan. "What do you suppose happened?"

"I can guess," Val said. "Dad happened. Bert Champion was tall, dark, handsome, and charming enough to turn any girl's head. But what I can't believe is that, in spite of everything, Aaron came home and stayed."

"His parents owned the land. Maybe they needed him. Or maybe he had nowhere else to go," Lexie said.

"Hey! What's going on here?" Tess stood in the doorway, her hands on her hips. "How can I sleep with all the chatter you two are making?"

Val rose and held out the box. "Sit down, Tess," she said. "We've got something to show you."

Tess shuffled through the pictures without comment, but the expressions that moved like shadows across her face betrayed her emotions. After she'd finished looking, she put the pictures in the box, closed the lid, and handed it back to Val. "I always wondered why Aaron never married," she said. "Our mother must've broken his heart."

"I always thought he kind of liked Callie," Lexie said. "He came over a lot more after Dad was gone. And he seemed pretty broken up when she died."

"Speaking of Callie," Tess said. "There's something I've been meaning to tell you—things I learned from the sheriff."

Stunned and perplexed, Lexie listened as Tess described the findings of the medical examiner and the crime lab.

"Why didn't you tell us sooner?" Val demanded. "We aren't children. We don't need to be protected from the truth."

"I know." Tess sighed wearily. "At first I just wanted to

bury her ashes and move on. But then I decided it wouldn't be fair to the two of you. You have a right to know."

"So you have even more reasons to believe that Callie might've been killed," Lexie said.

"Not reasons, just questions. It's not only that she was found on her back. The smoke in her hair, the smear on her shoe, and the missing bra—it all smacks of suspicious circumstances. Where did she go before she died? Who was she with, and why?"

Val shrugged. "The list is pretty short. Unless somebody we don't know about was on the property, it could've been one of the boys, or Aaron, or Ruben, or even Pedro. We may never find out. But we'll be more likely to see or hear something if we keep this to ourselves. Agreed?"

Her sisters nodded.

"I have another thought," Lexie said. "What action will we take if we do find out?"

There was a beat of silence. "I suppose that would depend on what happened," Tess said. "If a crime was committed, we'd have to notify the sheriff."

"And if it was just Callie sneaking out to meet someone?" Val asked.

Lexie shook her head. "I don't even want to think about that. I mean . . . she was like our mother."

"Hey, she was an attractive, sexy woman with practically no social life," Val said. "We can't rule that out."

"Whatever Callie was involved in, she ended up dead," Tess said. "If she didn't fall or jump into that arroyo, then somebody put her there. I was hoping we could put her death behind us and move on. But I was wrong. No matter how long it takes, we owe it to Callie, and to our family, to learn the truth."

* * *

Aaron arrived the next morning, the Kubota loaded with tools and plumbing parts. Lexie had ordered some grab bar kits and picked them up in town, but the frame on both sides of the toilet would have to be built from scratch with pieces of metal pipe cut to size and joined with elbows. Aaron had offered to do the job for free, but Lexie had insisted on paying him for time and materials. He hadn't objected. With the sale of his property still in limbo, he could probably use the money.

With Val on her way to town and Tess helping drive the bulls to fresh pasture, Lexie and Aaron had the house to themselves. As they worked together, Lexie showing him what she had in mind, handing him tools, and holding things in place, she found herself looking at him in a different light, seeing him as the young soldier who had loved and lost— and perhaps never recovered from his broken heart.

She'd spent enough time with Aaron to be comfortable talking. Why not ask him about the photos? They weren't really part of what the sisters had agreed to keep secret. And it might help her learn about the mother she barely remembered.

"Aaron, could I ask you about something personal?" She held the grab bar steady so he could mark the drill holes in the shower.

"Depends." He reached for the electric drill.

"While Val and I were moving things around, we found a box of old photographs—pictures of you and my mother, from the time you were kids. It was a surprise. I never even realized you were friends, let alone sweethearts."

The drill whined, biting into the shower wall, making

three holes for the long screws, then three more for the other end of the bar. "I can't believe she didn't throw those pictures away," he said. "But they must've meant something to her. Not that it matters, now that she's gone."

"All those years together. It must've hurt when she married somebody else."

Aaron was silent, leaning into the drill to make the last hole. Then the breath exploded out of him. "You're damn right it did. We had it all worked out, how we were going to get married when I came home, and how I could help her dad and take over the ranch one day. Instead, I served my country with honor and got shit for it."

It was an awkward moment. Any sympathy on Lexie's part would be insincere. If her mother, Isabel, had married Aaron, her family wouldn't exist. Still, she wanted to learn all she could.

"How did it happen?" she asked.

"About the way you'd expect. She'd promised to wear my ring and wait for me, but then Bert Champion hired on to run cows for her dad. Just a no-account cowboy without two nickels to rub together. But he had a pretty face and knew enough to move in on the boss's daughter. The right words, a little moonlight, and she forgot every promise she'd ever made to me. I came home to find that the bastard had stolen my girl, the ranch, and the family we'd talked about having. He took it all."

My father wasn't a bastard. Lexie bit back the words. She was learning things she'd never known, and she wanted Aaron to keep talking.

"He took it all and then the sonofabitch killed her—with that damned skittish horse—as sure as if he'd put a gun to her head. If Isabel had married me, she could still be alive. This house, and the family in it, would be mine."

His words were too much for Lexie. She had to defend her father. "My mother's death was an accident. Nobody killed her. And you could have moved on, Aaron. You could have found someone else and had a family of your own. Why didn't you?"

He gave her a startled look, as if he'd suddenly come to his senses and realized what he'd been saying. "Never mind that," he said, closing the door on the conversation. "Let's just get this job done. Hand me that number-two drill bit."

They worked for another hour with a minimum of talk. Lexie was accustomed to Aaron's silences, so she didn't feel as awkward as she might have. But the whole time she balanced and braced the metal pieces, and handed him what he needed, her thoughts were churning.

Aaron had never spoken about his connection to her family. But her mention of the photographs had triggered an avalanche of pent-up emotions. For as long as she'd known him, he'd been a good neighbor, dropping by to chat, to share a meal, or to help when needed, especially after her father's cancer diagnosis.

Until now, she'd never suspected his obsessive love for her mother or his deep, burning hatred for her father.

Your family owes me . . . The words of the cryptic note were branded in her memory. Could those words have been Aaron's? Could he, and not Callie, have been responsible for the malicious acts on the ranch?

But that didn't make sense. Bert was dead. Aaron might have gained some satisfaction from watching him suffer and die, but he'd have no reason to hate the rest of the family. And it was Callie who'd been found with the poison; Callie, who had reason to be resentful about the size of her inheritance. Motive, means, and opportunity. She'd had them all.

The work was finished by noon. Lexie paid Aaron out

of petty cash and invited him to stay for lunch, which would likely be canned soup and tuna sandwiches.

"Thanks, but I'll pass," he said. "I've got sprinklers to mend at home."

"Not quite like the old days, is it?" she couldn't resist saying. "We all miss Callie's great cooking."

"Not just her cooking." He gave her a forlorn look. "She was a fine lady and a good friend. I miss her every day."

"We all do."

Lexie watched him load the Kubota with tools and left-over parts and drive back toward his house. What a lonely, bitter man, she thought. His friendship with Callie had been the one bright spot in his life. Surely he wouldn't have harmed her.

But right now she had more important things to do than play detective. This coming weekend she would be driving to Tucson to pick up Shane and bring him back to the ranch. She wanted everything in his room to be spotlessly clean and arranged for his use. She would need to talk to the boys, to make sure someone strong was handy to help him out of the truck into his chair. And the plywood Aaron had laid down to serve as a ramp to the porch would need to be better supported. Maybe Ruben could take care of that before he and Pedro left for the rodeo.

It was her turn to fix lunch, so she hurried back inside and busied herself in the kitchen. With Shane coming, it wouldn't hurt to improve her cooking skills. One more thing to add to her growing mental list.

Could she really do this? The enormity of what she was about to face loomed over her like the crest of a huge, breaking wave. Shane. Here. Maybe for the rest of his life. And there would be no miracles, no magic cures. He would never be able to walk again.

He would be angry and frustrated with himself. He might even take his rage out on her. Could she stand it? Could she take it for what it was and understand?

She loved Shane with all her heart and soul. If he'd asked her to be his wife, she would have married him on the spot. But that wasn't what he'd set as a condition of his coming here. It would be hands off, no strings, no promises. Pride—that was all he had now. And that pride had built a wall between them.

In the hospital, she had taken his doctor aside and asked him about Shane's sexual function. She still remembered the doctor's words. *"It's too soon to say for sure. As far as we know, the nerves involved weren't damaged. But the key to that function is as much mental as physical. In other words, as long as he believes it can't happen, chances are, it won't. For a man, that can be the scariest thing of all."*

And that, Lexie sensed, was behind Shane's distancing himself from her. He was scared—scared to death of finding out that he wasn't able to make love to her.

The days, weeks, and months ahead would be a trial for Shane as well as for her. If she wasn't up to it, now would be the time to let him know. Otherwise, she would gather her courage and walk into the future with her eyes open, prepared to give him all the patience, understanding, and love her heart possessed.

After an all-night drive, Tess unloaded Whirlwind at Red Rock Arena in Gallup for the Wild Thing Bullriding Championship event. After seeing him fed and comfortable, she parked the rig in the lot and went in search of coffee.

Just outside the entrance to the park, she found a Starbucks, ordered a Grande black and slumped behind a corner table.

After twenty-four hours without sleep, she was feeling raw and irritable. She'd avoided the mirror in the restroom, but she probably looked the way she felt. Whirlwind wouldn't be bucking until this evening. Until then, she could catch a few hours of sleep in the truck. For that, it wasn't worth checking into a motel.

When her name was called, she picked up her coffee at the counter and returned to the table, this time sitting with her back to the room, as if to shut out the noise and chatter. She hadn't seen a bull riding event since Jack's death. It was something she needed to do. But it would take all her strength of will to watch without turning away—especially if some young rider went down under the hooves.

The coffee was almost scalding. She took careful sips until it began to cool. Little by little, as the bitter heat flowed down her throat, her body awakened to a brittle alertness.

"May I join you, Miss Champion?"

The sound of that resonant voice jerked the fragile knot of her nerves. Even before she looked up, she knew who was standing behind her. Brock Tolman was no stranger. They'd met briefly and casually over the years, at rodeos and stock contractor meetings. She'd seen him cross verbal swords with her father more than once. But this was her first one-on-one encounter with the man.

Her first impulse was to fling the hot coffee in his smug, insolent face. But that would accomplish nothing. Let him talk. Find out what his game was. That would be the smart thing to do. The less she reacted to him, the better.

Reining in her temper, she forced herself to speak. "It's a free country. You can sit anywhere you like."

"Thank you." He slipped into the chair on the opposite side of the table, his height and bulk filling the corner, making Tess feel almost small. He was dark and tanned, immaculately groomed, and dressed in a denim shirt and deerskin vest. Tess was suddenly conscious of her rumpled clothes, tousled hair, and eyes reddened from lack of sleep.

He took a sip of his black coffee. "I wanted to tell you how sorry I was to hear about your father," he said.

"My sister passed on your condolences. Just tell me what you want," she said.

"Just a conversation. I understand you've offered Shane a job, and that he's accepted."

"That's right."

"You can expect some pretty tough challenges—both for him and for you."

"Everything's a challenge these days. We'll manage."

"If things don't work out, there'll always be a place for him on my ranch."

"I'm sure he knows that." Tess tipped the cup to her lips. The coffee had cooled to lukewarm, and her restraint was wearing thin. "I'm aware that you bought my yearling bull from Alma Jensen. And I've guessed that you're behind the buyout on the hayfields near us and on Aaron Frye's property. Don't you have bigger fish to fry than the Alamo Canyon Ranch?"

A smile teased at the corners of his surprisingly sensual mouth. "I won't deny that. Maybe I just want us to be neighbors."

Her temper flared. "This isn't a joking matter, Mr. Tolman. Your raising the hay prices has put us in a bind. And something tells me it's only the beginning. What is it you really want?"

"I think you know. Sell me Whirlwind and you can have free hay for as long as you need it. Sell me your ranch, for a fair price, and you'll be able to stay in your house and raise your bulls on the land, with no financial worries."

Tess took a deep breath. "For starters, Whirlwind isn't for sale. And you already have his brother."

"His brother is an untried yearling. He may have the bloodlines, but only time will tell whether he can buck. And Whirlwind is just coming into his prime. If he continues to buck like he has this season, I can get him the events and riders that will put him in the running for Bull of the Year."

"That won't do us any good if he's yours—which he won't be."

"What's Chip Harris offering? I'll top it by twenty percent."

"Wait—Chip Harris made an offer on Whirlwind?"

One black eyebrow shifted upward. "Your sister didn't tell you?"

Tess stifled a curse. She knew that Lexie was dead set against selling the bull. But the fact that she'd kept Harris's offer to herself made things awkward now. "It must've slipped her mind," she said. "Lexie has a lot going on these days."

"As I'm well aware. But think about your ranch and what that land might be worth. Then think about what you could do with that much cash."

Tess rose, slinging the strap of her worn leather purse over her shoulder. "What the land is worth doesn't matter because we're not selling, Mr. Tolman. You may have taken lessons from the devil himself, but you won't be doing any business with us!"

With that, she turned away, stalked through the maze of tables, and headed for the door. As she reached it, the last thing she heard was his mocking laugh.

CHAPTER SIXTEEN

SHANE SAT BUCKLED INTO THE PASSENGER SEAT OF HIS OWN truck, his feet, clad in soft deerskin boots, resting uselessly on the rubber floor mat. Out of habit, he fixed his gaze ahead, on the long ribbon of asphalt that stretched across the cactus-studded desert. But he couldn't resist glancing at Lexie's stubborn profile, her hair fluttering back from her face, her graceful hands resting on the wheel.

Early in the drive, they'd made small talk. But now they'd fallen into a series of awkward silences. Amid the raging uncertainties, one thing was crystal clear. She was as scared as he was.

What if she'd taken on too much? What if bringing him to the ranch was a big mistake?

As if sensing his eyes on her, she gave him what was meant to be a reassuring smile. "It'll be all right," she said. "You'll see. We'll make it all right."

"Lexie, it'll be up to me, not you, to make things all right," he said. "I have to do this myself. If you see me struggling, let me struggle. It's the only way I'll learn and get strong. That's what they told me in rehab, and I agree with them. Understand?"

"I . . . think so."

"Good. You're my employer, not my mother." *And not my lover.* The last words were implied. Shane could tell from the tightening of her mouth that there was no need to say them. She was a smart girl, as proud in her own way as he was in his.

The hell of it was, he could scarcely look at her without remembering how she'd felt in his arms, her eager body welcoming him in, sheathing him in silken warmth, her little cries filling his ears as they climaxed together. Even the thought was enough to make him ache.

His doctor had discussed the issue of sex with him. *"Give yourself time,"* Shane had been told. *"Your body's had a powerful shock. As you recover, the function may come back on its own. If not, there are ways to help—injections, implants, devices like pumps. Above all, don't let yourself get frustrated and don't give up hope."* That much was easier said than done—especially when the thought of those alternative methods made Shane want to cringe.

Ahead, in the opposite lane, a raven, feeding on a road-killed rabbit, flapped upward to land on the crown of a saguaro. The grim but common sight reminded Shane that things had changed since his first visit to Alamo Canyon Ranch. The smiling woman who'd cooked breakfast for him was gone, and a new Champion sister had arrived from California.

"I confess I'm curious about your movie star sister," he said, shifting the conversation to neutral ground. "Is she like you or more like Tess?"

"Val?" Lexie shook her head. "She's more like somebody from a different family, or even a different planet. She's petite, gorgeous, enjoys shocking people, and couldn't care less about ranching. I told you she'd been in rehab."

"At least we'll have something in common," Shane joked.

"That's one way to look at it," Lexie said. "But, as you know, her rehab was for pills and alcohol. I guess that Hollywood lifestyle isn't as glamorous as the tabloids make it out to be. I've asked her about it, but if I even hint at questioning her, she clams right up. Whatever happened to her, I figure it must've been bad." Lexie slowed to let a ground squirrel scurry across the road in front of the truck. "Since she's not one for roping cows or mucking out the stable, we volunteered her for kitchen duty, with me as backup."

"How's her cooking?" Shane asked.

"Good enough, although she doesn't do breakfast, and she complains about not being able to find the fancy ingredients she likes. I'm hoping that with a man in the house, she'll be inspired to make more of an effort."

"I'll add that to my job description—inspire the cook."

She chuckled at his feeble joke. "Of course, we've been spoiled over the years. Nobody could cook like Callie did."

Shane's gaze wandered to the eastern horizon. The rocky, brown hills were beginning to look familiar. Lexie had already told him how her stepmother had died, and the sheriff's conclusions.

"She seemed so happy and full of life. I can't believe she won't be standing on the porch when we drive up," he said. "Does your family still think she sabotaged the ranch?"

"Some of us never did think that. We're still trying to find out what really happened. Tess has got her hands full, but Val and I have been playing detective." Lexie geared down and swung the truck onto the gravel road that led up to the pass.

"Any new discoveries?" Shane asked.

"Nothing that makes sense. Val thinks Callie might've been fooling around. That would account for the missing bra. But it's not like she had a great selection of men to choose from. Ruben doesn't strike me as a stud. Neither does Aaron. They're too old. I've known both of them all my life. And the boys . . . I know about teenage hormones, but I can't believe Callie would do something like that."

"You can't rule it out, especially since someone might have killed her."

"I know." Lexie sighed. "But Callie was like a mother to me. I can't even stand the thought of it."

They fell into silence again as the truck mounted the pass and began the zigzagging descent. From here, Shane could see the layout of the ranch, with its sprawling, red-tiled house, the sheds and stable, the bunkhouse, the tall windmill, and the small trailer where the foreman lived. He could see the paddocks, corrals, and pastures that spread over the high meadowland, and the patches of deep green where springs seeped out of the rocks. At the northeast boundary, he could see the arroyo, a ragged gash that looked as if it had been carved by some giant primordial claw. In the monsoon, it would channel the runoff and send it streaming down onto the reservation. Today it was bone-dry.

Compared to Brock's luxurious spread, the Alamo Canyon Ranch was nothing. But to Shane it was a refuge, a place to start over from nothing and build a life again— but only if he could find the strength, the patience, and the courage.

As Lexie pulled the truck up to the house, Shane saw three people waiting on the porch—the teenage boys he recognized from his last visit and a petite, red-haired woman in ragged jeans and a black tee. As Shane opened the door of the truck, she strode out to meet him.

"Howdy, cowboy. You must be Shane. I'm Val." She was as beautiful as Lexie had described her. But she was bone thin, and her smile reminded him of one he'd seen on a combat veteran with PTSD. She was wounded, he sensed. Like him.

Lexie had hurried around the truck. She directed her attention to the boys. "The wheelchair's in the back. Get it and set it up. After you help Shane out of the truck, you can unload his things from the back and take them to his room."

Shane stopped himself from protesting. The truth was, he'd needed help getting into the truck because of its height, and he would need help getting out and into the chair. In the rehab center, everything had been set up for him to get around on his own. But this was the real world. Pride be damned, there were some things he wouldn't be able to manage on his own.

The distance from the truck to the ramp wasn't far, but the chair's narrow wheels sank in the gravel, making for slow progress. And the ramp was so steep that Val had to jump behind him and help push him the last few feet.

Patience, Shane told himself. Today would be the worst of it. After that, little by little, the adjustments would come. But damn, he hated needing so much help.

At least getting around inside the house wasn't too difficult. Someone had moved the furniture to give him a clear path, and when he saw his bedroom and bathroom, Shane was relieved. With a few minor changes, he could manage fine here.

"Thank you," he said to Lexie, who'd come along to show him the way. "You've done a lot of good work here."

"I had help. We all want you to be comfortable."

"And the rest—clearing out my apartment, driving me. I'll owe you for life, Lexie. You've been an angel."

It was all he could do to keep from catching her hand, pulling her to him, and kissing her long and deep, as he ached to do. But he knew better than to try. And she had already stepped away.

When she spoke, there was a catch in her voice. "Get some rest. Supper will be in an hour, maybe longer, knowing Val. I think she's working on lasagna. Call me if you need anything."

With that, she walked out of the room. Shane listened as her footsteps faded down the hall. Then, gathering his resolve, he set to work unpacking and organizing the things he'd brought. The task would keep him busy till suppertime, at least. Without the use of his legs, everything seemed to take twice as long.

After a late supper, Shane had retired to his room, insisting he didn't need help getting ready for bed. Lexie sensed the reason. The intimacy of helping him undress and get into bed would be a strain on them both. And he would be all right, she told herself. Bedtime was something he'd learned to manage in rehab. If he really needed help, she could call one of the boys from the bunkhouse.

Since Val had cooked, Lexie had clean-up duty. She cleared the table, put the leftover lasagna and salad in the fridge, and started the dishwasher. That done, she opened two cans of cold lemon soda and wandered out onto the porch.

She found Val in the lounge chair, bare feet displaying flawless black polish on the toenails. Tess had found the nightly gatherings on the porch too bittersweet after Callie's death. But that hadn't stopped Val, and it hadn't stopped Lexie from joining her.

With a whoosh of breath, she sank onto a nearby chair. It had been a long day, making the nearly three-hour drive to Tucson, loading Shane and his gear, then driving back to the ranch. The worst of it had been the strain of making small talk as if nothing had ever happened between them—and doing her best to hide her shattered heart.

"Here you are. At least it's cold." She passed one of the sodas to her sister.

"Thanks." Val took a swallow and grimaced. "If it's all the same to you, I'd rather have a beer."

"You know better than that, Val. If you want, we could look for some non-alcoholic beer in town."

"Don't bother. Drinking that stuff is like kissing your ugly cousin." Val tipped the soda to her mouth again. "To get off the subject of ugly . . . that boyfriend of yours is flat-out gorgeous. I was drooling over him at supper. But before you get your hackles up, Lexie, I know he's taken. I like men, but I don't try to steal them from other women, especially my sister. Besides, I could see the way he was looking at you. Honey, you don't have a thing to worry about."

"Oh, Val! You don't know!" Lexie's words ended in a broken sob. "Before his injury, it was like we were on fire. But now . . ." She explained the situation and Shane's conditions for coming to the ranch. "Unless he can feel like a whole man—a man who can take care of his woman and satisfy her—"

"There are other ways to satisfy a woman," Val said. "I could name a few—including some that might make you blush."

"It's not that simple. He wants to be independent. He needs to know he's capable of earning a living and protecting his family. He's got this old-fashioned idea of what a man should be—and for him, it's that or nothing."

Val reached out, caught her hand, and held it tightly. "I don't know if you're asking for my advice. Lord knows I've made enough mistakes of my own. But here it is for what it's worth. Ready?"

Lexie nodded, blinking away a tear.

"It's just this," Val said. "Give him time. He's had his whole world turned upside down. Getting used to the new way of things is going to take weeks, at least, maybe months. Yes, it's going to be hard on you, keeping your distance. But think how much harder life will be for him. Right now, the most loving gift you can give that man is patience. If he loves you—and I truly believe he does—he'll come around in his own time."

"I hope you're right." Lexie sighed. "Right or not, I'd be a fool not to take your advice. I've been making this too much about me. I need to remember that it's about Shane— about giving him the space he needs to grow." She drained her soda and set the can on a side table. "Thanks, Val. I needed this little pep talk."

Val let go of her hand. "Well, as long as you're good with that, I have some other news. Today, while you and Tess and Ruben were gone, I did some detective work."

"What kind of detective work?" Intrigued, Lexie leaned closer to her sister.

"Snooping, for want of a better word. I went looking for any clue to where Callie might have gone the night she died."

"And what did you find?"

"Well . . ." Val shrugged. "Nothing, really. This is more about what I didn't find. I started with Ruben's trailer. You know he never locks it."

"That's because he doesn't have anything to steal. So what did you find?"

"Nothing, as I said. The place was immaculate, just a few dishes and a single set of flatware, a hot plate with a kettle, some instant coffee, a minifridge, empty, a twin-sized bed, a table and chair, a little TV, and the clothes in his closet. The bathroom's tiny—just a few necessities there. I went over every inch of space, including the drawers. The man doesn't have anything he doesn't need—and there was no sign that Callie had ever set foot in the place—no condoms, no Viagra, nothing."

"I never thought it was Ruben, anyway," Lexie said. "What about the boys?"

"I questioned them separately to see if their stories would match—they did. According to them, the only times Callie came into the bunkhouse was to pull the dirty sheets off the beds and leave clean ones. While she was there, she'd inspect the place to make sure it was shipshape and give them blazes if it wasn't. The boys had a nickname for her—The Sergeant. Evidently, they were terrified of her."

"So much for Callie the Cougar." Lexie had to smile, even though speaking the words gave her pain.

"Just to cover my bases, I went through the bunkhouse while the boys were working," Val said. "I found a couple of girlie magazines stuffed under the mattresses. But nothing more incriminating than that."

Lexie gazed at the flowing cloud shadows cast by the risen moon. "So maybe Callie wasn't fooling around. The sheriff's report didn't mention that she'd had sex. Don't they usually check for things like that?"

"I would think so," Val said. "They did say she hadn't been raped."

"But she still could have been murdered. Maybe she heard a noise outside, got up to investigate without bothering to put on her bra, and somebody surprised her."

"It's possible," Val admitted. "But you told me you didn't find that bra when you cleared out her things—just the clean ones in her drawer. And we haven't ruled out Aaron. You told me how much he hated our father."

"But he didn't have any reason to hate Callie. They were good friends," Lexie said. "I don't suppose you snooped inside Aaron's house."

"There was no way I could," Val said. "He was working within sight of the place all day."

"So, without checking his house, we've hit a wall. Short of an admission on his part, there'll be no way to prove he was involved with Callie—*if* he was involved at all."

"And there's nobody else we haven't cleared. If we don't find any evidence, we'll have to go with the sheriff's theory that Callie was sabotaging the ranch, and she fell trying to get rid of the rat poison." Val reached down and stroked the dogs, who'd settled next to her lounge chair. "Have you ever been in Aaron's house—I mean *ever?*"

"No, come to think of it," Lexie said. "I've known him all my life, but he's never once invited us in. Maybe the place is such a mess that he doesn't want anybody to see it. But what if he's hiding something?"

"We'll never know unless we look," Val said. "But we'll need to find the right time—not only when Aaron is safely away, but when everybody else is, too. We don't want to get caught going in there. Trespassing is against the law."

"So we'll wait. Once I happened to see him put a key under his doormat before he left. If that's something he usually does, we won't have a problem getting in." Lexie stood, stretched, and yawned. "Right now, I'm beat. I'm going to shower and make it an early night."

"Sleep tight. I'll be along." Val was a night owl. She could be expected to stay awake for hours yet.

Lexie went inside and headed for her room at the end of the hall. Passing Shane's door, she paused, listening.

At first, no sound came from the other side. She felt a pulse-flutter of worry. But then, as she pressed her ear to the wood, she could hear, over the pounding of her heart, the low, velvety murmur of his snoring. He was asleep.

Her hand rested on the doorknob. What could be wrong with slipping into the room just long enough to stand by the bed and look at him—even lean down and brush a kiss across his forehead? He was here, in her home, where she'd wanted him to be. Here, where she could see him and talk with him and love him, if only from a distance.

Her fingers tightened on the knob, then pulled away. Shane was determined to fight his battles alone. If she loved him, she would stay back and let him.

Steeling her resolve, she turned away and walked down the hall to her own bedroom.

Tess had managed to get a few hours of sleep in her truck. After cleaning up in a park restroom, she'd gulped down some coffee and hurried to the arena, only to learn that the program had been reordered. Whirlwind, who'd been scheduled among the early buckers, was to be the last bull out of the chutes. Riding him would be former world champion Clay Jeffords, currently number one in points on the PBR circuit.

Tess stared at the posted schedule, scarcely daring to believe her eyes. If Whirlwind bucked off the current world leader or gave him a high-point ride, the exposure would be phenomenal. On the downside, she'd planned to leave early and drive home overnight. Now, given the late finish and the need to allow rest time for the bull, she wouldn't be leaving Gallup till dawn.

After checking on Whirlwind in the pens, she found her

seat and settled in to watch the competition. Following Jack's death, she'd dreaded seeing another bull riding event. But, for the most part, she was able to block the nightmare memory and enjoy the sport. Only once, when a downed rider was solidly rammed by a bull's head, did she stifle a scream. But as the bullfighters closed in, and the young cowboy scrambled to his feet, she began to breathe again. She was going to be all right.

She'd looked for Casey among the bullfighters and was relieved not to see him. If he'd been here, and if he'd asked about Val, Tess would've been forced to lie. She didn't know what her sister might be hiding. That was Val's business. But if she didn't want her old love to know she'd come home, Tess would respect her wishes.

A stray breeze cooled Tess's face. The arena was an out- door facility, modern and beautifully set against a massive outcrop of red rock. With the moon and stars overhead and the night lights glowing, the effect was almost magical— except for the stress of thinking ahead, to the moment when Whirlwind would explode out of the chute with a world- champion cowboy on his back.

She would go down to the pens after intermission to make sure her bull was ready and to attach the flank strap when he entered the chute complex. For now, there was nothing to do but wait.

"Is this seat taken?" The deep voice made her nerves quiver like taut bowstrings. This was no coincidence. If Brock Tolman was here, it was because he'd planned to be.

"Suit yourself." Tess kept her gaze fixed on the arena.

"You must be looking forward to seeing Clay Jeffords ride your bull."

"I'm looking forward to seeing Clay Jeffords get dumped on his butt in the dirt."

Tolman's laughter boomed from deep in his chest. "Let's hope you're right," he said. "But either way, I want you to know I had a hand in it. Jeffords was looking for a challenging bull who could rack up the points. I suggested Whirlwind, so he made the request."

"I suppose I should thank you," Tess said coldly. "But Whirlwind still isn't for sale."

"I'm not here to talk about Whirlwind," he said. "I'm here to talk about Shane."

"For what it's worth, Shane isn't for sale, either. You think that just because you've got money, you can buy anything—or anyone—you want. But you're wrong."

A beat of silence passed before he answered. "You don't understand, Miss Champion. Shane was a sixteen-year-old runaway when I took him in. I care about him. And now that he's injured, no one is in a better position to help him than I am."

"Maybe he doesn't want your help. Maybe he wants to help himself."

"But I can get him what he really needs—the best doctors and trainers, the best equipment—"

Tess rose from her seat. "I'm not the one making his decisions, Mr. Tolman. All I did was offer him a job and a place to live. I'm not kicking him out on your say-so. Where Shane goes is entirely up to him. Now, if you'll excuse me, I'm going down to look after my bull."

"Go ahead." His voice rose slightly as she moved toward the stairs. "But think about this. I want what's best for Shane. Can your sister say the same? Or is she too starry-eyed to care?"

Tess pretended not to hear him as she made her way down to the pens. But the troubling words lingered in her mind like a curse. Lexie in love was a force of nature, sweeping away everything but her own desires. Had she made the best choice, persuading Shane to come to the ranch? Had Shane made the wisest decision in following her there?

Only time would answer those questions. But Tess couldn't shake the fear of a rough road ahead. If anything went wrong, someone was bound to be hurt.

Shane had laid out his clothes before going to sleep. Even aided by hand devices made to reach, hold, and pull, the process of putting everything on was maddeningly slow. But he was determined to show up for breakfast ready for the day.

And heaven help Lexie or anyone else who came in and offered to do the job for him.

He'd even managed to make the bed. Changing the sheets and laundering his clothes would have to be done for him at first. But with practice, he might be able to do those things alone. Becoming independent was his first goal. Only then could he think about taking care of someone else.

But he couldn't ask Lexie to wait—not for a time that might never come.

He rolled his chair down the hall and into the kitchen. The place smelled of coffee, bacon, and something burnt. Lexie, in ragged jeans and a pink tee, was mixing batter for the smoking waffle iron that stood open on the counter. As Shane rolled up to the table, she turned around and smiled— the smile he remembered from waking up to her face on his pillow.

I love you, Lexie. The words that came into his head were as natural as breathing. But he knew better than to say them out loud.

"Sorry about the smell," she said. "I've never made waffles, and I set the iron too hot."

"It's all right. I don't recall anyone ever making me waffles before—except the toaster kind." He moved to the single place setting, which was evidently for him. "Where is everybody this morning?"

"Ruben's getting the boys started, and Val's still in bed. You won't see her till at least nine o'clock."

Shane poured himself some coffee from the carafe on the table. "I like your sister," he said. "She's not what I expected—the Hollywood star."

"With Val, what you see is what you get. She was always a rebel, and that hasn't changed." Lexie poured batter onto the waffle iron and lowered the lid.

Shane helped himself to a strip of crisp bacon. "So when do I start earning my keep around here?"

"It'll be up to Tess to put you to work," Lexie said. "She took Whirlwind to Gallup this weekend, and she won't be back till tonight. Oh—but she sent me some great news. Last night Whirlwind bucked off Clay Jeffords in five seconds. The buck-off knocked him out of first place in the standings. Jeffords told the reporters he wants another ride. He said that he's not giving up till he lasts eight seconds on that bull."

"That's terrific. Great press for Whirlwind." Shane gave her a smile as she slid the waffle onto his plate. It hurt even more than he'd expected, that glimpse into the world he'd left behind—the adrenaline rush, the power of that massive animal's body bucking beneath him, the blast of the whistle telling him he'd won. It all came back with a raw pain that raised a lump in his throat. Never again.

But he would just have to live with that.

He smeared butter on the waffle and poured syrup over

the top. "Tess will have a lot to tell us when she gets home," he said.

"Not that Tess does a lot of talking," Lexie said. "Meanwhile, if you want, I can show you around the ranch. We can take the ATV. It goes anywhere—oh, and I've been checking online. We can order an adaptor kit to add hand controls. Once we get that done, you'll be able to drive it yourself."

"It's already taken care of," Shane said. "I ordered a new custom ATV with hand controls while I was in rehab. It even has a rack with a lift for loading and unloading the wheelchair. It'll be shipped to Tucson in a couple of weeks. All I'll need is somebody to drive the truck and pick it up."

"We can do that. It sounds great." But the enthusiasm had drained from Lexie's voice. She'd come up with a way to help him, and he'd shot her down. But that was the way things had to be, Shane told himself.

"A vehicle like that—it must've been expensive," Lexie said.

"I've got prize money stashed away—what? Are you asking me whether Brock paid for it? The answer is no. I haven't even spoken with Brock since I told him I was taking a job here. And it *will* be a job, Lexie. I won't be your resident charity case. If I can't be of real value to this ranch, I won't stay."

He'd hurt her. He could see it in her face. But what he'd said was what she needed to know. He loved her, but he wouldn't be dependent. He wouldn't be kept like a house pet.

"Finish your breakfast." Her voice carried an edge. "I'll have the ATV out front in twenty minutes. If you want a tour of the ranch, be on the front porch."

When she turned away, it was as if a door had closed between them.

CHAPTER SEVENTEEN

Three weeks later

SUPPER WAS A CELEBRATION AND A FAREWELL. LAST WEEKEND, in Phoenix, Whirlwind had bucked off yet another top rider. His average score of 44.5 had moved him into the top thirty ranked bulls. If he could keep performing well, he'd have a chance to make the PBR finals in November. But even with good scores, the final decision would be made by the PBR Director of Livestock, who had chosen the rookie bull for the circuit in the first place.

The two boys, Chet and Ryder, would be leaving at the end of the week to get ready for school. Lexie smiled as she watched them wolf down second helpings of Val's lasagna. The pair had been cheerful, hardworking, and responsible. She would miss them.

Tonight, as usual, the boys were peppering Shane with questions. In the weeks he'd been here, they'd tagged after him around the ranch like adoring puppies, talking constantly about the one subject that was most painful for him—riding bulls.

Shane had accepted their hero worship with patience

and good grace. But Lexie sensed that every time he spoke about the sport, he felt the loss, like grief over the death of a loved one.

As she watched him from across the table—enjoying the food and chatting with those around him, she couldn't help thinking how far he'd come since those awkward first days on the ranch. His work was going well. He'd long since mastered every task in the office. Even Tess, who seldom took advice from anyone, listened to his opinions. But Lexie knew that what he really wanted was to spend more time outdoors, with the animals.

Soon he'd be free to do that. The custom ATV he'd ordered would be ready for pickup in Tucson next week. Once he had it, he'd be able to drive himself around the ranch and on the backroads. After that, it would only be a matter of time until he owned a hand-controlled automobile with a wheelchair rack for highway travel.

He glanced up and caught her eyes on him. For a moment, their gazes met and held. Then Lexie forced herself to look away. The strain that had risen between them was still there, haunting and hurtful. They took care to be polite and gentle with each other. But the lines had been drawn—his out of pride, hers to protect herself from being hurt again. She loved him so much that even the sound of his voice took her breath away. But with his independence growing week by week, and no effort on his part to bridge the gulf between them, Lexie had resigned herself to letting him go.

"Who's ready for chocolate cake?" Val flitted out of her chair and back to the kitchen. Lexie rose with her and began to clear away the dinner plates. Her arm brushed Shane's shoulder as she reached past him. She steeled herself against the tingle of awareness.

Other changes were coming as well. The departure of the boys would leave the ranch shorthanded. But Pedro, Ruben's son-in-law who'd helped with the driving, had agreed to come and work full-time. His wife, Ruben's daughter Maria, would be coming along as cook and house-keeper. Next week, they'd be hauling their trailer up from the reservation to stand next to Ruben's and share the hookups. Relieved of her kitchen duties, Val would have to find new ways to be useful. She was still working out her plans.

After stacking the plates in the sink, Lexie helped Val serve the chocolate cake. She'd carried the last plate to the table and was taking her seat when Aaron struck his knife against his glass for attention. At the sharp ringing sound, the buzz of conversation stilled around the table.

"I have an announcement to make," he declared in a loud voice. "The sale of my property has finally gone through. I'll be going into Tucson to sign the papers and deposit the check on Friday. Then I'll be packing up for a move to Vegas."

There were murmurs of congratulations around the table. Tess looked sour but managed to be polite. Lexie and Val glanced at each other in alarm. They had yet to find a time when Aaron was safely gone, so they could check his house. Once he started clearing the place out, any evidence that might be there would disappear.

Friday could be their last chance.

Tess cleared her throat. "I know we're supposed to be celebrating. But as long as you're all here, I want to go over the plans for what's bound to be a busy weekend."

She glanced around the table. "On Friday, I'll be driving Whirlwind to Santa Fe. Ruben, you and Pedro will be taking four bulls to Prescott—we can decide which ones.

"Val—" She fixed stern eyes on her sister. "I'll need you to take the truck and drive Chet and Ryder to Ajo, where their parents will meet them. While you're there, you can pick up the shipment of Total Bull at the freight office and buy any other supplies we need. Got it?"

Val glanced at Lexie with a barely noticeable shrug. "Got it," she said.

"Shane and Lexie, you can stay here and keep an eye on things. The boys can do chores before they leave Friday morning. Val, can you help Lexie with chores on Saturday and Sunday?"

"Sure," Val said.

"I'll take the stable all three days," Shane offered. "I can muck out a stall and pitch hay as well as the next cowboy."

"That'll be great." Tess nodded. "So, is everybody good?"

"Right as rain." Val's lack of enthusiasm was clear.

Shane spoke up. "You deserve a round of applause for this great meal, Val. Come on, everybody, show some appreciation." He began to clap. The others at the table joined in until Val waved them into silence.

"Fiddle-dee-dee. All in a day's work," she said in a perfect Scarlett O'Hara imitation. "But I'll be damned if I'm doing cleanup."

Picking up her plate of cake and a fork, she walked out the front door and closed it behind her.

Half an hour later, with the table cleared and the dishwasher humming, Lexie headed for the porch to join her sister. Ruben, Aaron, and the boys had left. Tess was on her computer, and Shane was doing his nightly workout on Jack's old exercise machines. Lexie heard the familiar clink of the weights when she passed his closed door. The sound brought back bittersweet memories of her brother—even as it stirred images of the man who had shut her out of his intimate life.

Now that he was settling in, it appeared that Shane might have found a home here. But the barrier of polite distance between them remained the same, with no sign that it would ever change. Maybe she should be the one to leave. Why not? There was nothing to stop her. Certainly Shane wouldn't care.

Walking out onto the porch, she found Val in the lounge chair with the dogs curled at her feet. The night was warm and sultry. Insects buzzed around the porch light.

Lexie sank into a chair with a long sigh.

"What is it, girl?" Val asked. "Man problems? You can talk to me. I'm an expert."

"No . . . it's just, maybe I'm being selfish. I wanted things to work out with Shane. But nothing's changed. I know you told me to be patient, but he treats me like a sister, and I'm getting tired of it. Maybe I should just leave—go back to college, or move to Tucson and get a job."

"How can you even think like that?" Val asked. "This is your home. The family needs you. I never told you this, but the main reason Tess offered Shane a job was to keep you here. She was afraid that you'd go off with him, and she'd end up losing you. Hiring him was Callie's idea, and Tess agreed to it—that's what Tess told me. I'm not sorry about that—he's settled in and become a real asset to the ranch. But the whole idea behind this arrangement was to make you happy."

"Thanks a lot." Lexie's words dripped sarcasm. "Maybe Tess should just sell the place—bulls and all. Brock Tolman would buy it in a heartbeat. There's got to be more to life than shoveling manure and hauling bulls and pinching every penny."

Val rested a hand on Lexie's shoulder. "Give it time. I know I've said it before, but Shane wants the best for you—and until the best is what he can offer, he won't ask you to settle for less."

Lexie gazed into the darkness, saying nothing. Maybe leaving wouldn't be such a bad idea. The more she thought about it, the more sense it made.

"There's something else I need to talk to you about," Val said. "Something that's got me worried—about you."

"Go on."

"It's just this—" Val broke off as the screen door creaked open and Tess stepped out onto the porch.

"Mind if I join you?" she asked. "It's too quiet in the house."

"Sure. Pull up a chair." Val flashed Lexie a warning glance. Evidently, whatever she'd been about to say would have to wait.

For the past few mornings, Shane had been waking up with an erection. *Piss proud*—that was the old-fashioned term for it. It had little or nothing to do with arousal, and it went away when he relieved himself. The doctors had said it might happen, and that he should take it as an encouraging sign—a sign that physically, at least, everything was connected and working.

Not that he felt confident enough to make love. Lexie was the one woman he wanted. But his pride had alienated her; and even if she were to come to him in the night, the fear of failure would leave him humiliated. Even if he could function, why should she want him when she could have a man—any man she wanted—whose body was whole and unbroken?

Why should she love a *cripple?* Shane was doing his best to get used to the ugly word, to accept it as truth.

As he dressed, he willed himself to sweep the negative thoughts aside and focus on the day ahead. This would be the boys' last full day at the ranch. Tess had planned a special treat for them.

The two-year-old bulls were ready to face their first test with the bucking dummy—a small, weighted metal box attached to a strap with a remote-controlled release.

The ones that showed promise would begin a long period of training, with increasing weights, followed, finally, by a human rider. They'd be trained in chute behavior, loading and transport; and they'd be acclimated to the lights and noise of the arena before they were ready to compete. Those bulls that weren't inclined to buck would be auctioned off.

Today, with plenty of help, the two boys would be working with the young bulls. They'd be taught how to attach the dummy in the chute by dropping the strap down one side, hooking it from the other side, drawing it up and around the bull, and fastening it to fit. Shane and Tess would coach them on what to look for in a good bucker and how to pick the best. The boys would also be herding the bulls in and out of the chute. This important job would be a reward for a summer of feeding, watering, shoveling, and mending fences.

The bucking corral was attached by a gate to a paddock beyond the complex of sheds and pens. The distance wasn't far, but the ground was too rough and uneven for Shane's wheelchair. Lexie would be taking him in the ATV, which she would park next to the chutes, where Shane could coach the boys.

The plan suited Shane. His strained relationship with Lexie had worsened over the past weeks, to the point that she was avoiding him. In his pride, he'd hurt her in ways he'd never intended. He still loved her, still wanted her. But what if he'd already pushed her too far? What if she'd already washed her hands of him?

As far as he could see, the only solution was an honest conversation. Talking might only make matters worse. But that was a chance he'd have to take. At least the ride in the ATV would give him some time alone with her.

He was waiting on the porch when she came around the house in the ATV and stopped at the foot of the ramp. From that point, Shane could use his upper-body strength to transfer from the chair to the passenger seat of the ATV.

Lexie gave him an edgy smile. She looked pretty this morning, all in blue, with her hair in a ponytail and a straw Stetson keeping the morning sun off her face. Shane resisted the urge to sweep her into his arms, kiss her soundly, and end this standoff between them once and for all.

If only it were that easy.

"Thanks for picking me up," he said. "Since we've got a little extra time, would you mind driving up around the north pasture? I'd like to check on the cows and calves up there."

"No problem." She started the vehicle and headed up the narrow trail that skirted the pastures, circled along the property line, and ended at the bucking corral, where Tess, Ruben, and the boys were already setting up. The engine of the ATV was too loud for easy conversation. But Shane had a plan to get around that.

The sturdy wheels climbed the trail that led along the

fence line to the upper edge of the property. From here they could see much of the ranch and the livestock—the Hereford steers grazing in the grassy scrub that bordered the reservation, the pedigreed cows, their offspring, and the bucking bulls in the well-tended pastures.

As they came up on a level spot with a good view, he touched her arm. "Let's stop for a minute," he said. "We've got time. And there's something I need to say to you."

Lexie switched off the engine. She'd guessed that Shane hadn't really wanted to look at cows. Now here it was, the moment of truth—a truth that had been a long time coming. They were finished—as they had been from the day she'd brought Shane home to the ranch.

All she could do to salvage her pride was beat him to the final punch.

"I've got something to say to you, too," she said. "How about letting the lady go first?"

"Suits me. Go ahead." He smiled and leaned back against the seat. Lexie willed herself not to soften. He wouldn't likely be smiling by the time she finished.

"I've decided to go back to school," she said. "I left because Tess needed me. But now that Val's home and you're here, and now that Pedro's coming with his wife, I won't be needed anymore—not even by you."

His easy smile had changed to a look of surprise. "How long have you been thinking about this?"

"Quite a while, really. But I wanted to be sure before I told anybody. Last night I sent in my application. Everything should be in place for winter semester, at least, if not for fall."

He shook his head. "I feel like I've been bucked off out of the gate. I don't know what to say."

Say you don't want me to go, Shane. Say you need me. Say you love me.

But that wasn't going to happen. Her man had too much pride.

"You shouldn't have to worry about your place here," she said. "You've proven your worth to Tess. And once you're able to get around the ranch on your own, you'll be able to do even more. With a custom saddle and the right horse, you should even be able to ride again. You won't need me, or anybody."

He took a deep breath and exhaled slowly, as if mentally counting. "Lexie, I came here mostly because of you," he said.

She gave him a smile, blinking back the tears she didn't want him to see. "Well, we both know how that worked out, don't we?" she said. "Now, what was it you wanted to say to me?"

He turned away from her, his mouth a hard line. "There's no need for it now," he said. "All I can do is wish you the best. Let's get going. They'll be waiting for us at the corral."

The bucking trials took most of the morning. Of the thirteen two-year-old bulls that were bucked with the dummy, seven showed promise, some more than others. The rest would be sold at auction in the fall. The young bulls had no names, only numbers. The names would come later, when and if they were ready for competition.

Lexie left Shane in the ATV by the chutes and mounted up to help move the bulls in and out of the corral and rope any animal that threatened to misbehave. She'd already asked Val to drive Shane back to the house, sparing him the awkwardness of spending more time alone with her. They were finished. There was nothing more to say.

The hot summer wind dried her tears as she worked the corral. She remembered the red bull, so strong and full of spirit, who should have been bucking with the others today, instead of lying in the arroyo, his bones long since picked clean by scavengers. There was no way Callie would have unlocked the pasture gate and left it open. Somebody else had done that and more, and Lexie was going to find out who—starting tomorrow when she searched Aaron's place.

With people getting ready for the busy weekend, supper was a grab-and-go affair, with leftover lasagna and garlic bread available for microwaving and the last of the chocolate cake for dessert. When everyone had finished, Lexie cleaned up, pulled two cold lemon sodas out of the fridge, and went outside. She found Val, as expected, sitting on the porch, watching the last of the sunset fade above the pass.

"I was hoping you'd come out," Val said. "Sit down. We need to have a sisterly talk."

Lexie sank into a chair. "I hope it isn't about Shane."

"It isn't. Whatever's going on between you two is your business, not mine. But he doesn't want you to leave. He told me that much on the way back to the house."

"Well, he didn't say that to me."

"He wouldn't, you know. He's a proud man." Val popped open her soda, took a swallow, and grimaced. "When were you going to tell the rest of us that you're going back to school? Tess isn't going to like it, and I'm not so crazy about the idea myself."

"Tess doesn't run my life. Neither does Shane. I thought he was going to need me. But he doesn't want to need anybody, and I'm tired of trying to figure him out. That's why I have to leave."

"Do you love him, Lexie?"

"Does it matter? Is it worth loving someone who doesn't want to be loved?" Lexie brushed back a lock of her hair. "Never mind. You said you had something else to talk about."

"That's right. And I have a feeling you're not going to like it."

"I'll be the judge of that." Lexie shrugged. "Shoot."

Val poured the rest of her soda between the floorboards of the porch and crushed the can in her hand. "Last night at dinner, when Aaron mentioned that he'd be going to Tucson on Friday, you lit up like a Christmas tree. I could read your mind—you're planning to let yourself into his house and look for evidence."

"Of course, I am. Isn't that what we talked about?"

"It is. But I was thinking in terms of our doing it together. I won't be there to help you tomorrow. By the time I get home, Aaron could be on his way back."

"That's why I'm planning to go in early. Sure, I'd rather have you with me—especially as a backup witness in case I find anything. But I can do it on my own."

Reaching out, Val caught Lexie's hand and gripped it hard. "Here's the thing. I don't have a good feeling about this. I'm begging you, don't go into that house alone."

Bewildered, Lexie stared at her sister. "But we need to do this. With Aaron moving away, it could be our only chance."

"Then let him go," Val said. "He'll be out of our lives. Maybe we'll never know if anything happened between him and Callie. But she's dead, Lexie. She won't care. Sometimes you need to put bad things behind you and move on—nobody knows that better than I do."

"Well, you're wrong!" Lexie pulled her hand away and stood. "Callie deserves justice. What if she was innocent of those awful things? What if she was murdered? If I don't try to find out what happened, I'll never forgive myself."

"Listen to me, girl," Val said. "What if Aaron did kill her? If he were to find out you'd been in his house—and he could easily rig something that would let him know—he could come after you. Callie loved you. She wouldn't want that to happen." She paused. "Does Shane know what you're thinking?"

"No. And if you tell him, I'll never forgive you. But even if he knew, I wouldn't let him stop me."

Lexie turned toward the door. Val caught her wrist to stop her from leaving. "Please, Lexie," she said. "Think about what I've said. Justice isn't worth your life."

"I'll think about it—but no promises." Lexie crossed the porch and went back inside, closing the door behind her.

Val was right—if Aaron had committed crimes, especially if he'd killed Callie, sneaking into his house would be dangerous. But she couldn't let that stop her. She owed it to her beloved stepmother, and to her own peace of mind, to learn the truth.

By the time the sun came up on Friday, Tess and Ruben had loaded their bulls and left for the bucking venues. By eight-thirty, Val had made a quick breakfast for the boys and stashed their gear in the back of Shane's pickup, which she'd borrowed for the day. The two teens had hoped to ride in Val's red Cadillac convertible, with the top down. But since she needed to pick up supplies in Ajo, they would have to forgo that treat.

From the upper pasture, where she'd taken the ATV on the pretext of fixing the fence, Lexie watched the truck drive away, with Val and the boys in the cab. She'd avoided any encounter with her sister that morning. The last thing she needed was another lecture, or to find out that plans had been changed to keep her from checking Aaron's house.

From where she sat in the ATV, she could see all the way to Aaron's property. The battered red pickup he drove on his rare trips to town still sat in front of the house. He'd have to be leaving soon for his appointment in Tucson. Property closings could take time. Surely this one would not be scheduled late in the day.

Looking toward the ranch house now, she could see Shane, coming down the ramp in his chair. He'd be headed for the stable, along the path that had been swept smooth to ease the passage of his wheels. For him, cleaning the stalls and getting food and water for the horses would be slow work. But Lexie knew that he liked being able to do it. He was also getting to know the horses, in the hope that one could be trained to carry him with a custom saddle.

Touched by his strength, courage, and pride, she watched him labor toward the open stable door. He had insisted that he couldn't be a whole man for her. But he was more man than any she had ever known. She loved him so much— and even if she lost him, she would never stop.

She would love him for the rest of her life.

As Shane disappeared into the stable, Aaron, wearing a

sport jacket over his usual plaid shirt, stepped out of his house. After pausing to lock the front door, he walked to his truck, climbed into the cab, and drove out of the yard.

Lexie stayed where she was, her pulse racing as she watched the red truck climb the road to the pass. She couldn't make a move until he was out of sight. If she could see him, he could look back and see her.

And it wouldn't be a good idea to start up the ATV. The noise of the engine would bring Shane out of the stable to check on what was happening. She would have to get to Aaron's house on foot.

She watched the truck crest the pass and vanish. Just to be safe, she forced herself to wait a few more minutes. Then she climbed out of the ATV and set out across the pastures, down the slope toward Aaron's house.

Shane entered the first stall of the long stable. The horse, a buckskin mare, had been nervous about the wheelchair on his first few visits, but by now she'd grown accustomed to the strange mechanical contraption attached to the man. He talked to her and stroked her before he picked up the pitchfork he'd propped against the wall of the roomy box stall. Moving with care, he began forking up the dirty straw and pitching it into the wheeled cart he'd left outside the stall gate. Devising this process had taken time, trial, and error, and he was still trying to become more efficient. But he enjoyed working and being with the horses. It was one of the rare times he felt at peace. His latest long-term idea for the ranch was to add bucking horses to their rodeo stock. Bulls were ready for retirement after five or six years in the arena. A healthy bronco, for less investment, could buck for more than twenty. Tess was actually thinking it over.

He hadn't seen Lexie this morning. More than likely, she was avoiding him. The strain between them had been there since his first day on the ranch. For that, he could only blame himself. He'd needed space, but until yesterday, he hadn't realized how far away that need had driven her.

Was it too late to keep her from leaving? He didn't know what to do or what to say. He only knew that he loved and needed her—and that he couldn't stand the thought of losing her.

Heart pounding, Lexie stepped onto the porch of Aaron's house and raised a corner of the worn, dusty doormat. As expected, the key was there. When she lifted one end with a handy twig and picked it up with her fingertips, a shiver passed through her body. It wasn't too late to do the smart thing and leave. But if she were to turn back now, she'd never forgive herself. She had to do this for Callie.

Remembering Val's warning, she checked around the frame before opening the door. There it was—a small piece of cellophane tape that would pull loose when the door was opened—not a problem as long as she remembered to stick it back in place when she left.

Had Aaron expected someone to come into his house? But no, Lexie decided, it was just natural suspicion. After years of living alone, a man could develop some strange habits.

The key turned in the lock. She slipped it into her pocket, opened the door, and stepped inside.

In the dim light that fell through the closed venetian blinds, she could see that the place was a mess of junk and clutter. Why hadn't she brought a flashlight? It might have even been a good idea to bring a gun. She could've borrowed the pistol that was locked in the glove box of Shane's truck. But it was too late to think about that now.

As her eyes adjusted to the dim light, she could see more. Beer cans and snack bags cluttered the floor around the beat-up recliner that faced the TV. Stale odors drifted from the kitchen. Lexie resisted the urge to turn around and leave in disgust. She'd known that Aaron was solitary and maybe a bit eccentric. But she'd never guessed that he might be mentally unwell.

The kitchen was even worse. Dirty dishes and spoiled food cluttered the table and countertop. A foul odor seemed to rise from the cabinet below the sink. Trying not to inhale too deeply, Lexie opened the cabinet door.

A dead mouse lay swollen belly-up in a spot of powdery white substance that appeared to have spilled on the bottom of the cabinet. Was it rat poison? Lexie gagged and closed the cabinet door. She could feel the fear welling inside her like an icy flood. But she'd come this far. She needed to finish what she'd started before she panicked and fled.

The bed was rumpled, the covers thrown back. There was a closet on the far wall, its door missing. Nothing appeared to be inside but some clothes on hangers and some muddy-looking boots thrown on the floor. Dirty clothes were tossed over the back of a chair. The rest of the furniture consisted of a bureau on one wall and, next to the bed, a nightstand with a single drawer. If there were personal secrets to be found, the nightstand would be the place to look first.

Before opening the drawer, she checked the edges for more tape or anything else that might leave evidence of tampering. Finding nothing, she slid the drawer open.

Her eyes did a quick survey of the contents—tissues, a pen and notepad, a pack of Marlboros and a lighter, a bottle of prescription pills, an open package of condoms . . .

A glance at the bottle was enough to confirm that the pills were Viagra. Lexie's knees had gone weak. She would never have suspected Aaron of having an active sex life, yet the evidence was right here in front of her. But who was his partner? Assuming it was a woman, the choice was narrow. Either he was sneaking somebody in from the reservation or . . . it had been Callie.

The puzzle pieces were tumbling into place, almost too fast. If Callie had been sleeping with Aaron, and if she'd been here on the night of her death, then the missing bra—the bra that could be evidence of a murder—could be somewhere close.

If she'd lost it here, where would it go? Behind the bed, maybe? Or under it?

Forcing herself to stay calm, Lexie dropped to her knees and peered under the bed. Something pale was hanging from the box spring. She reached for it, caught it with her fingers, and tugged it free. It was a lacy white bra, size 38DDD—unmistakably Callie's.

Dizzy with fear and a strange elation, she was about to stand when she noticed something else on the floor, at the edge of the bed where it might have fallen. She reached for it, picked it up.

Her heart dropped as she held its weight in her hand.

It was Aaron's wallet, containing his driver's license, his cash, his credit cards, everything he'd be likely to need today. In his haste to get to his appointment on time, he must've dropped it out of his pocket while he was getting dressed.

Once he realized it was missing, he would almost certainly come back for it. He could already be on his way.

Lexie's pulse slammed as she scrambled to her feet. She had to get out of here.

She laid the wallet back where she'd found it, then rolled up the bra and stuffed it into the hip pocket of her jeans. Reminding herself to replace the key and the tape as she left, she strode back through the kitchen toward the living room. She would have to go out the front door, but after that she could cut around to the back of the house and up across the fields, to where she'd left the ATV.

Still plotting her escape, she entered the living room and stopped as if she'd hit a wall.

Aaron stood in the open doorway, a small but deadly-looking pistol in his hand.

"Well, Lexie, fancy finding you here," he said.

CHAPTER EIGHTEEN

LEXIE FROZE WHERE SHE STOOD. HER MIND SCRAMBLED for words that might save her. But Aaron's cold expression told her she wasn't going to lie her way out of this. She had only one reason to be in his house, and he would already know what it was.

"You aren't going to shoot me with that gun, Aaron," she said, masking her terror with bravado. "The police would find my blood spattered all over your living room. They'd find your bullets in my body and powder residue on your hands. The case would be a slam dunk."

She saw him hesitate, but he didn't lower the pistol. "Tell me what you're doing here, Lexie. I'm pretty sure I know, but I want to hear you say it."

She stalled, scrambling to gather her thoughts.

"Say it!" He snarled the words. This was the easygoing man who'd helped her drive and helped her with the bulls, the man who'd shown up for dinner at the house more often than not. She'd known him all her life. But she hadn't seen the real Aaron Frye until now.

She took a breath. "I came to look for the truth, and I

found it. Callie was sleeping with you. She was here on the night she died."

His laugh was rough, without humor. "So what? There's no law against a little healthy fornication. And since you're looking for the truth, I'll give it to you in spades. She'd been coming here for years, even while your dad was alive. Call it fair play or whatever the hell you want. He took my woman. I took his."

"But why did you have to kill her?" Lexie took a step into unknown territory. "Was it because she found out you'd been sabotaging the ranch?"

A smile twisted his mouth. "I didn't kill the blasted woman. We had a big fight about my selling the property. When I told her I'd be leaving, she threatened to kill herself. I told her to go ahead. I never thought she'd really do it. But I was wrong. I chased after her, tried to stop her, but . . ." He shrugged. "Too late. But it was her choice, not mine."

He was lying, of course. Callie had loved life too much to kill herself over a man. And even if she'd jumped into the arroyo on her own, she wouldn't have landed on her back.

But Lexie knew better than to contradict Aaron. She had him talking. She had to keep him going until she found a way out of here.

"What about the rat poison?" She challenged him. "I found traces of it under the sink. Are you going to tell me that Callie grabbed the box on her way out of the house, carried it to the arroyo and hung on to it while she jumped over the edge?"

Again, he responded with that flat, cold laugh. "Well, you've got me there, Miss Lexie, so I might as well fess up. Callie found that box in my kitchen by accident and threatened to tell the police if I tried to move away and leave her. That was when we started fighting. Afterward,

I saw her lying down there and figured that since she was dead, it wouldn't hurt to let her take the blame for the goings-on. I tossed the box down after her and left it for the cops to find."

But the sheriff had mentioned that Callie's fingerprints were the only ones on the box. How could Aaron have managed that—unless he'd wiped the box clean and used gloves or a cloth to press it against her dead hand before she went into the arroyo?

She decided not to mention that. Flattering him would be more likely to buy her time and information. "That was smart thinking, and it worked," she said. "Poor Callie couldn't say a word in her own defense. But there's one thing that doesn't make sense to me. Maybe you can explain it."

"Go on." His right hand had sagged with the weight of the pistol, but he still kept a firm grip. Making a dive for the weapon would be risky—too risky, Lexie decided. She might be fast enough to surprise him, but she was no match for his strength.

"Just this," she said. "I know you hated my father, and I know the reason. But why didn't that all end when he died? Why did you keep attacking the ranch—and our family? We were your friends, at least we thought we were."

"It's a fair question," he said. "But since you're not going to live much longer, why should I answer?"

His words confirmed her worst fears. Of course, he was going to kill her. He'd killed Callie for less than what she had on him now.

"It wouldn't be fair to let me go to my grave wondering," she said, playing along. "Besides, I have a feeling you might enjoy telling me."

He shook his head. "You always were a pesky little shit.

I'll tell you in the truck. Right now we're getting out of here. Put your hands behind your back. I might not want to shoot you here but if you don't cooperate, I can sure as hell break your arm."

Lexie didn't struggle as he snapped a plastic zip tie around her wrists. Her only chance of survival lay in getting him to drop his guard. Having her hands bound would make escaping more difficult, but she couldn't let it stop her.

"You don't have to do this," she said as he pushed her out the front door ahead of him. "I can give you the evidence I found. You can go and close on your property, take the money, and leave here for good. We can forget this ever happened."

"Shut up. You haven't offered me anything I won't get anyway." He used the gun to shove her toward the truck, which was parked a stone's toss away. Lexie didn't need to be told that he meant to drive to some remote spot in the desert and finish her.

Guiding her to the passenger side, he opened the door partway and ordered her to climb onto the seat.

"It's too high," she protested. "My arms—I can't grab anything to pull myself up."

"Too bad. Keep trying." He jabbed the muzzle of the gun into her back. He stood behind her in the opening between the door and the truck chassis, blocking any chance of escape.

Gasping with effort, Lexie managed to step up with one foot and push her body across the worn bench seat. If she didn't get away before the truck started, she'd have no way out. She sat up, adjusting her position as Aaron pushed the lock button down and stepped back to close the door. Whatever happened, she had to move now.

For a heartbeat, the heavy door was between her and the

man with the gun. Making a lightning turn in the seat, Lexie bent her legs like a cocked spring. With all her strength, she shoved her feet hard against the door, slamming it into Aaron's body.

As the door made contact, a gunshot rang out—but there was no time to wonder what had happened. Using her momentum, Lexie dropped to the ground and took off at a sprint. The sound of vile cursing reached her ears, but she couldn't look back. She was running for her life.

The distance from Aaron's house to the Alamo Canyon Ranch complex was almost a half mile. Lexie had captained the girls' track team in high school and even made All-State. But she was older now, and she was running in boots, with her hands tied behind her back. Even on the road, it was tough going. She was already out of breath.

She'd half expected to be shot at. When that didn't happen, she had to assume that Aaron was coming after her. Her only chance of getting away would be to find shelter. If she could get inside the ranch house . . . but no, with her hands tied, she wouldn't be able to open the front door. She'd be trapped on the porch. Her only option would be the open entrance to the stable. Maybe she could push the doors shut with her body or find a place to hide.

As she stumbled over a rock, almost falling, Lexie remembered. Shane had gone to work in the stable that morning. If he was still inside, she'd be putting him in danger, too. What could he do—unarmed and in a wheelchair—against a strong and desperate man like Aaron?

Aaron could kill them both.

From somewhere behind her, she heard the sound of the old truck—the grinding cough of the starter, then a roar as the engine caught. Lungs burning, Lexie pushed herself harder. She might be able to outrun Aaron, but she couldn't outrun a truck. He could crush her like roadkill and pass it off as an accident.

She was coming up on the stable—the only refuge she had. With the truck lumbering closer, she cut off the road and sprinted down the narrow, brushy slope, into the yard. Even in her panic, she remembered Shane. *Please don't let him be inside,* she prayed silently. *Please let him be safe.*

The truck followed her, lurching off the road and into the scrub. Lexie heard the engine roar, heard the whine of spinning wheels as the balding tires sank into the soft, red sand—stuck for the moment. Maybe she'd caught a break—but it wouldn't be for long, she told herself as she dashed through the open stable doors.

The stable was cool and dark inside. It had been built with a dozen roomy stalls in a single line, but half the stalls were empty these days. Lexie's sun-dazzled eyes peered into the shadows, all the way to the far end. There was no sign of Shane. She could only hope he'd finished his work and left.

From outside, she heard the door of the truck open and close. Aaron would be coming after her on foot. Even if she could do it with her hands tied, there was no time to close and bolt the heavy double doors. She needed to find a hiding place, fast.

The nearest stall held extra tools and tack—no cover there. The next stall was piled high with loose, clean bedding straw. The stall gate stood open. With her hands bound there was no way to close it from inside. Never mind; time was running out. Lexie burrowed feetfirst into the base of the pile, spilling straw down around her, leaving a tiny opening that would allow her to see. It wasn't the wisest plan—if Aaron found her, she'd be cornered—but right now it was all she had.

In the stillness, she could hear him walking into the stable, his footsteps rustling the spilled straw on the floor. But there was something odd about his gait, almost as if he were limping. As he stopped within view of the open stall, she could see what it was. A bloody rag was wrapped and tied around his upper leg. The gun must've gone off, hitting him in the leg when she'd kicked the door of the truck. He appeared to be in pain and losing blood, but that hadn't stopped him. It had only made him angrier. He was a wounded animal, desperate, dangerous, and intent on the kill.

Lexie held her breath as he came closer.

Shane had finished cleaning the stalls, but with little to do in the house, he'd decided to stay and spend time with the horses. Seated in his wheelchair, he was brushing down a powerful, black gelding when he'd heard someone come into the stable.

Was it Lexie? He'd almost called out to let her know he was here, but something—a prickling of his senses—held him back. Quietly, he lowered the brush and waited. A moment later, he heard a voice.

"Lexie? Come on out, little girl." The speaker was Aaron Frye. "I know you're in here, and you already know what's going to happen. You might as well give up."

Veiled by shadows, Shane ventured a wary look past the edge of the stall. Framed by the open doors behind him, Aaron stood near the entrance, a blood-soaked rag wrapped around his thigh and something in his hand that caught the faint light. Was it a gun? No. Shane's blood chilled as he recognized the object in Aaron's hand.

In a stable like this one, it was more dangerous than a gun. It was a cigarette lighter.

Panic flashed through his body. He forced himself to focus. Where was Lexie? How could he stop Aaron and get her out of here?

"You asked me a question, Miss Lexie," Aaron said. "Here's an answer you can take to your grave. I thought that seeing your father's miserable death would give me the revenge I wanted. But once he was in the ground, it wasn't enough. I didn't just want Bert Champion dead. I wanted to destroy everything he'd left behind—little by little, like the cancer that killed him. So I started small . . . a note on your truck, an open gate, a slashed tire, a dead bull . . . even Callie turned out to be part of it."

He paused, casting his gaze around the stable. "Now it's time for my master stroke—the stable, the horses, and you all at one time. No need to come out, Lexie. I've got that covered. All I have to do is light the straw, and this place will go up like a torch. Think about how it'll feel to burn to death. Think about the flames, the heat blistering your skin, the pain . . . You won't be so pretty when they find you." He clicked the lighter. A flame flickered in the dim light.

Driven by instinct, Shane moved. Yelling, he smacked his hand hard on the rump of the big black horse. With a shriek of alarm, the horse reared and bolted, bursting out of the stall and thundering toward the open door. Shane followed as fast as he could push the wheels. The pitchfork he'd used leaned against the wall. He grabbed it, balancing it across the arms of the chair. "Lexie!" he shouted. "Lexie, get out!"

Aaron stood in the horse's path. He tried to sidestep, but his wounded leg failed him. He stumbled to one knee. The horse clipped him as it galloped past. The lighter flew out of his hand, the flame dying as it fell.

Lexie, her wrists bound, had kicked her way out of the

straw pile. Straw clung to her hair and clothes. Rage flashed in her eyes. "You bastard!" She spat out the words as Shane held Aaron at bay with the pitchfork. "When I think about the things you did—and what you almost did here—I could kill you myself!"

Aaron's face was pale. Blood dripped from the dirty bandage on his leg. His eyes still smoldered with hatred, but he wasn't going anywhere. He was too weak, and getting weaker.

Still guarding Aaron with the pitchfork, Shane used his free hand to open his pocketknife and slice through the zip tie that bound Lexie's wrists. "Find some rope and tie his hands and feet," he told her. "Then you can use my phone to call the sheriff. Tell him to bring an ambulance."

Lexie found some rope in the tack room. Aaron didn't struggle as she tied his wrists behind his back. Even when she used a roll of horse wrap to cover the makeshift bandage and slow the bleeding before binding his ankles, he didn't speak. Only his glaring, defiant eyes held any resistance.

As Lexie spoke with the sheriff on the phone, her gaze lingered on Shane. She could see new pride in his expression, in the set of his shoulders and the tilt of his jaw. Something had changed for him. Today he had protected his woman and saved her life. That had to mean as much to him as it did to her.

She could only hope that it was possible for other things to change as well.

Shane lay awake in the darkness. It was after midnight. The house was silent. Even Val had quit rattling around and gone to bed. Faintly, from the porch, the dogs yipped at some wild thing in the yard, then settled back to guarding the house. The cool night breeze wafted the scent of sage through the screened window.

Over and over, Shane's mind replayed the day's events—the drama in the stable, the flickering lighter, the plunging horse, and Aaron's look of hatred as he was rendered helpless.

Most of all, Shane remembered Lexie—the terror that had gripped him when he'd heard Aaron's threat, not for himself but for her. If Aaron had touched his lighter to the straw where she was hiding, she would have died horribly, within seconds. He remembered the sight of her, crawling out of the hay with fury in her eyes, and how relief had almost overcome him as he realized she was safe. And then she'd wrapped Aaron's leg to slow the bleeding. How much courage and compassion had it taken for her to do that? She was amazing, his Lexie, and today he'd nearly lost her.

It had taken forty minutes for the sheriff to arrive with the ambulance. Waiting together, with Aaron lying between them on the stable floor, they'd said little. But their eyes had met often, trading unspoken questions.

While the paramedics tended Aaron's wound and readied him for transport to a hospital, Lexie told her story to the sheriff, who shook his head, praised her detective work, then scolded her for her reckless behavior. "You're lucky to be alive, young lady," he'd said. "If this cowboy—" Here he'd nodded at Shane. "If he hadn't been in the stable, the whole place would've burned, and you with it."

As the ambulance was getting ready to leave, Val had arrived home. Scolding and fussing like a mother hen, she'd ushered Lexie inside to clean her up and make her rest.

Shane had stayed outside to coax the spooked horse back into its stall, which took some time.

For the rest of the day and evening, he and Lexie had had precious little time to talk. Val had been a constant presence, hovering over her sister and demanding to know every detail of what had happened that morning.

Sitting across the table at supper, Lexie's gaze had been tender and questioning. Shane had ached with the need to talk to her, to tell her how much he loved her and how sorry he was that he'd kept her at a distance. Would she forgive him, or had he hurt her so deeply that she would never trust him with her heart again?

He'd waited, hoping for the right moment. But it hadn't come. He would have to find it tomorrow.

In the stillness, he heard the bedroom door open and close. A pale shape flitted through a shaft of moonlight. Shane's heart leapt. Could this be happening?

"Lexie?" he whispered.

"I'm here." Her voice was as soft as the wind. Maybe he was dreaming.

"Are you all right?" he asked.

She stood next to the bed. "I can't sleep," she said. "Thinking about what almost happened today—I was so scared, Shane. I'm still scared. I . . ." She hesitated, taking a breath. "I think I need you to hold me."

Heart pounding, he raised the covers and shifted to make room for her. Clad in a silky wisp of a nightgown, she slipped into bed beside him. He wrapped her in his arms, her body trembling, her skin like soft, warm satin against his.

And as he held her close, feeling her love and trust, all that he had yearned for, hoped for, and feared to lose forever became possible.

EPILOGUE

Seven weeks later

A WAXING CRESCENT MOON HUNG LOW IN THE EVENING sky. Its light shone through thin clouds, casting mottled patterns across the landscape. The windmill creaked softly, its vanes turning in the light breeze.

The three women sat on the porch, the light above the door turned off to discourage flying insects. The day had been long and tiring. Tess and Lexie had spent most of it with the beef herd, making sure the steers were ready for shipment. Tomorrow the animals would be loaded into a cattle truck and hauled to a feed lot, where they'd be fattened for auction.

Val, who'd always claimed she was allergic to cows, had spent the day painting the living room. She'd made it her project to refurbish every part of the tired old house, giving it a fresh new look in time for Lexie and Shane's late-November wedding. The work had a long way to go, but she appeared to be enjoying every minute of it.

Still dressed in her paint-spattered work clothes, she

tilted a can of Diet Coke to her lips. "Damn!" she muttered, lowering the can. "What I wouldn't give for a beer!"

"Don't even think about it, sis," Tess said. "One sip, and you'd be on your way down that slippery slope. That's why we don't even keep the stuff in the house."

Val pulled a face at her sister. Tess ignored her. Lexie giggled. From inside the house came the faint thump of Shane's weight machine. He never missed his nightly workout. His last checkup at the clinic in Tucson had shown that he was making great progress. By now, he could drive around the ranch and backroads in his hand-operated ATV, and he'd ordered a custom saddle for riding. He was determined to live a full life. But he would never ride bulls again, and Lexie knew that sometimes that reality still hurt.

"I still miss Callie," Lexie said. "I'd give anything if she could be here to see my wedding."

"We all miss her," Tess said. "But thanks to you, at least we know she was innocent of any crime."

The sisters had ordered a simple marker of pink marble and laid it where Callie's ashes were buried. Their stepmother had been far from perfect, but Callie had always acted with love toward her family.

Tess kicked off her dusty boots and stretched her long legs. "So what does everybody think of today's big news?" she asked.

The call had come that morning from the PBR Director of Livestock. Whirlwind, who'd bucked off nearly every cowboy who settled on his back, would be going to the World Finals in Las Vegas.

And there was even more good news. Shane had been hired by the sports network to sit in as a commentator. Lexie knew he was pleased. Even if he couldn't ride, he could still be a part of the PBR family.

"We've all got to be there," Tess said. "Even you, Val."

Val's expression froze. "Not me. I'll stay home and tend the farm, thank you."

"But why?" Tess asked.

"You know why. At least Lexie does."

"Don't be a wuss, Val," Lexie said. "You're bound to run into Casey sooner or later. You might as well get it over with."

"No," Val said, crushing the can in her fist. "Just no. I don't even want to talk about it."

Lexie took a deep breath. "Well, since you don't want to talk about anything else, I have some news—something I haven't shared with anybody but Shane."

Her sisters stared at her. "What?" Tess asked.

Lexie grinned. "I'm pregnant!"

ACKNOWLEDGMENTS

Special thanks to Jeff and Wendie Sue Kerby Flitton of Bar T Rodeo for their gracious hospitality and invaluable help in researching this story.

Read on for an excerpt from the next novel
in Janet Dailey's Champions series.

WHIPLASH
The Champions

From **New York Times** *bestselling author Janet Dailey comes the latest Champions novel, set on the Alamo Canyon Ranch, where a legacy bull rearing operation is run by three sisters—women who aren't afraid to compete in a man's world, or to take on something as wild as love—and win.*

When Val Champion returns to the family ranch, she's ready to put her past behind her. Her dreams of a Hollywood acting career have become a nightmare of fear. But once she sees rodeo man Casey Bozeman facing down a bull in the arena, she knows she's no safer at home. Face to face with her first and only true love, Val can't deny her still powerful feelings for Casey. Feelings she can never act on again . . .

Val's the one who got away, the woman who broke his heart so hard he still feels the sting. But there's no denying Casey's still drawn to the fiery beauty. And there's no way he can stand by when the high stakes Professional Bull Riding finals in Vegas bring out the danger Val's been running from. Suddenly the rugged cowboy is willing to risk it all for her once more, even if it means facing down those secrets lurking in her unforgettable eyes . . .

CHAPTER ONE

Las Vegas, Nevada
Early November

CASEY BOZEMAN PLANTED HIS FEET IN THE THICK DIRT that covered the floor of the vast T Mobile Arena. As he waited for the first chute to swing open, he willed himself to ignore the lights, the noise, the TV camera crews, and the crowd of 20,000 people who'd come to watch the World Finals of the PBR. His mind was laser focused on one job—protecting the rider who would explode out of the gate astride 2,000 pounds of bucking bull.

A glance to either side confirmed that his teammates, Joel Hatcher and Marcus Jefferson, were in place. Like Casey, they were dressed in loose-fitting athletic gear with protective vests underneath. The team of bullfighters, as they were called, had worked together for the past five PBR seasons. They trusted each other with their lives. But it was a given that, whatever the cost, the rider's safety came first.

Farther out in the arena, a mounted roper waited with his lasso ready. If a riderless bull was headed the wrong way, it would be his job to rope the animal and herd it back to the exit gate.

The announcer's voice blared over the public address system, introducing the first rider and bull, in sync with the images that flashed onto the huge display screens. In the gated chute, twenty-year-old Cody Woodbine, ranked fifth in world standings, was lowering his body onto Cactus Jack, a surly, white-faced behemoth with blunted horns like the front end of a '69 Cadillac.

Casey had faced Cactus Jack before. Some bulls, the good ones, just wanted to dump the cowboy and head back to the pen. Others had murder on their minds. Cactus Jack was the second kind.

Inside the chute, the bull was body-slamming the thick steel bars, a move that could break a rider's leg. One of the men, perched on the chute's side rail, shoved a wooden wedge down next to the huge animal to hold him in place. Others pulled the bull rope tight around the bull's body, just behind the shoulders. Cody Woodbine thrust his gloved left hand into the rope handle and wrapped the rope around the handle's base. In the arena, Casey shifted and danced to keep his muscles loose. His teammates did the same. They had to be ready for anything.

The rules were always the same. At the rider's nod, the gate man would pull a rope to open the chute, starting the all-important clock. With one hand gripping the rope handle and the other hand in the air, the rider would have to stay on the bull for a full eight seconds. For a successful ride, both the bull and the rider would be scored on the basis of fifty points each. For a buckoff, only the bull would be scored.

It was a simple system, but fraught with dangerous surprises.

All eyes were on Cody Woodbine as he hitched forward

on the bull until he was sitting almost over his hand. At his nod, the gate swung open, freeing a ton of raw fury to surge into the arena.

Streaming snot and manure, Cactus Jack leaped and twisted, then went into a bucking spin to the right—bad news for a left-handed rider; but the young cowboy hung on as the digital clock ran up the time, displaying each second by tenths.

From the back of a bull, eight seconds could seem like forever.

The three bullfighters circled the kicking, spinning bull, ready for a dismount or a buckoff. Casey could see that Woodbine was losing his seat, leaning too far right as he struggled to outlast the clock. But the determined cowboy kept fighting, barely hanging on.

The eight-second whistle blasted. Woodbine had done it. But the young rider was in trouble. As he tumbled off to the right, his left hand twisted under the rope handle and caught fast. He hung against the side of the bull, flopping like a rag doll as Cactus Jack bucked and spun.

Casey flung himself at the bull, his left arm supporting Woodbine, his right hand working at the twisted rope. Joel and Marcus darted in to slow the beast, getting in his face, even grabbing a horn in an effort to distract him.

Seconds of spinning, jolting terror crawled past. At last, Casey felt the glove loosen. He pulled Woodbine's hand free. The cowboy tumbled to one side and rolled clear of the pounding hooves. Dragged away by Marcus and Joel, he was safe. But Casey had gone down with him, and Cactus Jack was looking for somebody to hurt.

As Casey struggled to rise, the massive head filled his vision. The horns caught his padded vest with enough force to toss him high over the broad back. As the roper closed in, Casey's body glanced off the bull's side and crashed to earth.

Watching the event alone on closed circuit TV, Val Champion swallowed a scream. She pressed her hands to her face to block her view of the screen, but she could still hear the announcer's voice over the cheers of the crowd.

"It's an 85.5 for Cody Woodbine on Cactus Jack. But he's going to need that shoulder checked. From here, it looks like it might be dislocated." There was a pause. "And Casey Bozeman is back on his feet, shaken but ready to go. Those bullfighters are tough hombres. They've saved a lot of lives. And now, coming up is our next ride."

Lowering her hands, Val sank onto one of the two beds in her room at the Park MGM Hotel. Casey was all right. He would live to face the next bull. And the next. But she wouldn't be watching. She couldn't stand it.

She and Casey were ancient history. She wasn't supposed to care about him anymore. But heaven help her, she did. And caring hurt. It hurt so much that she never wanted to care again.

Hell, she needed a drink. She needed more than a drink. But she'd been clean and sober for the five months she'd been out of rehab. She had vowed to stay that way. Besides, her sister Tess would kill her if she smelled the faintest whiff of alcohol on her breath.

The Champion family had come to Vegas bringing two bulls from their Arizona ranch—Whirlwind, a rising star in the rankings, and his younger brother, Whiplash, here as a last-minute alternate.

The rest of Val's family—big sister Tess, and adorably pregnant little sister Lexie, with her wheelchair-bound husband, Shane, were down in the arena watching the event live. Val had tickets, too. But she'd gotten cold feet. Pleading a headache, she'd locked herself in the room she shared with Tess and opted to watch Round 1 on the big screen TV.

She'd told herself she could handle this. But watching Casey almost die had been enough to convince her she'd misjudged. She'd be smart to sell her tickets for the remaining four nights and spend the money on a flight back to Tucson and a long Uber ride to the family's remote mountain ranch.

Standing, she switched off the TV, turned off the lights, and walked to the window. The darkened room offered a view of the nearby T Mobile Arena, lit up like the Fourth of July. Northward, as far as Val's eyes could see, Las Vegas glittered like an endless dumping ground for used Christmas lights and gaudy costume jewelry.

Tacky but strangely beautiful, it called to her with a siren's seductive voice. The hotels and casinos, which she knew by sight, whispered names that resonated like islands in a tale from Sinbad the Sailor. *Bellagio . . . Mirage . . . Aria . . . Paris . . . Venetian . . .*

Val turned away from the window. Out there, beyond the glass, was everything she'd left behind, everything she'd run away from to save her body and soul. Four months ago, she'd come home to her family and the ranch, hoping they could make her whole again. She was doing better now. But something was missing. She'd realized it the moment she saw Casey on TV.

Casey. Her first love.

The man she could never be with again.

Connect with Us

Visit us online at
KensingtonBooks.com
to read more from your favorite authors, see books
by series, view reading group guides, and more.

for sneak peeks, chances to win books and prize packs,
and to share your thoughts with other readers.

facebook.com/kensingtonpublishing
twitter.com/kensingtonbooks

Tell us what you think!

To share your thoughts, submit a review,
or sign up for our eNewsletters, please visit:
KensingtonBooks.com/TellUs.